Praise for Michael Gilbert and *Anything for a Quiet Life*:

"Gilbert is as wise and witty a writer as the mystery, thriller or any hybrid thereof as we've been privileged to read."
—*Chicago Tribune*

"A charming collection."
—*The Kirkus Reviews*

"Gilbert, an accomplished mystery and espionage novelist, continues to amaze and entertain with these nine short stories."
—ALA *Booklist*

"This collection delights by virtue of Gilbert's fanciful plotting."
—*Publishers Weekly*

Also by Michael Gilbert available from Carroll & Graf:

The Queen Against Karl Mullen

ANYTHING FOR A QUIET LIFE

MICHAEL GILBERT

Carroll & Graf Publishers, Inc.
New York

First Carroll & Graf hardcover edition 1990
First Carroll & Graf paperback edition 1991

Carroll & Graf Publishers, Inc.
260 Fifth Avenue
New York, NY 10001

ISBN: 0-88184-715-1

Manufactured in the United States of America

CONTENTS

1

ANYTHING FOR A QUIET LIFE

The four-door family saloon slowed as it reached the crest of the downs. Jonas Pickett pulled it into a lay-by and got out. Claire climbed out too, and they stood for a moment looking down at the township of Shackleton-on-Sea.

"You can see all the town from here," said Jonas. "The new housing estate, and what they call the industrial zone – though there doesn't seem to be a lot of industry in it yet – they're both a bit further back. We'll see them when we get round the next corner."

"It's rather snug," said Claire. "Squeezed in between those two arms of the cliff. Like a cuckoo in a nest that's too small for it. It looks as though a really fierce storm would bring the sea rolling in and wash it all away."

"About six hundred years ago it did just that. The old town's under the sea. They'll tell you they sometimes hear the church bell ringing down under the waves. It's a sign that something terrible's going to happen."

"It's a lovely little town," said Claire. "I don't believe that anything terrible ever happens in it."

"I hope not," said Jonas. "I've come here for peace and quiet, not excitement."

"In that case," said Claire, evidently not for the first time, "I can't see why you didn't simply retire here. What was the point of opening an office?"

Jonas said, "Sam would never have forgiven me if I'd retired."

"Sabrina wouldn't have been happy about it either," agreed Claire.

They got back into the car and drove on down the twisting

road, between hedges of dusty thorn and elderberry. A final turn took them out, past the church, through a maze of tiny streets, and on to the Esplanade, where the sea sparkled in the June sunlight.

Shackleton was not a fashionable resort, like its neighbours Brighton and Hove, but it was clearly quite a prosperous place. A marketing centre, Jonas guessed, for the agricultural hinterland. A lot of small hotels and decent-looking boarding houses. A bit of light industry in the background. There would be two different populations: the visitors who crowded the beaches and the pier in the summer months; and the local residents who lived on the money they brought, and resented the noise they made.

At the far end of the Esplanade, where the Shackle stream runs out to sea, Jonas turned back again into the town. The High Street was full of cars and shoppers and dogs, and he saw that stalls were already being set up in the central square for the next day's market. A turn to the left took them into a quieter street, parallel with the High Street. It was a mixture of shops and houses. One house, rather bigger than the others, was set back behind a small paved courtyard, with an alley running down beside it. It was a Georgian building with bow windows, three white steps up to the front door and a dolphin bell-pull.

"Don't tell me," said Claire. "I guess it was the old doctor's house. It's got that unmistakable look."

"You're quite right," said Jonas, "and now it's the new lawyer's house. Sam has got the plate up already, I see."

It was a brass plate, worn with much polishing.

Jonas Pickett, Solicitor and Commissioner for Oaths

"Are you going to live here?"

"I've got the top two floors. Sam's got the basement. The office is the bit in between."

"A bachelor establishment," said Claire thoughtfully. "What about Sabrina and me?"

"She's got rooms for both of you with the vicar."

"That sounds all right. All we need now is a few clients."

During the first month there were no clients but a lot of callers. Men who came to put the finishing touches to Jonas's flat and men with filing cabinets and desks to complete the fitting out of the office. One whole morning was occupied with the installation of an impressive safe. Travellers called hoping to sell them office accessories. They were mostly sent away empty-handed by Sam Conybeare. They did not stop to argue. Sam was a mountain of a man who had once performed remarkable feats of strength and daring in a circus. Jonas had rescued him from his wife, who was nagging him to death, and he had devoted himself to Jonas's welfare ever since.

People dropped in to pass the time of day. Thirty years of legal practice in the south of England had given Jonas a wide circle of acquaintances. Among the first to arrive was Major Appleby, the headmaster of St Oswald's, one of the three preparatory schools in the neighbourhood. He told Jonas, "There used to be eight when I started up here after the war. Times are getting harder every day. If I have to shut up shop you shall handle the sale." Jonas thanked him and said he hoped it wouldn't happen.

Their first professional visitor was not a client. He arrived on a Friday morning in the middle of July. He introduced himself to Claire, who examined his card which identified him as Christopher Clover, of Smardon and Clover, solicitors, whilst he examined Claire with approval. She was worth looking at.

She said, "Shall I tell Mr Pickett what it is you want to see him about?"

"Just a friendly visit. One professional man to another. If he's busy I could come back."

"I'll find out," said Claire, in the cool voice which matched her appearance.

Jonas said, "Of course. Show him in. Ask him if he'd like a cup of coffee."

Mr Clover said he would just love a cup of coffee, and what a lovely old house it was, wasn't it?

Jonas had brought down some of the furniture from his office in London. There were chairs upholstered in red leather. There was a huge roll-top desk occupying the space in front of the bow window. On the walls there were portraits, in oil, of severe-looking legal gentlemen. The general effect was undeniably impressive. It certainly impressed young Mr Clover.

He looked at the pile of dockets and papers on the desk and said, "Well, you seem to be busy. Perhaps I oughtn't to be interrupting you."

"Don't be misled," said Jonas. "These are hangovers from my previous practice up in London. The young gentlemen I bequeathed it to find there are some matters that they still need help with. I see from your card you're in practice here yourself. That's good. You can give me your professional view of Shackleton."

"Well," said Mr Clover, "it's a nice place. Splendid climate, and friendly people. But legally, I should say it's pretty tightly tied up."

"I'm glad to hear it," said Jonas. "I didn't come here to work myself to death."

Mr Clover looked at him doubtfully. He said, "Well, we've been here for two years, and I don't mind telling you it was hard grafting at first."

"Who's the opposition?"

"Well, Porter and Merriman look after the nobs. I mean, people like Sir James Carway and Admiral Fairlie and old Mrs Summers. R. and L. Sykes handle most of the litigation. That's the local bench and the County Court at Brighton. Bledisloes do the commercial and company work, such as it is."

"I don't suppose that I shall cross swords with any of them," said Jonas. "My specialities are Bills of Exchange, Copyright and Patents. And Church property. Particularly Welsh Church property. A curiously complicated field since Disestablishment." Thinking that he detected a look of relief in young Mr Clover's eye, he added maliciously, "Of course, nowadays one must be prepared to tackle anything. My partner, Mrs Mountjoy, seems to revel in the run-of-the-mill stuff."

After Christopher Clover had left, Claire put her head round the door and said, "I may have got a client for you."

"What sort of client?" said Jonas cautiously.

"He's a young man – not all that young really – youngish. I met him at the tennis club. When I first joined he was new too, so we arranged a few singles."

"Very natural," said Jonas.

Claire looked at him suspiciously, then she said, "He's not the sort of man who talks a lot, but I gathered that he's down here for the summer, living in a caravan. He was in that big caravan park beyond the golf course, out on the Portsmouth road. But he had to get out two or three days ago. There was some trouble."

"What sort of trouble?"

"The person who told me about it didn't really know. But the police turned up, and there was a bit of an argument. When I next saw him at the club I said if he needed a lawyer he'd better come and see you."

"Has he a name?"

"His name's Rowe. Dick Rowe."

"And did he say when he proposed to call?"

"I think," said Claire, who was looking out of the window, "that that's him coming now."

"Then we had better admit him."

He wrote on the pad in front of him, 'Rowe', 'caravan' and 'Trouble?'.

At the moment when Claire opened the front door and ushered Mr Rowe into the reception room, the door on the far side opened also, and Mrs Mountjoy came out, followed by her bad-tempered rough-haired Scots terrier, Bruce. 'Like owner, like dog,' Jonas used to say, which was unfair to Sabrina. True, she favoured an untidy hairstyle, but she was more abrupt than bad-tempered.

Bruce growled at the newcomer, and then made a dart for his ankles. Instead of retreating, Mr Rowe bent down and scooped Bruce up with a firm hand under each of his forelegs. Bruce looked disapproving. This was not the reaction he had expected. Mr Rowe held him for a moment, moving the fingers of his left hand. Then he said, "Yes. I thought I noticed a slight stiffness. There's a lump under his right foreleg."

"Oh dear," said Mrs Mountjoy. "You don't mean – "

"Not serious. Not yet, anyway. But you ought to have it cut out. A vet would do it with a local anaesthetic."

He put down Bruce, who scuttled back behind Mrs Mount-joy and glared at the newcomer through the tangles of his hair. Claire said, "Better come in, Dick, before he changes his

11

mind." She ushered Mr Rowe into Jonas's room, and closed the door behind him.

"And who in the world is that?" said Mrs Mountjoy.

"That," said Claire, "is our first client."

The description which occurred to Jonas when he saw Rowe was 'average'. He was of average height, of average build, and had a very average face. He saw what Claire had meant when she had first said 'young' and then corrected it to 'youngish'. Rowe certainly gave a general impression of youth, but where a young man's face is open, and lit with the joyful expectation of what life has to offer, this face was closed. It was more than closed. It was sealed.

"Sit down, please," said Jonas. "My secretary tells me that you had some problem."

"Problem?" said Rowe. He sounded surprised. "Not that I'm aware of. I just wanted to make a will."

"That shouldn't be too difficult." Jonas ran over in his mind the details he needed. "First I'd better have your full names."

"Richard Athelston Rowe."

"And address."

"Since my movements are uncertain, it had better be my London bank. The London and Home Counties Bank."

"Right." Jonas scribbled busily. "Executors?"

"The bank has agreed to act as my executor."

"Splendid. Then the next thing is, who are to be the beneficiaries?"

"I wish to leave everything to Claire Easterbrook."

Jonas had almost written this down before the impact of it struck him.

He said, "You mean, my secretary?"

"Yes." And, as Jonas paused, "Is there some difficulty?"

"If you had wanted to bequeath your estate to me," said Jonas with a smile, "there would have been considerable difficulty. Solicitors aren't supposed to draw up wills in favour of themselves. But members of their staff? I suppose there's no objection."

"Good."

Jonas still hesitated. Then he said, "You mustn't think me impertinent, but I gather that you have only known Miss

Easterbrook for a month. Are there not other people, members of your own family . . . ?"

"I have no family."

"None at all?"

"None at all. I am unmarried. My father and mother are dead. They were only children. I have no brothers or sisters. I understood that if I died without a will my property would go to the state. That seemed to me to be one good reason" – a very slight smile twitched the corner of his mouth – "for making a will."

The accent was puzzling. There was the faint suspicion of a brogue, allied to a broadening of the vowels which Jonas associated with educated Americans. He said, "You must excuse me for having been startled by your proposal. In the way you put it, it seems quite logical. Might I ask if Miss Easterbrook is aware of your intentions?"

"No. And I see no reason to inform her. Unless" – again that very slight smile – "my will should become effective. If that happens, of course, she'll have to know."

"Then it will take a little longer, because I shall have to type it myself. When it's ready, where shall I get in touch with you?"

There was a slight pause before Rowe said, "As I mentioned just now, my future movements are a bit uncertain. Could I call on you to sign the will in three days' time? Say Thursday morning, about midday?"

"That should be sufficient time even for an inexpert typist like myself," said Jonas.

Later that day he discussed their client with his partner Sabrina Mountjoy, from whom he had no secrets.

"He's certainly got his wits about him," she said. "I mean, noticing that Bruce was limping, and diagnosing what was wrong with him. I saw the vet at lunchtime, and he's going to operate this evening."

"He struck me as a remarkable man altogether," said Jonas. "A man with no family, no face, and a curious reluctance to disclose his present address. Although, as it happens, I think I know it."

"How come?"

13

"When old Major Appleby, of St Oswald's, came to see me last Thursday, he mentioned that a stranger had called on him and asked permission to park his caravan for a few weeks in the spinney at the far end of their football field. From his description I think it was Rowe. He liked him and was prepared to say 'yes' but was worried about local authority repercussions."

"What did you tell him?"

"I said that out of sight was out of mind."

"That doesn't sound to me like legal advice."

"I didn't charge him for it," said Jonas.

As Mrs Mountjoy was going she said, "I've just realised it. Of course, your new client doesn't exist."

"What on earth do you mean?"

"He's a legal fiction. Don't you remember? John Doe and Richard Roe."

She departed, cackling. Jonas started to type.

That was on Monday.

On Tuesday night Jonas slept badly. This was something that happened about once a month. Jonas thought that it might be something to do with the weather. The first heavy storm since their arrival had swept up the Channel that afternoon, and it had been raining on and off ever since. After a few hours of dozing he was jerked back to wakefulness by the feeling that something was wrong.

The rain had stopped, the clouds had blown off, the stars were showing, and the night was very still. What he had heard had been a sharp crack, and it had come from somewhere below him. He looked at his watch. Half past two. He got up and sat for a moment on the edge of his bed, thinking. Then he pulled on a sweater, pushed his feet into a pair of old slippers and started downstairs.

His living quarters were on two floors, bedroom and bathroom above, dining room, kitchen and living room below. He went into the dining room, which was immediately above his own office. There was no repetition of the crack which had woken him, but he could hear a succession of much smaller noises which suggested that someone was moving about. He hesitated no longer. He had no great opinion of burglars – mostly they were cowardly people whose one idea, if disturbed, was to get away. There was a poker in the fireplace. Jonas picked it up and made his way down to the hall.

Definitely there was someone in his office. Now he could hear a desk drawer being opened and shut. The crack which had woken him must have been made when the intruder forced the front of the desk. He threw open the office door, and clicked down the switch.

No result. Bulb taken out? In the half light through the bow window he could make out the figure of a man, who was behind the desk and had been using a torch, which was switched off as Jonas appeared. For a moment nothing happened. Then, to his relief, he heard steps coming up from the basement. Sam was joining the action.

Jonas said, "You'd better come quietly. There are two of us."

The man was out from behind the desk by now. He advanced towards Jonas steadily and without speaking. As Jonas swung the poker, something hit him with a horrid force in the muscle of his right arm. He dropped the poker. A knee drove into the bottom of his stomach. As he went down, crowing for breath, the door at the back of the room opened and Sam appeared, outlined against the light from the passage behind. The intruder hurdled Jonas, reached the hall door three steps ahead of Sam, jerked it open and made for the front gate, where a car stood, parked without lights. At the gate he paused for a moment.

Jonas, who had crawled as far as the open front door, croaked out a warning. Whether Sam heard it, or would have heeded it if he had heard it, is an open question. In fact, at that moment he slipped on the wet flagstones and went down.

There was a soft but unpleasant sound as the gun went off. The bullet went over Sam, who was on his back, through the open door, over Jonas who was on his knees, and smacked into the barometer which hung at the end of the hall.

The next moment the intruder was in the car, which was already moving. By the time Sam had got to his feet and lumbered to the gate it was thirty yards away and going fast.

Jonas said, "Watch it, Sam. Don't let him get another shot at you." He had got some of his breath back. The car was disappearing round the far corner.

Sam said, "I wanted to see if I could get his number, but it's covered with mud. Crafty sod."

"We'd better telephone the police."

The policeman who arrived on a bicycle ten minutes later was large and red-haired. He told them that his name was Roberts, and it was clear from his manner that he was out to be reassuring. Jonas did not want to be reassured. He wanted the intruder caught. Roberts said, sure and they were probably tough lads from Brighton. People did shoot other people in Brighton. Not in Shackleton. Had anything been taken?

An examination of the office showed that the contents of the desk had been disturbed. Drawers had been opened, and papers scattered.

"It's quite mad," said Jonas. "I don't keep money in my desk. I keep it in the bank."

"Maybe he was after looking for the key of the safe."

"It's possible. He'd have been out of luck. I keep it in my bedroom. Hello!"

"Is something missing, then?"

"The only thing that seems to be missing," said Jonas as he sorted out the mess, "is three sheets of paper. They were my third effort at typing out a will."

"That's a curious thing to steal, sir. However, there doesn't seem to be a lot we can do about it tonight. Why don't you come along in the morning and have a word with the skipper?"

Jonas looked at the pleasant, not over-intelligent face of PC Roberts, and agreed that it might be well to have a word with the skipper.

Detective Superintendent Queen listened patiently to what Jonas told him. He said, "It's true that we get a few tough characters in here from Brighton and Portsmouth from time to time."

"But what possible interest could they have in the papers in a solicitor's desk?"

"I believe Roberts suggested they might have been looking for the key of the safe."

"Then why did they steal three pieces of paper?"

"Yes," said Queen thoughtfully, "that does seem odd. I didn't quite follow about that. Were they valuable at all?"

"Their only value was that they'd taken me an hour to type out. It was a will."

"Very odd. For a local person?" Seeing the look on Jonas's face he added, hastily, "I wasn't wanting to know what was in the will, you understand. Just the name. I thought it might give us a lead."

"I suppose there's no harm in mentioning his name. It was a Mr Richard Rowe. And he's not local. Just a visitor."

As Jonas noted the reaction of Superintendent Queen to this he suddenly remembered Claire telling him that there had been trouble involving the police at the caravan site. He had not been clear, from what she had said, if the arrival of the police and Rowe's departure had been connected.

Queen said, "Would you excuse me for a moment, sir," and went out, closing the door behind him. It turned into a long moment. Jonas could hear the rumble of voices from a nearby room. He was beginning to get impatient when Queen reappeared. He said, "I wonder if you would mind coming along and having a word with the boss."

The boss, he gathered, was Chief Superintendent Whaley, head of the uniformed branch at Shackleton. He had already heard a number of things about Whaley, not all of them complimentary. He was a big man, with a strong black moustache and a colour in his cheeks that might have indicated short temper or high blood pressure. Or both, Jonas reflected. However, he seemed genial enough and waved Jonas to a chair.

He said, "You're new in Shackleton, Mr Pickett."

"The very latest thing in lawyers."

"We're always glad to see a London man opening up down here. Shackleton's an expanding place. There should be work for all."

"I hope so," said Jonas.

"We get a lot of co-operation from firms like Porter and Merriman and the Bledisloes."

"I'm glad to hear it." Jonas noted the omission of R. and L. Sykes. If they defended in the Police Court there could be understandable enmity there.

"It makes things easier all round. After all, you're an officer of the court. I'm an officer of the law. We're both on the same side."

Jonas thought, he wants something, and is winding himself up to ask for it. Like a clock getting ready to strike.

"The fact is that I'm going to ask you a favour. Rowe came to see you. I gather you were making a will for him."

"I can't comment on that."

"Of course not. Professional confidence. I understand that. I'm not in the least concerned with how Mr Rowe planned to dispose of his property. It's only" – it came out with a sudden rush – "do you happen to know his present address?"

"I do," said Jonas.

"Then could you – ?"

"I imagine there could be no harm in letting you have it."

"Very kind of you."

"It is, care of the London and Home Counties Bank."

The colour in Whaley's face deepened slowly. He said, "I think you realise, Mr Pickett, that that was not what I wanted. I meant his address in Shackleton."

"I'm surprised at you, Superintendent. I couldn't possibly disclose Mr Rowe's whereabouts without his consent even if – " he paused fractionally, and then said, "even if, as you yourself pointed out, it was not a matter of professional confidence."

There was a long pause. Then the Superintendent said, "Tell me, why did you change your mind?"

"Did I?"

"What you were going to say was, 'I couldn't tell you Mr Rowe's address, *even if I knew it.*' Then you stopped because it had occurred to you that this would not be true. From which I assume that perhaps you do know his address."

"You add mind-reading to your other accomplishments?"

The Chief Superintendent ignored this. He said, "I can't force you to let me have this information, but I have to warn you. It can prove to be a dangerous piece of knowledge."

"And what he meant by that," said Jonas to Claire later that morning, "I haven't the least idea. If the police are after Rowe, knowledge of his whereabouts might be dangerous for *him*. But why should it be dangerous for *me*?"

"Search me," said Claire. "If he wants to find out where

Rowe's hiding, why doesn't he get his chaps to do something about it?"

"Such as what?"

"Follow him home from the tennis club."

"I don't know. There's something about this that doesn't add up. I think I'll pay a call on Major Appleby."

St Oswald's Preparatory School for Boys stood among trees in ten acres of smooth Southdown turf. He found the Major in one of the classrooms, correcting exam papers. He said, "You want a word with my caravanner? You'll find him in the copse behind the rifle range. I warn you, you'll have to look pretty hard. He's tucked himself well away."

Jonas walked through the patch of woodland behind the miniature range without seeing anything but trees and bushes, and had concluded that the headmaster had misdirected him, when, on his return journey, he noticed a small fold of netting among the bushes, between two trees. Looking closer, he saw that a section of camouflage net had been artfully interwoven with bracken at the bottom and small, leafy boughs at the top. Peering through it he could just make out the shape of the caravan.

A voice behind him said, "Can I help you?"

Rowe had come out from a tree behind which he must have been standing. When Jonas spun round, he said, "Well, if it isn't Mr Pickett," but there was not much more friendliness in his voice.

Jonas opened his briefcase, and said, "I've brought you your will. Perhaps you'd like to look it over. If it's what you want we could get Major Appleby and his wife to witness your signature."

Rowe held the will in his hand, without looking at it. He said, "Would you tell me how you knew I was here?"

"The Major's an old friend. When he called in on me the other day he mentioned that he had been asked to accommodate a caravanner. I guessed from his description that it was you."

"I see. I hope you didn't pass on that inspired guess to anyone else."

"That's the second time today," said Jonas, "that someone

has suggested that I might pass on information about one of my clients to third parties. I'm getting a bit tired of it."

Rowe looked at him steadily for a moment, and then said, "No. Naturally you wouldn't. Stupid of me. Let's go in and get this business done, shall we?"

The Major was in his study, with a young girl and an elderly spaniel. He said, "My wife's out, but my daughter Penelope can act as the second witness. She's over eighteen, and said to be of sound mind."

Penelope smiled tolerantly, and said to Rowe, "I do believe Shandy is better already." Hearing his name the spaniel thumped his tail on the floor. "It must have been what you said, one of those nasty corn spikes got between his toes."

Rowe squatted down by the dog, and lifted the bandaged paw. The dog did not try to pull it away, but licked his hand.

"It'll be all right now the poison's out," he said.

When the will had been signed and witnessed, Rowe said, "If you'd care to come back to my caravan we'll settle up. Would you like a cup of tea, or is it too early for a drink?"

"Never too early for that," said Jonas. The caravan was neat and well organised. Jonas said, "I can see you're an old campaigner. You've done a lot of this."

"A fair amount. Water?"

"Just a drop. What are your plans for the future?"

"A bit indefinite. Ice?"

"No, just water."

The warning-off was clear. Don't talk about the past. Don't talk about the future. It rather limited possible subjects of conversation. In the end it was Rowe who broke the silence. He said, "I don't know what your methods of book-keeping are, but could I suggest that you enter this fee that I'm paying under some such heading as 'Sundries' or 'Miscellaneous'?"

Jonas thought about it. He said, "Actually, we haven't set up a lot of book-keeping yet. You're our first client. So I suppose it'll be all right. Very well. You shall be a 'Sundry'."

"Excellent," said Rowe. The faint smile which hardly seemed to penetrate the mask of his face appeared once more. "I think that Sundry is a very appropriate description of me at this precise moment. As I told you, I shall shortly be moving on. I'll try to keep in touch with you. If you don't hear from

me after, say, six months, have a word with my bank manager.
At the Westminster branch."

Jonas promised to do this. He had come to St Oswald's on
foot, and as he walked back into the town he was thinking
about his first client. Sabrina had called him a legal fiction. He
was certainly an elusive character. All that he really knew
about him was that he seemed to have a talent for dealing with
dogs.

It was market day, and the streets of the old town were
crowded with cheerful Sussex farmers, their wives, families
and live and dead stock. When he reached the office Claire was
getting ready to shut up shop.

She said, "We had another visitor this afternoon. A man."

"You don't think – "

"No. Definitely not the sort of man who would burgle the
premises. Rather nice, I thought. Tubby and middle-aged.
Might have been an army man. Name of Calder. He left his
card. It's on your desk. He said he might call back later, on
the chance of finding you still here."

"Client number two, perhaps," said Jonas. "We're looking
up. Where's Sam?"

"He's gone down to the Post Office. There was a message
about some registered packet that's gone astray. I couldn't
quite understand what they were saying. Sam's gone down to
sort it out."

When Claire had departed, Jonas sat for a moment staring at
the card. It was not very informative. Middle-aged? Possibly a
retired officer. There was the sound of a car drawing up, and
footsteps on the flagstones of the courtyard. The newcomer
came through into the hall, opened the door of Jonas's room
and came in without knocking.

He was neither tubby nor middle-aged. He was large and
thick, and moved with the bouncing tread of an athlete. He
said, "Don't let's have any trouble. You're an old man. I could
hurt you badly, and I'll do it if I have to."

Jonas started to say, "What on earth – " but got no further.
The man came round the desk, caught the end of his tie in one
hand and the knot in the other and started to throttle him.
Jonas plucked at the man's hands with his own. He might as
well have tried to move a steel clamp. He was fighting for

21

breath, and the room was swimming round him. He could see the man's face in a mist. He thought he was smiling.

The pressure relaxed. The man said, "See what I mean? Now come along." He picked up the circular ruler from Jonas's desk. "If you make any trouble, I'll crack both your kneecaps. You won't walk for six months."

He linked his left arm with Jonas's right arm, and they walked out of the house together. Anyone seeing them would have thought they were very close friends.

They got into the car that was waiting outside. He and the big man sat together on the back seat. Jonas thought it looked like the car he had seen driving away the night before. He had recovered control of his voice, and said, as the car moved off, "I suppose it's not the slightest use asking you what all this is about."

"Well, now," said the man. "I can't see any reason not to tell you what our intentions are. It might be sensible, really. Save you from doing anything heroic, like. We're not going to kill you. We're not even going to hurt you, unless we have to. Turn left here, Danny."

"Then what are you going to do?"

"We're taking you off to a quiet place, to ask you a few questions. You give us the right answers, we keep you there long enough to check up that you've told us the truth. Then we let you go. Understood?"

Jonas understood perfectly. They would ask him where Rowe had hidden his caravan. And he would tell them. No doubt about that. Then one of them would go off to find out if he had told them the truth. If he had, they would let him go. Or would they? He rather doubted it. If they intended to let him go, would they have allowed him to see their faces, listen to them talk, note the number of their car? Jonas was surprised to find that he could weigh up the potentialities of the situation as if it was a legal problem which concerned one of his clients.

By now they had reached the area of small streets between the church and the market. When they swung round to the right, Jonas knew that they had taken the wrong turning. That road was a dead-end, running up to the churchyard wall. There were two women standing on the pavement talking.

The driver said, "We'll have to go back."

"No trouble," said the big man genially. He dipped one hand into his pocket, took out a gun and pushed the muzzle into Jonas's side so hard that it made him gasp. He said, "You do anything stupid, and I'll pull the trigger. It won't stop us from getting away, but you won't have any stomach left. Think about it."

Jonas said, "I'm not stupid."

"Stay that way."

The driver had got the car reversed. The two women watched the manoeuvre incuriously. They drove off slowly, turned out of the street, and headed down a road which, as Jonas knew, would bring them out near the market-place.

Market day, too, thought Jonas. They'll run into trouble there, for sure.

The trouble came as they turned the corner. It was a herd of bullocks, driven by a farmer with a red face. He had been in trouble already with the motorists, whose cars were blocking the end of the street. The bullocks were filtering through this barricade, using the pavement on both sides of the cars. One of the bullocks on the offside pavement had just avoided treading on a baby-chair. The woman who owned it was telling the farmer, in pungent Sussex, what she thought of him and his bullocks. A sympathetic claque of bystanders were supporting her. One of the cars in the block ahead had started to move. The driver of Jonas's car turned down the window and said to the farmer, "Shift those bloody cows over, can't you?"

There was no hope of backing. A van and a car were already blocking the road behind him. But he had seen that, as the rearmost of the cars in front moved, he could squeeze past the other two by using the nearside pavement.

The farmer, attacked from a new point, swung round and told the driver what he could do to himself. The driver ignored him. He had already started to edge forward. The gap in front of him was widening.

A bullock swerved across his bow. He sounded a blast on his horn.

This was a bad mistake. A frisky Southdown bullock can take just so much and no more. It reared up on to its hind legs, performed a skittering dance, came down alongside the car, and pushed its head through the open window. The big man half rose in his seat.

Jonas felt the pistol shift away. His left hand was already on the door catch. He tugged the door open and rolled out into the gutter.

By this time there was a crowd on both pavements. Two men helped Jonas to his feet. When he looked round, the car had gone, squeezing past the block in front.

"Well," said one of the men. "That's a nice way to treat you. They might have stopped to see if you'd hurt yourself."

"I think they were in too much of a hurry to stop," said Jonas. "Thank you. I'm quite all right now."

A woman said, "Your trousers are going to need a bit of cleaning."

Jonas wasn't worried about his suit. He was glad that he still possessed a stomach. When he got back to the office he found Sam, angry at having been sent on a pointless errand. "There wasn't no parcel," he said, "and what have you been doing to yourself?"

"It's a long story," said Jonas. "I'll tell you when I've had a bath and changed."

As he was coming downstairs the front door bell rang. To Jonas's relief Sam was there to answer it. He had had enough of strange callers.

The newcomer was middle-aged and tubby. He looked as if he might have been an army man. He said, "My name's Calder. I left my card with your secretary. Do you think we could have a word?"

"Yes," said Jonas. As they went into his office he breathed to Sam, "Stay handy." He was past taking chances.

Mr Calder looked appreciatively round the room before settling himself down in the visitor's chair. He said, "There was a nasty smash out on the Portsmouth road just now. It'll be on the evening news, I expect."

Jonas stared at him.

"The car ran into a roadblock. Ran into it quite literally, I mean. Tried to crash through it. Silly thing to do. Went out of control, hit a telegraph pole and caught fire. Two men in it, both dead. I'm sorry about that."

"If it's the men I'm thinking about," said Jonas, "I'm not in the least sorry they're dead."

"I suppose that's understandable," said Mr Calder. "But we were sorry about it. We'd have liked at least one of them more or less undamaged. We had some questions we wanted to ask him."

Jonas was not sure whether his visitor's matter-of-fact manner was comforting or alarming. He said, "I suppose we're talking about the same car. The one I got out of."

"Correct. Actually I'm not quite clear how you did get out of it. I gather there was a bit of a fracas."

"A bullock put his head through the window."

"Very disconcerting," said Mr Calder, and started to laugh. He suddenly looked much more human. He said, "We owe you an explanation. If I tell you some of the background, you'll realise what it was all about. Dick Rowe's an Ulsterman, but his mother was American, and he lived for some time in the States. When his mother and father died he and his brother came back."

"He said he hadn't got a brother."

"That's right. His brother was shot by the IRA. That's when Dick came to work for us. He posed as an American sympathiser. Helped with running arms and explosives. Got into their confidence. It was information from him that led to the arrest of the people responsible for the last two bomb explosions in London. Very dangerous job. Of course they got on to him in the end, and we had to pull him out."

Jonas thought about his client. He said, "He did look a bit impassive. Was that plastic surgery?"

"That's right. New face, new identity. We fixed him up with a job in the States. A partnership in a veterinary practice."

"He'd be good at that," said Jonas.

"The trouble is that arrangements like that take time. We have to work through our friends on the other side. Reciprocal assistance. Meanwhile we had to put Dick on ice. He was target number one for the opposition. We thought the best plan was to supply him with a caravan and let him spend the summer here. We chose Shackleton because it looked nice and peaceful."

"That's why I chose it," said Jonas.

"On the off-chance that Dick might need help we alerted your senior policeman, Chief Superintendent Whaley, to the position. I needn't tell you that he was meant to keep it totally under his hat. But he had to go and tell someone else. In strict confidence, of course. And someone else told someone else."

"The only time I met our Chief Superintendent he didn't strike me as a very discreet sort of person."

"My own boss," said Mr Calder dispassionately, "who is also Dick's bank manager, has expressed the opinion that Whaley ought to be first skinned and then filleted. He not only talked. He tried to put a police guard on Dick. Thus pointing him out plainly to the opposition."

"That was why he pulled out of the caravan park."

"He not only pulled out. He sent for us. We've got quite a large team down here at this moment."

"Large enough to organise a few roadblocks."

"Oh, quite," said Mr Calder with a smile. "I was glad you weren't in the car when it happened. You'd been bothered enough already."

This seemed to Jonas to be an understatement. He said, "I suppose when they burgled my office they were looking for information about Rowe. They thought there might be an address in his will. Which reminds me. I suppose Rowe isn't his real name."

"No. Do you think that might invalidate his will?"

"I suppose it might."

"I *could* give you his real name."

"No," said Jonas firmly. "When he gets to America he can make a new will. And use an American lawyer. I wish him well, but I don't want to know anything more about him."

Claire opened the door, said "Sorry. I didn't know you had a visitor. But it was a bit urgent."

"It's all right," said Mr Calder. "I'm just going."

"What is it now?" said Jonas resignedly.

"We've got a new client. A Mrs Lovibond. She's waiting outside. She wants to consult you about something."

"Certainly."

"The thing is, there may be a bit of trouble about this. She's one of Chris Clover's star clients."

"Then why is she coming to me?"

"I gather she saw you roll out of a car, and felt sorry for you."

2

BLACK BOB

The moon was throwing a cold clear light over the field. It was called the Top Field, because it was the northernmost of the seven which made up Maggs's Farm, and stood a little higher than the other six. Under the hedge which bordered its upper end something was moving, slipping in and out of the shadows. It might have been an animal but, when it appeared for a moment in the full moonlight, it could be seen to be a boy.

Tommo was a young tearaway who lived with his mother in a farmhouse two miles up the road. She had long given up any attempt to control him, and her neighbours all prophesied that he would come to a bad end. What he was doing, at three o'clock on that particular morning, was setting snares for rabbits. They holed up under the bank among the roots of the thorn bushes and would start coming out at first light. Tommo reckoned to pick up three or four. Later in the day he would offer them for sale to their rightful owner, Farmer Maggs.

He was not the only occupant of the Top Field.

A dark cloud was drifting along the upper edge of the pasture; moving, stopping and moving on again. This was Black Bob, Farmer Maggs's most valued possession. He was a splendid animal, not grossly over-bred like some of the bulls which won rosettes at the Smithfield Show ('Can't hardly carry their own weight,' said Maggs. 'They have to wheel 'em up to the cows on a trolley.'). Black Bob was one of the smaller, lighter, Southdown strain, but was still a formidable hunk of muscle and aggression, moving over the grass with the ponderous certainty of a Sherman tank.

Tommo watched him without fear. Black Bob would never

charge into a thorn hedge, and if he did make any such move, Tommo could wriggle through the close-growing roots as easily as the rabbits he was trapping.

Black Bob knew that he was there, a trespasser in his private kingdom. But he knew that he was unassailable. He gave a brief snort to mark his feelings and moved off down the field.

Tommo had scooped out a little hole in the dust at the foot of the bank. He was a great deal more comfortable there than he would have been in the sordid heap of rags in his mother's back kitchen. As soon as it was light he would see what luck his snares had brought him, and would move down with his catch towards the farmhouse. He liked to wait until Maggs had left on his morning round, when he could deal with Mrs Maggs, who was more generous and less suspicious than her husband.

On this particular morning he had not long to wait. He saw Maggs come out, not dressed for farm work, but wearing a dark suit and carrying a bulging leather case. Tommo was not to know it, but he was on his way to Shackleton, to call on his solicitor, Jonas Pickett. It was a visit which was to have consequences for all of them.

"Well, Mr Maggs," said Jonas. "It's not a simple question. Not by any means."

The contents of the leather case were spread on his desk. Some of them were modern documents, neatly typed and bundled together with tape. Others were huge old-fashioned deeds, handwritten on parchment.

"When I bought the farm," said Maggs, "the lawyer from Hoole, old Michelmore, he was the one who looked after our family business, but he's dead now, he said, 'No need to keep any deeds that's more than thirty years old, you can use 'em for lampshades if you like.' But Mrs Maggs, she wouldn't hear of it."

"I'm glad of that," said Jonas. "I think it's a crime to destroy old deeds."

"That's what Mr Westall said. He said, tear them up and you're tearing up the history of the county. I let him have the old deeds to look at. Truth to say, he kept them so long I thought he'd forgotten all about 'em, but when he came back, he was in a real taking, I can tell you."

Jonas knew of Mr Westall, although he had never met him. He was one of two acknowledged local antiquarians. He had written a treatise on historic and prehistoric Shackleton. Jonas had borrowed it from the vicar, and found it a curious work, being partly based on genuine research among the local archives, and partly designed as an attack on the theories of his rival in this field, Professor Templeman from Sussex University.

"When he brought the deeds back he had a big book with him, some sort of local history."

"Clayborne's *History of West Sussex*," suggested Jonas. "I've got a copy here." He fetched down the fat red and gold book from the bookshelf.

"That's the one," said Maggs. "That's the very book. He read me some things out of it, all about King Henry the Eighth it was. From what he told me, he wasn't the sort of joker we learnt about at school."

"Bluff King Hal? He was a lecher and a bully."

"That's right. And it wasn't just his nine wives. I expect they got no more than they deserved. It was what he did to all those monasteries. Did you know there used to be one a few miles north of here? You'll not see one stone standing on another now."

Jonas had found the place in the book. He read out, " 'In 1520 the Bernadine Cistercian Abbey of Fyneshade was visited by the King's Commissioners. The Abbot, Robert Beaufrere, had been warned of their coming and before their arrival had caused all the ornaments to be removed from the chapel and the Abbey building and buried. They had been replaced by common artefacts of wood and iron.' "

"That's right," said Maggs. "That's what he told me. The King had the abbot and his – what was he called?"

"His sacristan."

"Right. He had the pair of them taken up to London and put in the Tower, and they tried to make them tell where all these treasures had been put. But no matter what they did to them, and they really worked them over, they couldn't make them talk."

"That's right. They both died under torture rather than tell where the abbey treasure was hidden. The abbot was a strong man. There's a lot about him here." Jonas was turning the pages of Clayborne. "We don't know much about the sacristan. All we're told is that his name was Legrand."

"Ah," said Maggs. "But that was the point. That's what old Westall was going on about. It's what he'd found in my deeds. They don't go right back to those times, of course, but it seems that one deed tells you what was in an earlier one. You'd understand about that, sir."

"Recitals, yes. Go on."

"Well, it seems the farm belonged since way back to a family called Lengard, and he made out that this was really the same as Legrand. It was just that people weren't so fussy about spelling in those days."

"It's a possible variation," said Jonas. He was beginning to see what Mr Westall was getting excited about. "And your farm's not far from the site of the abbey."

"Little more'n a mile across the fields."

"And if the farmer, in 1520, was a relative of the sacristan, his farm would be the logical place for them to bury the abbey treasure. Yes, I see. It's plausible. And Mr Westall wants to wander over your property with a metal detector and see if he can turn anything up?"

"That's right, sir. First thing I thought was, why not? Won't do no harm. He'd have to be a bit careful in the Top Field. I've kept Black Bob in there ever since he upset that picnic party. Well, you know about that."

It had been the first occasion on which Maggs had consulted him. A family, with little knowledge of country ways, had thought they could share one of the lower fields with the bull. Luckily they had got out over the fence unhurt, and Black Bob had contented himself with trampling on a transistor and other belongings which they had scattered around, and had finished by sitting down on their picnic basket. They had wanted compensation. Jonas had told Maggs to ignore them. "They were trespassers. They've got no rights. They won't sue you."

This had proved to be an accurate prediction.

"Howsomever," said Maggs, "my wife wasn't so sure about

this metal detector. She said, 'You go and have a word with Mr Pickett. He was right about the picnickers. He'll tell you what to do.'"

"Well," said Jonas, "as I said, it's not a simple question." He referred to some notes which his partner, Sabrina Mountjoy, had made for him. He referred all difficult legal points to her and very rarely found her wrong. "Things are classed by the law as treasure trove, *if* they were obviously hidden with the object of recovering them later, *if* the owner can't now be traced, and *if* they turn out to be gold or silver."

"Not much doubt is there? This'd be treasure trove all right, or most of it."

"Quite so. And that's where the snag comes in. If they *are* treasure trove they belong to the finder. It's only if they *aren't* treasure trove that they belong to the owner of the land."

Maggs said "Ah," and then "Oh." His mind was moving over the new possibilities. "So if they turned out to be diamonds or rubies or such, they wouldn't be treasure trove, and I'd get them. But if, what's more likely, they were gold and silver, old man Westall would collar the lot."

"Right."

"Then what I do is I tell Mr Westall, you keep off. And I get myself one of those metal detector things and look for the stuff myself."

"How big is your farm?"

"Five hundred acres, just under."

"You realise that it'll take you about a year to cover it all properly."

"I'm in no hurry," said Mr Maggs.

But Mr Westall was in a hurry.

The following morning a telephone call was followed by the arrival of Jack Merriman, junior partner in the firm of Porter and Merriman. Jonas had played golf against him and had concluded that if his law was as erratic as his putting he could be a dangerous adviser.

Jonas said, "I don't think you've met my partner, Mrs Mountjoy. I believe that you want to discuss the law of treasure trove, so I thought I'd have her in on it. She knows much more about it than I do."

Merriman smiled politely and plunged straight into business. He said, "I gather you advised Maggs not to let Mr Westall have access to his farm."

"I told Mr Maggs that if any searching was to be done it might be better for him to do it himself."

"I expect you know that using a metal detector is quite a skilled job. Mr Westall has considerable experience in that field. He'd be much more likely to find the abbey treasures – always supposing they are there to be found."

"And when he found them?" said Jonas drily.

"He would be quite willing to sign an agreement that any reward paid by the museum would go to Maggs."

"Yes. I thought about that," said Jonas. "But I gather there could be some difficulty in policing such an agreement."

"Overton," murmured Mrs Mountjoy.

"Quite so. I expect you remember the Overton Farms case. The finder handed over some of the items he had unearthed, but pocketed the really valuable ones."

"I hope you're not suggesting –" began Merriman.

"I'm not suggesting anything," said Jonas. "I'm sure that Mr Westall's interest is antiquarian and historical. I was simply pointing out that no paper agreement can ever be entirely watertight. My real point, however, was much simpler. The land belongs to Mr Maggs. If he doesn't want Mr Westall on it, he's entitled to say so."

"I'm not sure about that," said Merriman, in the manner of someone about to produce a trump card. "Basically all treasure trove belongs to the Crown. I take it you'd agree with that."

"Agreed," said Jonas cautiously. "The finder gets a reward from the museum equal to its value."

"And if there is reason to believe that treasure can be found in a certain place, then every effort should be made to recover it."

"That may be so."

"And to prevent treasure being unearthed is regarded by the law as a ground for the prosecution of the owner of the land."

Mrs Mountjoy bestirred herself. She was a large woman, and possessed a deep and authoritative voice. She said, "I take it,

Mr Merriman, that you are referring to the offence known as Concealment of Treasure Trove."

"Precisely."

"It was abolished in 1968. See Section 32(i)(a) of the Theft Act of that year."

"Oh?" said Mr Merriman rather blankly.

Another putt missed, thought Jonas. When Mr Merriman had taken himself off he said, "Good work, Sabrina. That finished him. I suppose you weren't pulling his leg?"

"Certainly not. He would have known it himself if he'd kept up to date with his law."

But Mr Westall was far from finished. He turned to the press. The editor of the *South Down News* had already published several learned articles from Mr Westall's pen, some of them rather hard going for his readers. The one he received the following week was more to his taste. "Good stuff," he said to his second-in-command. "Should start something."

> There is, apparently, a legal right to act the part of the dog in the manger. Although I cannot claim to have proved it conclusively, I have established a strong possibility that a number of priceless artefacts of gold and silver, probably adorned with precious and semi-precious stones, lie buried in a defined area north of the town of Shackleton. Yet the owner of the property has seen fit to refuse to allow even a simple preliminary examination which would confirm or refute this theory. Apparently the law supports him . . .

There followed several paragraphs dealing with the history of Fyneshade Abbey and comparing the stupidity of the law with the unselfish zeal of your true antiquarian. Jonas had just put down the newspaper when the telephone rang. It was Mr Maggs. He had read it, too.

"My wife says I ought to sue him for libel."

"Don't think of it," said Jonas. "It's probably what he wants. If no one takes any notice, it's a damp squib."

Someone did take notice. The next number of the *South Down News* contained a letter from Professor Templeman of Sussex University. It was written with a practised pen, dripping acid.

> I was fascinated to read the effusion in your last week's issue from our *soi-disant* antiquarian expert, Mr Westall. He spoke, with bated breath, of artefacts of gold and silver adorned, if we are to believe him, with precious stones! What Mr Westall appears to have overlooked is that Fyneshade Abbey was a Cistercian Foundation under the rule of St Bernard. As even schoolboys know, that rule permitted the use, as ornament, of nothing but iron. I fear the treasures must be dismissed as a figment of Mr Westall's over-heated imagination. There is, however, another angle to it. King Henry the Eighth's Commissioners, unlike Mr Westall, would not have been ignorant of such elementary facts. They would have realised that the riches of a prosperous, long-established community like Fyneshade would have been in the form either of currency or gold and silver in bar form . . .

"And that really will stir people up," said the editor.

It certainly stirred Mr Westall, who rang up his solicitor.

"On the whole I should advise against an action for libel," said young Mr Merriman regretfully. "Fair comment on a matter of public interest, and all that sort of thing."

"It's not fair comment," said Mr Westall. "It's outrageously unfair. However, if you say so – "

The ripples did not stop there. The national press began to show interest. Antique ornaments might not evoke great public concern. Bullion was another matter. Jonas had a word with the friendly Detective Superintendent Queen. He said, "I expect you saw what was in last week's *South Down News* about the abbey treasure."

"It's in the *Express* and the *Mirror* this morning," said Queen. He sounded unhappy.

"I imagine that every amateur treasure-seeker in the country will be queuing up to have a look for it."

"And a lot of not-so-amateur villains," said the Inspector. "I've made arrangements to have a car doing regular patrols.

That's all right by day, but it's a long perimeter to watch by night."

"Treasure-hunting by night wouldn't be easy. It's not a quick job."

"Let's hope we don't have any trouble," said Queen. "We've got enough on our plate already."

Two days later, at ten o'clock in the morning, when Jonas had just settled down to deal with his post, Claire announced a visitor. It was Dr Makepeace. Jonas knew Dan Makepeace and liked him. He was coroner for the district, one of the new type, qualified in law as well as medicine. He said, "Since you're acting for Mr Maggs, you won't be surprised that I'm calling on you."

"Delighted, certainly, surprised, too. I wasn't aware that my client had been killed, or had killed anyone."

"As a solicitor," said Dr Makepeace, "you ought to know better than to say a thing like that. Do you suppose that coroners are only interested in dead bodies?"

"A slip of the tongue," said Jonas. "I suppose it's the treasure."

"Certainly. Historically it's the duty of the coroner to look after all the interests of the monarch. Buried treasure – "

"Of course. And stranded whales."

"We don't get many of them. But treasure, that's something else altogether. It'll be my duty to keep a close watch on how things develop."

"You *and* the police. Excuse me." His telephone had rung. He picked up the receiver and said, "I'm busy. I can't deal with it now." Then, with a change of tone, "Oh, I see. Yes. Yes, of course. As a matter of fact Dr Makepeace is with me. I'll tell him." He replaced the receiver slowly, and said, "That was your officer. You'd better put on your other hat. There's a dead body in Maggs's Top Field."

"Dead by violence?"

"Yes," said Jonas. He sounded upset. "It's a clear case of murder, and the murderer is known. Black Bob caught an intruder in Maggs's Top Field last night and – dealt with him. Rather thoroughly. Maggs would like me to be there to look after his interests. Your officer is on his way up there."

"My car's outside," said Dr Makepeace. "We'll go together."

By the time they got there the police photographers had done their work and the body had been removed to one of Maggs's barns and laid on a trestle table under a tarpaulin. The coroner's officer, a stolid ex-policeman, indicated it to the coroner, but seemed disinclined to approach the table himself. When the coroner had lifted the tarpaulin, Jonas understood why, and went outside to regain control. A superficial glance at what was lying on the table suggested that Black Bob had stamped or jumped with sharp hooves several times on the body, and once at least on the face.

Dr Makepeace said, "We shall have to rely on the clothing for identification."

Chief Superintendent Whaley, who was there with Superintendent Jack Queen, nodded his agreement. He, too, seemed unwilling to make any closer inspection. He said, "We've telephoned the pathologist from Portsmouth. As soon as he gives the word we'll have – that – taken down to the mortuary. When we have his report, we may be able to get somewhere. And you – what's your name? Tommo. Don't go too far away. We'll need a statement from you."

Jonas saw that a boy was trying to efface himself in a corner of the barn. Maggs said, "My wife'll look after him, Superintendent. He'll be handier here than at his home. You can telephone us when you want him."

"All right," said Whaley. "I'm getting back to the station. And Jack, I think you'd better stay here for the time being."

Queen nodded. He said, "Leave me two men. When this news gets about we'll have a job keeping people out of the Top Field."

"Keep them out of my farm altogether," said Maggs. He sounded angry.

As the crowd started to disperse, Jonas said to Maggs, "If you've got Tommo's story, I'd better hear it as soon as possible."

"My wife got most of it from the boy before the police arrived. If that Superintendent frightens him he won't get nothing out of him at all. He'll just clam up. We'll walk up to the field."

When they got to the Top Field there was a policeman guarding the gate, but the field itself was empty.

"I moved Black Bob down to one of the barns," said Maggs. "I daren't let anyone else handle him. He's in a wicked mood. Not that you can blame him, really, with his hide full of shotgun pellets."

"He'd been shot?"

"Shot at. Young Tommo was under the top hedge. Sleeping out, he says. Rabiting I don't doubt, though he won't admit it. It must have been between three and four in the morning. Not starting to get light, but not too far off it, when he heard a car stopping in the road – a big car, by the sound of it. Maybe a van. He didn't see it. He heard people getting out, and the door slamming, and about ten minutes later – and I can tell you he was surprised – he saw three men coming into the field."

"You mean they'd got through that hedge?"

"*And* the wire fence. But there's more to it than that. Come and have a look."

They walked across.

When the local authorities had widened the road at this point, they had not only compensated Maggs handsomely for the land they had taken. They had built him a fence of stout diamond mesh along the new verge. This ran outside the old thorn hedge, itself a formidable barrier.

"Professional work," said Jonas.

The intruders had cut a neat square in the fence, folding back the flap, and had then carved their way through the thick roots and branches of the old thorn hedge to make a sort of tunnel.

"They wouldn't have done that in a hurry," said Jonas.

"Have another look," said Maggs.

When he got down on his knees at the opening of the tunnel he saw what Maggs meant. He said, "You mean they were reopening a tunnel that had been made before. I can see the old cuts now. All they had to do this time was to chop away stuff that had grown since they were here on the previous occasion. How long ago would you think?"

Maggs examined the cut ends and the new shoots. He said, "Thorn's not a quick grower. Not like elder. I'd say two years, maybe less."

"It looks as though they knew that all they had to do was cut the fence and do a little hedging."

"They may have known about fences and hedges. They didn't understand my black prince. They knew he was there, right enough. That's why they brought a gun. They thought they could scare him. So when he moved over to have a look at them, they loosed off. I'd guess when the pellets hit him he just went mad. Tommo didn't care much for talking about the next bit, but the end of it was one man badly hurt – a broken arm it sounded like – and another man helping him. They got away because Bob was attending to the third man who was lying on the ground."

"And the others just left him there, and drove off?"

"That's what Tommo says. He was scared blue. He slid off home, but his mum saw there was something wrong and got the story out of him and sent him back to tell us. We rang up the police."

Jonas said, "As far as you're concerned, of course, there's nothing to worry about. They were trespassers, and worse than trespassers. They broke into your property, armed."

"I thought I was probably in the clear," said Maggs, but he sounded relieved. "It didn't seem to me that they were ordinary treasure-hunters. To start with, they didn't have one of those metal detectors you were talking about."

"You're sure of that?"

"Certain sure. When Bob got at them, all they wanted to do was get clear. Anything they were carrying they dropped it. When I came up this morning I found a pick and a spade and – I don't know what you'd call it – a long rod it was, measured off in feet and inches. The police, they took them all away."

Jonas thought about it, and the more he thought, the odder did it seem. He said, "It looks as though they not only *knew* the treasure was there, but had been told where to dig, maybe by the people who cut the original hole in the hedge."

"It certainly looks like it," said Maggs.

"You clear off." This was to a young man in a trench coat who had crawled through the gap in the hedge.

"Be a sport," said the young man. "Give us a story for the *South Down News*. We're ahead of the London boys for once."

"I haven't got no story for you," said Maggs. "And if you don't clear out, you'll find yourself in trouble, I can tell you that."

The policeman was already advancing across the field. As the young man backed reluctantly out of the tunnel, two more cars drew up on the road outside. One had a notice 'Press' on the windscreen. The other had a blue light on top.

"Dead heat," said Jonas. "We'd better be getting back to the house before they start pestering Mrs Maggs."

The editor of the *South Down News* said to his faithful staff of two, "It's *our* story, and the way I'd like to run it is this. Do some research in the libraries. Portsmouth and Brighton will be best. They've got sections dealing with local history. And have a word with Mr Westall. He'll be keen to help. I believe that the abbot, Robert Beaufrere, was a well-known man. I don't mean that he was popular. Rather the contrary, from what I've been able to find out. But a *strong* man."

"You think it's his spirit still protecting the treasure? His curse will be on anyone who tries to disturb it? That sort of thing."

"Lovely," said the editor. "Work it up."

"I don't understand it," said Whaley, "and I don't like it."

"It's odd whichever way you look at it," agreed Queen. "If these people had been normal treasure-hunters they'd have brought the proper equipment with them. They didn't need to, because I'd guess that someone had *already* used a detector and located the site. They knew they wouldn't be allowed to lift the stuff, so they came back at night to dig it out."

Whaley said, "It's possible, but it's got snags to it. If someone had already been over the ground with one of these detectors and had located the treasure, how did he keep clear of that bull when he was doing it?"

"Maybe it was that young Tommo. He seems to know how to dodge in and out."

"He's a slippery customer," agreed Whaley. "But I don't somehow see him as a treasure-hunter, do you? And there's another difficulty. If he was hunting for it, how'd he know it was in that field? There are half a dozen other fields in Maggs's

Farm. All that old Westall ever proved – if you can call it proof – was that it could have been in one of them."

"There's another odd thing, too," said Queen. "The pathologist is still working on the body, what's left of it. But we've got a preliminary report on the clothes. You saw it?"

Whaley nodded, "Nothing in the pockets. An expensive suit, but all tailor's tabs cut out. No laundry marks." The two men looked at each other. The same thought was in both their minds.

"They were professionals," said Whaley, "and ten to one they came from London. As soon as we've got the prints we send them up to Central to see if they're on record. Then, maybe we can see where we're going. All we can do meanwhile is keep people off the farm and hope the thing dies down."

"The press are bound to splash it."

"Shackleton used to be a nice, quiet place," said Whaley. "A bit of healthy noise in July and August with the summer visitors and the funfair on the Lammas, but nothing to get upset about. But ever since that solicitor fellow arrived from London it seems to have been one thing after another."

"Jonas Pickett, you mean. You don't think he's behind this?"

The Chief Superintendent considered the possibility, and shook his head. He would like to have blamed Jonas, but could see no way of doing it.

"I don't see how we can tie him into it," he said regretfully.

The headline, in the largest type available to the printer of the *South Down News*, said, 'BLACK BOB LIVES'.

Robert Beaufrere, the formidable Abbot of Fyneshade, the man who defied King Henry the Eighth and died in the Tower of London rather than give up the treasures of his abbey to that despoiler of the monasteries, was known throughout the countryside as Black Bob. Can it be a coincidence that when modern vandals threatened to lay hands on the silver and gold and precious stones, to preserve which he suffered on the rack, a modern Black Bob should step into his place and mete out justice to the robbers?

Inserted here were photographs of the bull in the ring at the Lewes Show, and an engraved portrait of Abbot Beaufrere. Both looked tough customers.

"Good stuff," said the editor, "but have we any proof that the country people called the abbot Black Bob? It seems a bit disrespectful."

"Not actually," said his assistant, "but it will be very difficult for anyone to prove that they didn't."

Whaley read the article, but paid less attention to it than he might have done on account of a telephone call which he had just had from Scotland Yard. It came from a Chief Superintendent Morrissey, who was known to him by name as head of the London District Regional Crime Squads, which picked men who dealt with serious and violent crime in the Metropolitan area.

Morrissey said, "Those dabs you sent us off the man the bull trod on. They belong to a chap called Darkie Haines. He's got a record as long as your arm. Everything from GBH downwards. A very dangerous character."

"He met a more dangerous character that night," said Whaley.

"Yes. I saw a copy of the pathologist's report. Your animal did a thorough job. Pity he didn't get a chance to stamp on the other two as well. Now this is only a guess. But Haines normally operates with Lefty Summers and Mick Gavigan. They're both hangers-on of Catlin's mob. And Lefty's in hospital with a broken arm."

Whaley said, "It seems to add up, doesn't it?"

"It adds up," said Morrissey. "I'm not sure if I like the answer or not, but I'll send down my number two, Jock Anderson, to have a word with you. And the farmer. He could be useful if he'd agree to play along."

"Before he'll do anything," said Whaley sourly, "he'll want to talk to his solicitor."

"Why not?" said Morrissey. "They're not all crooks."

"I'm not saying he's a crook. A chap called Pickett. Used to practise up in London."

"You mean old Jonas Pickett."

"You know him?"

"We had one or two encounters in the line of business," said

Morrissey. "He always played straight down the fairway as far as I was concerned."

"If your people know him," said Whaley, "it may make things a bit easier."

Jock Anderson turned out to be a young-looking, pleasant-mannered Scotsman.

He found Mr and Mrs Maggs having tea, and joined them at the table. After eating four of Mrs Maggs's scones with South Down butter, jam and cream on them, he said, "I would imagine you've had a bit of contact with the press lately?"

"Contact! I'll say I've had contact. It's got so I can't hardly poke my nose outside the farm but they're yammering round asking for what they call a statement. Promising me money for it. One of 'em, from a London paper he was, he got into the house through the scullery window. I gave him a statement with the thick end of my walking stick."

"They're a pest," agreed Anderson. "But I wondered if there might be one of them you could talk to. Maybe the lad from the local paper. He wouldn't be so uppity as the others."

"Young Richards," said Maggs thoughtfully. "He's not so brash as the ones from London. I expect I could talk to him. But what's the point of it? I haven't got nothing new to tell him."

"That's just it," said Anderson. "I could suggest something which he'd be glad to print. Let me explain what I've got in mind."

"It seems daft to me," said Maggs. He had driven down to talk to Jonas.

"Let me get this straight," said Jonas. "He wants you to let it out to the local press – preferably accidental like – that you're so fed up with all this fuss that you've decided that the only way to stop it is either to find the abbey treasure, or prove that it isn't there."

"Right."

"And the way you're going to do this is to tell Mr Westall that you've changed your mind. He and his friends can start prospecting right away."

"Not right away. He was very particular about that. It's

Wednesday today. I was to let him start as early as he liked *on Monday morning*, and then go on until he'd covered the whole farm."

"Not until Monday. I see." A glimmering of what was in Jock Anderson's devious mind was beginning to dawn on Jonas. He said, "I suppose that is one way of settling the matter. I'm told he's an expert with this particular apparatus, and if he brings a party of fellow enthusiasts with him, they ought to be able to cover the area fairly quickly. Of course, we'd have to get him to sign up the sort of agreement he was talking about before he started."

"It's not that part of it I mind so much. It's the other bit."

"Let me guess," said Jonas. "You've to let it be known that after, shall we say, Saturday night, the police will no longer be guarding the farm."

"That's right. And I hope it makes more sense to you than what it does to me. What he suggested was that I'd had an argument with the police about paying for their help. They'd wanted to charge me five pounds an hour for having a policeman on duty. And time and a half for the weekend. So I said, if that's the way you feel, you can take 'em away. I'm quite capable of looking after my own fields."

"Plausible," said Jonas, his admiration for Jock Anderson increasing. "And I take it you were to tell the reporter that this was *strictly* confidential, and not for general publication."

"That's right. But you know how it is. People get talking."

"I know just how it is. I admit it seems an odd thing to do, but I've got a feeling that if you co-operate, it could be very helpful."

"Helpful to who?"

"To you and the police."

"Well," said Maggs, with a grin which exposed some ill-cared-for teeth, "if you say so. You've always advised me right up to now. But I'd like you to be handy, just over the weekend, in case I need you in a hurry."

"My dear Mr Maggs," said Jonas, "I wouldn't miss it for the world. I'll be available in my office, or my flat, from Saturday morning onwards."

Saturday passed peacefully. It was seven o'clock on Sunday

evening when Jonas's telephone rang. It was Mr Maggs. He sounded more excited than worried. He said, "Could you come along, Mr Pickett? I'm sure I don't know what's going to happen, but I'd like you to be here when it does happen."

"I'll drive right up," said Jonas.

"Not right up. Arrangements are you leave your car in Joe English's yard. That's about half a mile down the by-road west of my place."

"I know it," said Jonas. "What then?"

"Then you walk. But not along the road. There's a track that goes through the woods, and comes out near my house. Joe'll show you."

It was dusk by the time he reached Maggs's place. The approach route had been carefully chosen. It ran for the most part through woodland and the lie of the land hid it from observation. Maggs had the door open and whisked him inside as soon as he arrived.

He and Mrs Maggs seemed to be alone in the house.

"I saw five cars in Joe's yard," said Jonas. "Where are the men?"

"They've moved off to take up their positions," said Maggs. "All afternoon they've been coming in, quiet-like, by twos and threes. They've got searchlights with them. And rifles. They're expecting trouble, no question."

Mrs Maggs said, "I liked that young Scottie. Very well spoken, he was. You'll take a bite of supper, Mr Pickett, I expect."

"That would be splendid," said Jonas. "I guess we've a long night ahead of us."

"Better comfortable in front of a nice fire," said Maggs, "than squatting in a damp ditch."

It was two o'clock by the illuminated dial on Jock Anderson's watch when the cars arrived. They stopped a long way short of the field, but he was listening for them, and he heard them. Then there was half an hour of silence. "Playing it cautiously," he said to the Sergeant, who was in the ditch beside him. "Afraid there may be a trap, but think they can spring it."

The Sergeant grunted. He suspected that he was catching a cold and was glad that the moment for action had arrived.

"Pass the word to take up action posts, but no lights until I give the signal."

There were five men, and they came across the field in a purposeful bunch; the two on the flanks were carrying shot-guns. Two had spades, and one a measuring line. There was enough light for the watchers to see them at work. A line was laid down from one of the gate-posts in the inner fence, and the digging started.

It was easy going, because it was clear that the earth at that particular spot had already been disturbed. After twenty minutes' spadework a halt was called, and one of the men got into the shallow excavation and stooped to lift what was in it. A second man got in beside him to help. Six boxes had been unearthed and laid on the grass when the lights came on from two corners of the field.

"There are fifteen men here," said Anderson. He had rejected the loudhailer. His voice was clear, and there was a flat undertone of menace in it. "We are armed, and if there is any trouble, our instructions are to shoot. Drop those guns."

When he finished, there was a long moment of complete silence and immobility.

Anderson said, "In case you might be thinking of making a run for it, I should tell you that your cars have already been taken over."

The man standing beside the excavation, who seemed to be the leader, said something. The shotguns were dropped and the police closed in.

Later, Anderson said to Maggs, who had come up in defiance of orders to the contrary, "I think we'd better leave things as they are until it's light. We'll need to take photo-graphs of things as they've been left, and then maybe do a bit more digging."

"It's much too late to go to bed," said Maggs. "So why don't you come in and have a hot cup of tea, with maybe a drop of something in it?"

This seemed to everyone to be an excellent idea. Two men were left on guard, and the rest came down to the farmhouse, where the fire was revived, a kettle put on, and bottles produced.

"Do you think," said Jonas, "that you could now tell us

what it's all about, and what's been dug up? Not, I gather, the abbey treasure."

"May be more valuable than that," said Anderson. "I'm not too sure what the price of gold is today, but those six boxes are crammed with gold bars."

Light began to dawn. Jonas said, "Of course. The Heathrow robbery."

"Lifted from the bullion store fifteen months ago. We were sure it was the Catlins, but we couldn't pin it to them, for there was no trace of the loot. We kept them under surveillance for months after the robbery. They were laughing. They knew they were safe. I'd surmise they came off the motorway, at the junction north of here, drove along until they saw a nice thick hedge, tunnelled through it, and buried the stuff. Lucky for them the bull was in the lower field at the time. Then all they had to do was wait until the heat was off. Only – "

"Only," said Jonas, and the full humour of it was beginning to strike him, "suddenly they read in the papers that the place they've buried it is about to be given a going-over by a gang of amateur treasure-seekers."

"Aye. They had to get it out. That bull stopped them the first time. This time they'd got no option. They may have suspected it was a trap, and they came prepared for trouble."

"So why didn't they put up a fight?"

Anderson thought about it. He said, "That robbery was a brutal job. They crippled three of the security guards. One of them's in hospital still. I expect they thought that if they started anything we'd shoot their legs off."

"And would you have done?"

"That question," said Anderson, in his dominie's voice, "is what you might describe as academic."

At first light they all made their way up to the Top Field. It was whilst the photographs were being taken that the treasure-hunters arrived: a party of four men and two girls, equipped with metal detectors, and led by Mr Westall in person.

He looked with dismay at the open pit and the boxes beside it. He said, "I hope you've been very careful when removing whatever you've found. Old artefacts can so easily be damaged when handled by unskilled persons."

Anderson said to Jonas, "I think you'd better explain it to him, sir."

"I'll try," said Jonas.

It took ten minutes. Five of the treasure-seekers listened to him. One of the girls had wandered off on her own. A police van had been run up on the path between the fields and the last of the bullion was being manhandled on to it when she gave them a hail. She said, "I've never used one of these things before, but it seems to be getting excited."

Attention was switched from the open pit to the place where she was standing at the bottom of the field. The other girl said, "I expect you're using it wrong." Mr Westall walked over, used his own instrument, and said, "No, there's definitely something here."

He had taken pegs from his pocket and was marking out an oblong site. "Perhaps we could borrow those spades?"

The police seemed keener on helping than on giving up the spades, and the amateur treasure-hunters soon became glad of professional assistance. If there was anything there it was buried deep.

From time to time Mr Westall encouraged them by announcing a strengthening of the signals. It was when they were fully four feet down and the lifting of the earth was becoming a real physical effort, that they heard what they had all been waiting for. A spade struck on something that was neither earth nor stone.

Mr Westall jumped into the pit with a flurry of anxious advice. "Hands only, now," he said. "No more spades. We must use hands."

Slowly the object in the pit took shape. They could see that it was a box, perhaps six feet long and two feet wide, formed of stout oak planks bound with strips of iron. The wood had stood up to the passage of time better than the metal which was rusted and fragile.

"Two of you at each end. Lift it very gently. That's it."

The box was laid on the edge of the pit. Mr Westall looked at it proudly. He said, "Really, we shouldn't try to open it here. It ought to be taken to a place where it can be dealt with properly."

He realised, however, that the feeling of the meeting was against him.

"Well, then," he said, "we might just look. But carefully. I beg of you."

The edge of a spade was placed under one of the planks and the top lifted like a lid. Whatever it was inside was covered with several thicknesses of leather. As Mr Westall peeled them off, everyone leaned forward. The police photographers had their cameras focused. What lay in the box was a surprise to all of them.

It was an iron crucifix.

Staring down at it Jonas was aware that he was looking at a miracle, created by a master-craftsman, some forgotten genius of the Middle Ages. The face of the man on the cross was in no way formalised. It was the face of a real person. Or of two persons in one: the divine compassion of the man who had suffered the agonies of crucifixion and had forgiven his tormentors; the strength of the man who had died on the rack rather than reveal where his greatest treasure was hidden.

3

VIVAT REGINA

Mrs Grandfield was standing at the window of her breakfast
room. The sun was shining from the blue sky of a midsummer
day. It was cheering the hearts of the holidaymakers who
crowded into Shackleton-on-Sea during the summer months.
They had been disappointed by the bad weather of the previous
week; and had now hurried to the beach, the parents to doze
in deck-chairs, the children to build sandcastles or waste their
money at the row of stalls which lined the Esplanade.

All these people were happy. Mrs Grandfield was not
happy.

The pleasures of the crowd meant nothing to her. Her
house, Old Priory Lodge, with its ten acres of garden, its
paddock and its meadows, lay nearly a mile from the town on a
little-used side-road. From where she stood she had a bird's-
eye view of her domain. She could hear the puttering as their
gardener-chauffeur, Clegg, drove his motor mower across
their smooth lawn. She could see the well-stocked flowerbeds
and the neat yew hedge at the foot of the lawn. To right and to
left lay her property. Only over the hedge, where the side-road
moved away from the curve of the hill, was an acre of common
land. On it, only too clearly visible, was the cause of her
discontent.

Six gypsy caravans.

To someone less personally involved the sight might have
seemed attractive. They were motor caravans, but their body-
work had been built in the old-fashioned gypsy style with
windows and chimneys and, in two cases, an open balcony at
the back. Some almost naked toddlers were playing a game
which seemed to consist of climbing up and falling off the

front steps of one of the larger caravans. In the background two older boys were tinkering with an ancient motor-car.

"Probably stolen," said Mrs Grandfield.

Charles Grandfield who had come into the room at that moment, said, "What's that, Nora? Stolen? What's been stolen?"

"I was remarking that the car those two gypsy oafs were dismantling had probably been stolen."

"What makes you think that?"

"They're all thieves and liars. A feckless, shiftless crew, they've got no right to be here."

"It's common land, my dear."

"How do they know that? Mr Porter once told me that any unfenced land beside the highway belongs to the corporation. Since you're chairman of the council, doesn't that mean it belongs to you?"

"I'm not quite clear about that," said Mr Grandfield. "But since it seems to worry you I'm going to find out. I'm seeing Porter this morning, and I'm going to have a word with the Chief Superintendent. There may be some local by-law they're infringing."

"I'm sure that Whaley will be helpful if he can. They're like rats. Once you let them in they're all over the place. Two of the older boys spend all their time on the beach handing out deck-chairs to old ladies, who are probably afraid not to tip them. And the old creature who seems to run the gang has a booth on the front and pretends to tell fortunes."

"The Queen of the Gypsies," said Mr Grandfield with a slight smile. "Yes, I have heard about her."

"In the old days she'd have been tried as a witch and burnt at the stake."

"We can't quite do that sort of thing now. But don't worry, you may find that the law has a card or two up its sleeve."

When he reached the police station he found that Chief Superintendent Whaley was away on leave, and he had to deal with Detective Superintendent Queen whom he found to be less immediately co-operative. He sympathised with Mr Grandfield's feelings, but pointed out that until the gypsies broke the law they were hardly a police problem.

"Actually," he said, "they seem to be quiet sort of folk. We haven't had any complaints from people in the town."

"What about those two boys, who wander about on the beach extracting money from people for handing out deck-chairs – which are corporation property, anyway?"

"Oh – you mean Ben and Billy," said Queen. "Do you know, when my wife took the kids down to the beach the other day she was so pleased with the new arrangement that she gave – Billy, I think it was; you can hardly tell them apart – five pence over and above the hire fee."

"For what?"

"For fetching her deck-chair from the store and setting it up where she wanted. And, I rather suspect, for smiling whilst he did it. The old arrangement was that you had to fetch it yourself from that old storekeeper, who looked as if every day was a wet Monday."

"I reckon those two boys are potential dangers."

"Well, we'll keep an eye on them," said Queen. "If they step out of line you can be sure we'll clamp down. But in my view the gypsies are a lot less objectionable than that terrible fun-fair which turns up in August with a merry-go-round and steam whistles and makes the whole place almost unlivable in for a whole month. If you could use your influence on the council to get *them* refused a licence you really would be doing us a good turn. Some of the stall-holders who come with them are very doubtful citizens."

This was a skilful, and successful, effort to divert Mr Grandfield from his immediate grievance. He said, "I know what you mean, but it's not an easy problem. The council's split on it. Agreed the fair's a nuisance, but it brings in a lot of trade, and that makes the commercial lobby on the council support it. However, I'll think about it."

A steam whistle a mile away was a lot less objectionable to Mr Grandfield than gypsy caravans a hundred yards from his dining room window.

Having reached an age when most solicitors would have been considering retirement Jonas Pickett liked to take things easily. His practice in Shackleton had grown considerably during the twelve months he had been there, but he found that he could usually deal with his mail by mid-morning. He then devoted half an hour to coffee and gossip with whichever members of his staff had time to spare. That morning it was his secretary, who seemed to be suffering from a suppressed joke.

She said, "You'll never believe it, but Sam's had his fortune told."

Jonas said, "You mean Sam actually paid a visit to the Gypsy Queen?"

"Paid it, and paid for it. He's a complete convert."

"What did she tell him?"

"She read his past and his future in a milky glass globe. She said that she saw him, in his youth, performing prodigious feats of strength on different fairgrounds."

"Since she has herself been following the same circuit for many years she'd be likely to know about that."

"You mustn't start to sow doubts in Sam's mind. If you do, he won't have faith in her predictions for his future."

"Which were?"

"She said that he is going to be lucky in love."

Jonas guffawed. "What an admirable prediction. It could mean anything. Good technique, though. Let's persuade Sabrina to visit the gypsy's lair."

The fact that he referred to his partner by her first name was an indication that their conversation was informal. In the same way, Claire called Mr Pickett 'Jonas' when they were alone, but 'Mr Pickett' when third parties were present. By such conventions the decencies were preserved.

"If you think she's a fraud," said Claire, "you ought to visit her yourself. Then you could expose her."

"There are several excellent reasons for my not doing so." Jonas ticked off the reasons on his fingers as though Claire was an opponent in court who had put forward a weak argument. "First, I don't think she's a fraud. I think she's a very astute performer. Secondly, if you attempted to assert that the sort of vague predictions she makes rendered her subject to the law you'd have to prosecute all the so-called astrological experts who daily fill the less reputable organs of the press with their nonsense. Thirdly, and finally, I could not, myself, consider taking any action against her since she is my client."

"If she's your client, why don't I know about it?" said Claire indignantly.

"Because it all happened when you were up in London at the end of May. She came to see me, because she wanted to be quite sure, before they moved their caravans on to this particular piece of ground, that they couldn't be turned off it. I wish all my clients were as prudent. Most of them consult me *after* they've done something stupid."

"And they can't be?"

"Not as long as they behave themselves. Old Priory Lodge belonged to Colonel Croxton. It had been in his family for generations. Grandfield was his nephew, or some such relation. He got it because both Croxton's sons were killed in the war. Just before he died the Colonel dedicated this little patch of land by the road to the corporation on condition that they made it available to travellers. I got a copy of the deed from the town clerk. It was drawn up by Croxton's London solicitor, Marcus Apperly. Very competent man. Must be retired or dead by now."

"Then I suppose he was just a bit older than you," said Claire. This was unkind, but she was still ruffled by their earlier exchanges.

"A *lot* older," said Jonas firmly. "He stipulated in the deed that the council should draw up regulations for the use of the site, which he would approve. Provided that campers and other people who used it obeyed the regulations they couldn't be turned away. As a matter of fact, since the corporation set up that camp-site near the sea, with piped water, electricity and all modern conveniences, I gather the Priory Lodge site has been very little used. Mostly by scouts and occasional hikers."

Claire said, "I've never seen it mentioned in any of the publicity handouts. Is there a notice board or something drawing people's attention to it?"

"I don't think there is."

"Then how did the Gypsy Queen know about it?"

"I expect she saw it in her magic globe," said Jonas.

At about this time, Mr Grandfield was getting much the same advice from Mr Porter. Porter and Merriman were the oldest and most respected firm of lawyers in Shackleton and Cedric Porter, son of old Ambrose Porter, was now senior partner. He spoke with a massive authority which belied his comparative youth.

He said, "I have studied the terms and conditions laid down by Colonel Croxton in his deed of dedication. I will not conceal my view that he was ill-advised to leave these conditions as imprecise as they are. To take one point, they impose no actual time limit on the travellers camping there."

"Good God," said Mr Grandfield, "do you mean that those gyppos can put up there permanently?"

"I would suppose that after a period – a considerable period – it would be possible to commence an action to eject them on the grounds that the deed refers to 'travellers' and this would not be an apt description of people who had used the encampment for, say, six months."

"Six months," said Mr Grandfield, "for Christ's sake. My wife will be a raving lunatic long before that. Is there *nothing* we can do?"

"If they break the regulations, or make themselves objectionable in some way, an order for their removal could be made."

"But suppose they behave themselves. That old witch who calls herself the Queen. She's seen a copy of the rules. She got them from Pickett."

"From Jonas Pickett? Indeed."

The way in which Mr Porter said this indicated his opinion of the latest addition to the legal firms in Shackleton.

"The others seem to regard her as their leader. If she tells them they've got to keep the rules, they'll keep them."

"There is another possibility. I do not imagine that these people are particularly wealthy. The offer of a suitable sum of money might induce them to move off somewhere else."

"And come back again a month later and look for another payment."

"Bribery is essentially deplorable and rarely successful," agreed Mr Porter, "but I can think of no other solution at the moment."

Mr Grandfield refrained from comment on this pronouncement. A further possibility had occurred to him, but it was not one he could discuss with his solicitor.

As he left the office he remembered that he had promised to buy his wife a dozen eggs, and he made his way along the crowded main street to the big supermarket which had recently opened up on the corner site. Since Mr Grandfield had only the one purchase to make he ignored the trolleys and made his way straight to the grocery counter, where he picked up two cardboard cartons, each containing, according to the label, six eggs, new laid, large size. One of the cartons seemed to be coming apart so he placed it very carefully on top of the other and turned to make his way back to the entrance.

As he did so two trolleys whizzed past him abreast of each other, one of them nearly running over his foot. He recognised the youths who were propelling them. One was Ben and the other was Billy. Both were grinning.

"Watch where you're going," he growled.

"Sorry, guvnor," said Ben. "But it's those outsize feet of yours."

"If we'd known you was here," said Billy, "we'd have had the floor cleared."

An assistant walked up to see what was going on.

"I advise you," said Mr Grandfield loudly, "to keep a close eye on this couple, and to check their purchases very carefully."

Claire, who was shopping on the other side of the counter said, equally loudly, "And I should advise you to take no notice of such a slanderous and uncalled-for statement. As a senior councillor I should have thought you'd have known better."

Mr Grandfield had been turning gradually redder. Now he lost his temper entirely. He said, the words frothing as they came out, "I suppose you're angling for work. Well let me tell you that if you or your shyster employer choose to start proceedings against me for slander you may find you've bitten off more than you can chew."

He turned on his heel and made for the door, forgetting, in his fury, that he had to pay for the eggs. The young lady on the pay desk shouted after him, "Excuse me."

Mr Grandfield swung round, slipped on the polished floor and came down with a crash. The fragile egg-box disintegrated.

*　　*　　*

"It was a splendid sight," said Claire. "Eggs everywhere and people rushing up, some to help, but mostly to stare. It was like a bun fight in a Salvation Army hostel."

On her return to the office she had found Jonas and Sabrina arguing about a Bill of Sale. They suspended the argument and listened with interest.

"He's a silly little man," said Mrs Mountjoy.

"He's more than silly," said Claire. "He's vicious. Do you realise he actually accused Mr Pickett of being a shyster?"

"Did he, though?"

"In front of a dozen witnesses."

"You could found an open and shut action for slander on that, Jonas."

"No," said Jonas firmly. "I've spent thirty-five years keeping my clients out of court. I don't intend walking in there myself."

"Billy and Ben weren't helping matters. They both joined the scrum round the fallen hero, and managed to break the other box of eggs."

"That wasn't wise," said Jonas. "And I hope the Queen tells them so. She's a remarkable woman. You ought to go and see her, Sabrina."

"I have," said Mrs Mountjoy. "I was so impressed by Sam's account that I went down first thing this morning. You have to get in early these days to get a session. There's usually a queue."

Claire said, "Most of them just come to look at the blackboard."

"Blackboard?" said Jonas.

"She's got one outside the booth. Every morning she chalks up a Message from the Stars for Today. Sometimes it's just general stuff. Politics or the stock exchange or what the weather's going to do. But she had a real scoop when she gave them the winner of the Derby. Everyone's been following her tips since then."

"She did that?"

"Well, more or less. Her message was 'You'll need dark glasses to look at the Derby winner'. Which, you remember, turned out to be Sunshine. Good odds. Third favourite. Twelve to one."

"I seem to remember," said Jonas, "that the favourite was Searchlight and the second favourite was Arc Light."

"You mustn't be cynical about her," said Mrs Mountjoy. "Some of these old women have got a real gift. Insight or foresight, I don't know which. You ought to consult her yourself."

"You haven't told us yet what she predicted for you."

"She didn't actually predict anything, but we had a very interesting talk. She really is a remarkable person. In any classification of humanity I'd put her several classes ahead of Mrs Grandfield."

"You mean she's a lady?"

"That's an old-fashioned description. But, yes, I think so. She's got all the gypsy patter and slang, but occasionally, when she forgot to act, I thought there were signs of a good education somewhere in the background. Do you remember Matthew Arnold's poem – the one about the scholar gypsy?"

"Vaguely," said Jonas. "Was that the one about the student who got fed up with Oxford and decided to spend the rest of his life studying gypsy lore and living with them?"

"Right – and I shouldn't be at all surprised if that isn't what this old girl did. If she's in her fifties now and really has been with them for twenty or thirty years she must have been quite young when she – I don't know quite how to describe it – "

"Dropped out."

"No. Drop-outs are negative characters. She struck me as a thoroughly positive person. She told me about the other members of her little tribe. Three complete families. An older pair, with no children. A father and mother with a lot of kids, and a widow with the two boys, Ben and Billy."

"Is the old girl related to them?"

"She was a bit uncommunicative about that. But there's no doubt she's the boss."

"The Queen."

"In view of certain recent developments," said Mrs Mountjoy drily, "it might be more appropriate to describe her as the Prime Minister."

The plan, which had been at the back of Mr Grandfield's mind when he left Mr Porter's office, was simple if old-fashioned.

When you can't buy someone off, scare them off. The humiliating scene in the supermarket had stiffened his purpose. And he had the right person for the job. Clegg, in the course of a varied career, had been, so far as anyone knew, a soldier in the Commandos and a chucker-out in a night-club. He had also, quite possibly, had a number of less reputable jobs. Mr Grandfield had never enquired. Old Priory Lodge was an isolated property, and it suited him to have a man who could look after it and be responsible for its security. He and his wife liked to go to bed early. Clegg had a room on the ground floor at the back of the house and attended to the locking up.

When he got home Mr Grandfield explained to Clegg what he wanted.

"Throw a scare into them?" said Clegg. "Yes, I guess I could do that. They're none of them much more than a shilling in the pound. I'll walk down now."

The only person visible in the gypsy encampment when Clegg got there was Billy. He was sitting on one step of the caravan he shared with Ben, reading a copy of the local newspaper. He looked up as Clegg approached, grinned, and said, "I see the price of eggs is going up."

Clegg moved up until he was within easy reach of Ben, and said, "I've got a message for you and the rest of your crowd."

"I'll pass it on," said Ben.

"It's very simple: get out before you get into real trouble."

"What sort of trouble might you have in mind?" said Ben.

"These caravans of yours. They'd make a nice bonfire, wouldn't they? Suppose someone happened to be careless one night, with a tin of petrol and a match?"

"I've heard of that sort of thing happening," said Ben. "Nasty dangerous stuff, petrol."

"Next point," said Clegg, moving in even closer. "I've got friends round here. Fishermen, some of them. Rough types. You know. They might feel that you lot needed a lesson."

"A lesson in what? Manners?"

"This sort of lesson," said Clegg. He swung with his right. It was a quick vicious blow, but it met only the air.

Ben had slipped off the steps on the far side. Now he moved out into the open. "Talk about lessons," he said. "Someone ought to give you a lesson in boxing, Granpa. When you're going to hit someone you don't want to send them a postcard telling them you're going to do it."

Clegg lumbered out after him. He recognised that Ben was much lighter on his feet than he was, but he hadn't half his weight or muscle. All he needed to do was to get his hands on him. The best tactics would be to provoke him. He said, "All right, my boy. Stop running away, let's see if you can hit."

Ben came dancing towards him. Clegg took a step back to give himself distance. It was a mistake. Billy had come up quietly behind him and was crouched on the ground. Clegg fell over him and landed flat on his back.

Before he could get up Billy had grabbed his hair, pulling his head back and Ben had landed on his stomach with a thump that drove all the breath out of him. He now had a knife in his right hand, and the point of it was resting on Clegg's exposed throat.

"Well," said Billy. "When does the lesson start?"

Clegg said nothing.

"Come along," said Ben. "We haven't got all day."

"Let him up," said the Queen.

Billy let go of Clegg's hair and Ben removed himself. Clegg scrambled to his feet. He said, "It's lucky you turned up, lady. If that boy had touched me with his knife he'd have been in bad trouble; as it is I could have him for assault."

"Stop talking nonsense," said the Queen. The tone of command was so compelling that Clegg, who had opened his mouth to speak, shut it again.

"You made a threat. I heard it. A threat of arson. That's an indictable offence. I expect your master sent you to do it. Now get back to him and give him this message. If he wants trouble, he can have it. But we shan't start it. You understand? All right. Off you go."

Clegg felt that he must assert himself, but could think of nothing to do or say. He turned on his heel and stalked off.

Ben and Billy looked serious. Ben said, "What do you think he's going to do now?"

"What a silly question," said the Queen. "We can't possibly tell what he's going to do. On the other hand, we can make our own plans. I've had an idea."

As she explained her idea Ben and Billy stopped looking serious and started to grin.

Billy said, "That'll tickle him up."

"Something has got to be done about it," said Mr Grandfield. "I won't tolerate it. I'm being made a public laughing-stock."

"I don't quite understand," said Mr Porter cautiously. "What blackboard are you talking about?"

"If you don't know about it" – Mr Grandfield was starting to get cross – "you must be the only person in Shackleton who doesn't. This person – this person, who calls herself the Gypsy Queen has got a blackboard outside her booth on the front. She chalks up some nonsense every day. The Voice of the Stars."

"A lot of newspapers – " began Mr Porter.

"I know, I know. To start with it was harmless nonsense. It was an advertising stunt. It attracted customers. Now it's not harmless at all. She's using it to pillory *me*."

"In what way?"

"When I heard about it I got my gardener to go down there. He copied down the last two or three. Apparently it's been going on all week."

"Have you got them there?"

Mr Grandfield produced some pieces of paper and Mr Porter studied the pronouncements from the stars. Each one started in the same way. 'Big Chief Great Meadow he say – ' followed by a short message. The first was 'Pride Cometh Before Fall.' The second, 'Who Walketh Softly does not Trip.' The third, 'Egg on Face Causes Ridicule.' Legal training enabled young Mr Porter to remain serious. He said, "The first two – er – texts appear to be generally accepted axioms. The third one, I confess, I don't entirely understand."

Mr Grandfield said, "They all relate to an unfortunate incident in one of the shops. I had bought some eggs, and tripped and fell as I was carrying them to the door."

"I see." Mr Porter re-studied the messages. "And you think they refer to you?"

"Of course they do. Big Meadow. Grand Field. It's perfectly obvious. People were sniggering about it at the Rotary Club yesterday. It's – it's slanderous. You've got to stop it."

"It's a difficult problem. To start with, since the words are written, they would constitute a libel, not a slander. And it is true that the definition of libel is an untrue statement which causes hatred, ridicule or contempt."

"Ridicule – exactly."

"But which of these statements would you say was untrue?"

Mr Grandfield stared blankly at the paper. In the end he said, without attempting to conceal the fury in his voice, "Are you really telling me that there's nothing I can do about this?"

"You could report it to the police, I suppose. But I hardly see what they could do."

"Thank you – for nothing," said Mr Grandfield and stormed out. In his hurry he left the papers behind him. As Mr Porter read them again he allowed himself a single cautious smile.

On Wednesday at nine o'clock in the morning, the station Sergeant came into Chief Superintendent Whaley's office and said, "It's Mr Grandfield, sir. Wants a word with you."

Whaley groaned. He had been talked at by Mr Grandfield on the Monday and telephoned twice on the Tuesday. Personally he liked and approved of the chairman of the council, but his patience was being tried. He said, "I suppose it's those damned gypsies."

"I understand it's something more serious this time, sir. There's been a robbery."

"A robbery." Whaley felt more cheerful. This was something he could deal with.

"When and where?"

"Last night, sir. At Old Priory Lodge. Superintendent Queen has already gone out there to take charge."

"Show Mr Grandfield in."

Mr Grandfield said, "I knew something like this would happen." Like the Chief Superintendent, he sounded almost glad that matters had been brought out into the open. "They've gone too far this time."

"Have you any reason to suppose that it was the gypsies who did this?"

"Of course it was the gypsies. It was a grudge job. They took the only things I really minded losing. The Croxton silver. A tray, two salvers, a loving cup, two cream jugs, a set of forks and spoons. All marked with the Croxton cypher. There was a lot of other silver, but it hadn't been touched. If it wasn't done out of spite why should a thief take the marked silver, and leave the unmarked stuff?"

"That's certainly odd," said Whaley. "Very odd. Leave it with us."

That afternoon he discussed it with Superintendent Queen.

"It was a simple job," said Queen. "A pane of glass cut out of the dining-room window, which opened on a catch. The silver was in an unlocked cupboard in the sideboard. People who keep valuable stuff like that really deserve to have it stolen."

"I believe they had great confidence in that man of theirs. Clegg. Did he hear nothing?"

"He seems to have slept through it. Not that there would have been a great deal of noise."

"No prints?"

"Only the ones you'd expect."

Both men thought about it.

"It's plain to see what's in Mr Grandfield's mind," said Queen. "There's no love lost between him and the gypsies. They were on the spot. They *could* have done it."

Whaley said, "The only real indication that it was them and not a bunch of professionals from Brighton or Portsmouth is that they took the marked silver and left the unmarked. Professionals would never have done that."

"There is one thing more. We've had a communication. Someone must have pushed it through the letter-box very early this morning. It was here when we arrived."

The message was written in pencil in block capitals. It said, 'THE SILVER IS AT THE BACK OF THE GYPSY'S STALL.'

"I suppose it means that stall she tells fortunes from."

"I imagine so." Queen said it without enthusiasm. In the course of his career he had received many anonymous letters. Most of them had led to nothing but trouble. He said, "Hardly enough to justify a search warrant."

"I'm afraid you're right," said Whaley. "Yes, what do you want?"

It was the station Sergeant. He said, "I thought you ought

63

to see this entry, sir." He had the Station Incidents Book in his hand. "Constable Seddon put this in when he came off duty this morning."

Whaley looked at the book. It was a volume in which officers recorded all matters, important or unimportant, which came to their attention during the course of their duty. It was an innocent-looking book, which had caught and convicted an uncommon number of criminals.

Whaley read the entry and said, "I'd better hear it from Seddon himself. He should be back at the station by now."

Constable Seddon was a middle-aged man, running a little to fat, happy in his work and devoid of ambition. He said, "It was when I was patrolling the Marine Parade. The bit that runs along behind all those little shops and booths. It was pretty dark, but about halfway down, on the left, I thought I saw someone climbing over the railing. I shouted to him to stop, and he took to his heels."

"Him? It was a man?"

"Yes, sir. I'm sure it was a man. But that's about all I could see. I'm afraid" – Seddon smiled self-deprecatingly – "that he was a lot faster than I am. When I got to the end of the passage I could just see him pedalling off on his bicycle. Up the road. The one that goes past the golf club."

"And past Old Priory Lodge," said Whaley.

"That's right, sir."

After Seddon had gone, Whaley said, "If we're going to act at all we'll have to act quickly. If one of those boys lifted the silver and deposited it in the old girl's back room you can bet it isn't going to stay there long."

Queen nodded agreement. He said, "We'll need a warrant."

Whaley considered the three magistrates who made up the Shackleton bench. Colonel Rattray was chairman. He was a bit of a stickler for forms and precedents. Mrs Crossman had recently been appointed and was an unknown quantity. He said, "Laurence Deickman's our best bet. Apply to him. And if he gives you the warrant we'll execute it at once."

At six o'clock that evening two detectives called on the Queen. She had just dealt with her last customer and was locking away the black cloth and the white globe with its carved stand in a cupboard at the back of the room.

When they showed her the search warrant she stood quite still. Her eyes, a piercing blue in her sunbrowned face, were fixed more on the men than on the paper they held. When she said nothing they shifted uncomfortably. One of them said, "You understand, lady, just doing our duty."

She said, "I understand perfectly. Of course you may search where you like. There's only this cupboard in here. It's unlocked. And nothing in the back room but two old tables and some empty cardboard boxes."

The Croxton silver was in a sack, under a pile of cardboard boxes.

At about half past seven Sam Conybeare, answering the bell, discovered two distraught boys on the doorstep. He listened to them, blocking the door with his massive body. He said, "Mr Pickett's in his flat upstairs. He's changing to go out to dinner. He could see you tomorrow."

"You don't understand," said Ben. "They've taken her away. They're locking her up."

Sam could feel the anguish in the boy's voice. He said, at last, "All right. You can come up. One of you. The other stays here."

Jonas listened to what Ben had to say, cancelled without much regret a dinner date with Ronald Sykes and walked round to the police station.

Queen seemed to be expecting him. He said, "Certainly you can see your client if you want. She's made no statement of any sort. She's been charged with receiving stolen goods and will appear in front of the magistrate tomorrow."

"Are you opposing bail?"

"Normally, of course, we should. Receiving's a serious offence. In this case we've decided not to. We don't think she'll run away, and if she does, she won't get far."

"And if she does," said Jonas to himself, "it'll be a convenient admission of guilt." Aloud he said, "I shall certainly advise her not to do anything so stupid."

He found the Queen in one of the cells below the police station. She was examining her bed critically. She said, "I've slept on harder places than this. I suppose I'll manage. I'd welcome one more blanket."

No extravagant denials of guilt. No protests. Jonas wondered how much it would take to disturb the serenity of this remarkable woman.

He said, "You're charged with receiving stolen goods, knowing them to have been stolen. It's the second bit that's important. I take it you'll plead not guilty."

"I certainly had no idea the silver was there. Anyone could open the back door of my place. It has a lock of sorts but a child could fiddle it. I never worried. There was nothing in the place anyone would want to steal."

"All right," said Jonas. "I won't bother you any more tonight. The police say they won't oppose bail, so you can come and talk to me about it as soon as they let you out."

But the talk they had on the following morning took them very little further. The Queen persisted in her placid denial that she knew anything about the silver. Jonas said, "We'll fight this at the committal, and try to persuade the bench that there's no case to answer. It's their job to prove that you knew the stuff was there, not yours to prove you didn't."

"I'm sure you'll do your best."

"You realise that the strongest card in their hand would be if you ran away."

"I'm too old to run," said the Queen.

When she had gone Jonas summoned a council of war. He said, "I'm convinced the police have got some card up their sleeve. If they'd nothing to go on but guesswork they'd never have got a search warrant. Someone saw something that night. If we can find out and latch on to it, we might be able to cast enough doubt on the case to get it thrown out. I don't know quite how we're going to set about it."

"I can tell you one thing," said Sam, who had attached himself to the conference. "You'll get a lot of help. Nobody likes the Grandfields, and the idea's already beginning to get about that it was a put-up job. I met Clegg twenty years ago on the south coast circuit. No one trusted him and I think he's got some form."

"Proving that Clegg's been to prison isn't going to help the Queen. Clegg isn't on trial. What we want is an independent witness. Search round, all of you, and see what you can rake up."

Three weeks later, on the eve of the hearing, he was forced to admit to the Queen that he'd achieved nothing. He said, "I'll do what I can for you in the Magistrate's Court, but I'm afraid it'll go up to the Crown Court. I'd better brief counsel for that."

It was at this moment that Claire put her head round the door and said, "I apologise for interrupting, but there are two young men who say they must see you at once. They're very pressing. I doubt if I can keep them out."

"Then let them in," said Jonas. He had a shrewd idea who they would be.

Ben and Billy marched in resolutely. They stood in front of Jonas's desk like two boys in the headmaster's study. They avoided the Queen's eye.

Ben was the spokesman. He said, "We've decided to come clean. Billy and me. We took that silver. We dumped it at the back of her place, just to get it under cover. She'd no idea it was there. Next night we were going to take it on to Brighton and get rid of it."

"How?" said Jonas.

Ben seemed disconcerted for a moment. Then he said, "We know people there who handle that sort of thing."

"I see," said Jonas. There was a fairly long silence, whilst the two boys fidgeted. Then he said, "All right, go along with my secretary, dictate a full statement to her, and sign it. I'll see that it gets in front of the bench tomorrow. It'll be the end of the case against your Queen. But it'll be the start of a very serious matter for you. You understand me?"

Ben and Billy nodded.

When they had followed Claire out he said to the Queen, "Do you believe that?"

"Not a word of it."

"If they go on with this, it's going to mean bad trouble for them. You realise that?"

"What a pair!" said the Queen. She gave a throaty chuckle. "And they're doing it for simple love of me. Tell me, Mr Pickett, if you found anyone who was prepared to do that for you, wouldn't you consider that your life hadn't been entirely wasted?"

Jonas said, "You might be right about that. But – "

"Of course, I shan't let them do it."

"How are you going to stop them?"

"I shall tell them I don't need them. I've got a very good defence without them. If you'd got me clear away at the Magistrate's Court I shouldn't have used it. If I'd been sent on for trial at the Crown Court, I suppose I should have had to. Now I'm afraid we'll have to use it at once."

She spoke for ten minutes while the expression on Jonas's face turned from surprise to incredulity and from incredulity to comprehension.

As soon as the Queen had departed Jonas summoned Sabrina. She was not a woman who smiled often, but when she understood what Jonas was saying there was an expression on her face which, in a younger woman, might have been described as a grin. She said, "By God, if only we can prove it."

"There's a time element in this," said Jonas. "I don't want to ask for an adjournment, but it only gives me one day to locate our witness and persuade him to give evidence. I shall have to start the search in London, and I'm going up at once. If I'm not back by the time court opens you'll have to hold the fort. You can spend a bit of time cross-examining Mr Grandfield."

"Yes, indeed," said Sabrina.

"Now, Mr Grandfield," said Mrs Mountjoy, "I'd like to ask you a few questions about the subject matter of this charge."

"About the silver? I thought I'd described it fully. I could do it again if you like."

"Not a description. I was interested, at the moment, in establishing your title to it."

"I'm not sure that I understand."

"The charge here is one of receiving stolen goods. The stealing is alleged to have been a theft of *your* property. I was therefore starting from the beginning, and establishing that it *was* your property that was taken."

"Are you suggesting that I stole it?"

"I am not suggesting anything," said Mrs Mountjoy, "and we should get on more quickly if you refrained from flippancy."

Mr Grandfield looked at the bench to see if they were going to support him. The chairman said, "I think this line of questioning is legitimate, although I cannot, at the moment, see where it is going to take us."

Mr Grandfield said, "Then I'll answer the question. The silver is a collection known as the Croxton silver. I inherited it, some twenty-five years ago, from my uncle, Colonel Croxton."

"When you say that you inherited it" – Mrs Mountjoy was studying a document – "is that strictly accurate? I have here a copy of Colonel Croxton's will. It does not, in fact, mention you at all."

The reporters looked interested, the magistrate looked up, and the frown on Mr Grandfield's face deepened. He said, "Need we go into all this?"

"Now that the point has been raised," said the chairman, "it might be as well to settle it."

The audience was with him. They scented the possibility of a family scandal. It was known that the old Colonel had loathed his young nephew.

"Oh, very well," said Mr Grandfield crossly. "There was no need to mention me by name in the will, because the property was entailed. It came to me as the nearest male descendant. That was after both the Colonel's sons had been killed in Burma."

"But the entail would only have covered real property, wouldn't it? And I see that the personal effects – that would include the silver – were left specifically to his niece Clarissa."

"Yes."

"Then how did they come into your possession?"

"Clarissa had gone abroad a short time before the Colonel died. No one knew what had happened to her. After seven years I, and everyone else, assumed that she must have died abroad."

"And the silver went to you as next of kin?" Mrs Mountjoy had dragged out her questions to the best of her ability, with one eye on her watch. A telephone call from London, received just before the court opened, had informed her that Jonas would be back by eleven o'clock – it was now nearly half past.

The chairman started to say, "That would surely – " but

was interrupted by the arrival of Jonas, followed by a spry, white-haired old gentleman.

Jonas said, "I must apologise to the court for not being present at the commencement of these proceedings, but I had the most urgent business in London. If you have no objection I will continue the cross-examination of this witness myself."

"That's entirely up to you," said the chairman. He was looking at the old gentleman, who had seated himself at the end of the solicitor's bench. He had a feeling that he had met him before but was unable to place him. Mr Grandfield clearly knew him. He had not taken his eyes off him since he had come into court.

"In fact," said Jonas, "I have only one more question to ask the witness. Mr Grandfield, do you, or do you not, recognise the lady in the dock?"

"Recognise – " said Mr Grandfield. "I – can't – "

At this point his voice seemed to stick.

"Come along, Charles," said the Queen briskly. "I know it's nearly thirty years, but I haven't changed all that much, surely?"

Mr Grandfield opened and shut his mouth, but still no sound came out.

The chairman said, with admirable self-restraint, "Do I understand, Mr Pickett, that you are in a position to prove the identity of the prisoner?"

"If I might call my witness."

Mr Grandfield seemed thankful to leave the box. The white-haired old gentleman took his place, recited the oath with practised briskness, and said, "My name is Marcus Apperly. I was, until five years ago, the senior partner in the firm of Apperly and Hulbert. We acted for Colonel Croxton. I drew up his will and was well acquainted with his family, or with such of them as were left after the war. In particular his nephew Charles Grandfield, and his niece" – he shot a quick glance at the Queen who smiled encouragingly – "Clarissa Oldshaw."

"And you recognise her?"

"Certainly. And even if I was not in a position to identify her, I have been shown papers which are, I think, quite conclusive. I'll be happy to produce them to you, sir, in due course. I should like to add that, in addition to making his will, the Colonel asked me to draw up the deed by which he dedicated an acre of his land to travellers. He had already heard that his favourite niece had some romantic intention of joining the gypsies, and I think he hoped that, if she did so, some time, maybe long after his death, her caravan might come to rest on one of his fields."

There was a long silence. No one seemed to know what to say next. In the end Jonas said, "I take it, sir, you would agree that if we can produce proper evidence of this, there is no question that the charge can stand."

"I would entirely agree," said the chairman, "that no one can be convicted of receiving stolen goods when they turn out to be their own property."

Late that afternoon Jonas and Mrs Mountjoy sat in conference with Mr Apperly and the Queen, now to be known as Clarissa Oldshaw.

Mr Apperly said, "I've had a word with Grandfield's solicitor, Cedric Porter. He's a pompous young ass, but he fully appreciates the position his client is in. If they'd gone to the court for a formal presumption of Clarissa's death we might have had to go back to get it reversed. As they didn't, there's no need. The furniture, the pictures and the silver will have to be handed over to Miss Oldshaw."

"Not a lot of room for them in my caravan," said Clarissa.

"I'll be happy to arrange their sale. One of the pictures is a small, but unquestionable Stubbs and two of the equestrian pictures are Herrings. They are in fashion at the moment and will realise a lot of money. It should be quite sufficient to enable you to buy a house and be comfortably off for the rest of your life."

Clarissa considered it. Extraordinary eyes, thought Jonas. An uncanny, piercing blue, like sword-blades.

"All right," she said. "Sell the lot. Except the loving cup. I'll keep that. I'll turn respectable and settle down in East-bourne, among all the pussies."

"It will be a change after your previous existence."

"Don't talk about it as though it was an ordeal, Marcus. I wouldn't have missed it for the world. I've learned to speak

Polski, Romany and Basque. And the people I've met – you've no idea. I'd write a book about them, only no one would believe it."

"Maybe," said Mr Apperly severely. "I still think it was imprudent. However, there's one other point. I hear that Clegg has disappeared. Which is fair proof that what we thought was true. He did plant the silver in your place. Maybe the Grandfields put him up to it. Maybe they didn't. But in any event you clearly have a case against *them*. They brought a criminal charge against you, which turns out to be unfounded, and had you taken into custody. I imagine they'd be glad to pay handsomely to have it settled out of court."

"No," said Clarissa. "No. It's not worth bothering about." She was staring out of the window. "They'll both be dead inside the year."

It was, in fact, almost exactly a year later that the Grandfields were killed in a crash on the Portsmouth motorway; a combination of a lorry with inefficient brakes and an icy road. When Miss Mountjoy showed the newspaper report to Jonas she said, "I warned you not to be cynical."

4

THE REIGN OF TERROR

Jonas was sitting on a bench at the end of the pier watching the seagulls.

He was not, as he was fond of explaining to his friends, a retired solicitor. He was a retreating solicitor. Having made as much money as a bachelor of modest habits was likely to use in the rest of his lifetime, but not wishing to rust in idleness, he had abandoned a successful practice in north London and set up a modest office in Shackleton-on-Sea.

The trouble was that it was becoming too damn successful. He was beginning to turn away new clients. And human nature dictated that the more clients he turned away, the more flocked to consult him.

He had been firm on one point. On a lovely summer's morning he was not going to kick his heels behind his elegant office desk. After some argument he had compromised with Claire, and had agreed to carry with him a horrid little gadget called a radio-pager.

Claire had devised a code.

One bleep meant come back before lunch, there are papers to sign. Two meant an unexpected client. Three was an emergency.

"And I mean a real emergency," said Jonas. "Like the office burning down. Not that a mouse has appeared in the muniments room, or Sam has brained some over-persistent salesman."

The second contingency was the more likely. Sam had a short-fused temper which he vented from time to time on everyone except Jonas, who now abandoned his inspection of the seagulls and examined the pier. It was a palatial structure, a bit out of scale with the rest of the town. All right at Brighton, thought Jonas. But they could have done with something a bit more modest in Shackleton. It had a concert hall for the pierrots who came each summer and an amusement arcade with a miniature roundabout for young children and a ghost train for children of all ages. Also rows of space-age games and a few elderly slot-machines which had fascinated Jonas when he discovered them.

Originally they had been operated by the insertion of a penny. Nowadays you had to buy a metal disc which cost you five pence. When this was inserted exciting things happened. Gravestones rose in churchyards, bats flitted round belfries and skeletons emerged from the cupboards in a haunted house. One of the most popular was the Reign of Terror. In this a guillotine descended on the neck of an aristocrat and old women waved knitting needles in ecstasy.

Worth all the space-age games put together, thought Jonas.

The amusement arcade was open from two o'clock in the afternoon until nine o'clock in the evening, from May to October. A compromise to suit the permanent inhabitants of Shackleton, many of them elderly, who considered that the pier was a place for walking, fishing and thinking about life. They pointed out that they had to put up, in August, with Bailey's Circus on the Lammas. Four weeks of pandemonium. Enough was enough.

Jonas agreed. He disliked disturbances of any sort, human or mechanical.

His radio-pager gave two bleeps.

He said, "Blast," got up and started back through the crowd which was beginning to thicken. A squat man with a squint snapped a camera at him and said, "Fifty pence for a lovely picture to put on your mantelpiece."

Jonas said, "Take that damn thing away."

The man grinned. "No offence, Granpa. I thought the kids might like a picture of the old man."

Jonas ignored this impertinence and pushed his way out into the street.

At the office he found two men, both of whom he knew. He had helped Farmer Maggs when there was trouble over his bull, Black Bob. With him was Mike Landless, proprietor of the South Wind Restaurant.

"I told Mike you looked after me all right," said Maggs. "So when Mike had this bit of bother I thought I'd bring him along and inter-jooce him."

"No introduction necessary," said Jonas. "I've eaten a lot of good dinners cooked by Mr Landless."

The South Wind was in the street behind his office.

"Nice of you to say so," said Landless, who was a tubby middle-aged Londoner. "I hope we can keep it up. Perhaps I'd better explain. It's not only me, there's a lot of us in it, almost all the main restaurants and hotels in the town."

Jonas had some idea of what was coming. He had heard the stories that were beginning to circulate.

Landless said, "It's these people from FSP who've been going round."

"Food Sales Promotion? Headquarters in Brighton?"

"That's the crowd. Their reps have been calling on us. They know that most of us buy our supplies locally. I get a lot from Mr Maggs here. New potatoes and mushrooms and asparagus and raspberries and strawberries and such. The idea was, would I switch all my orders to World Wide Suppliers? I told him, thank you very much, but I was well suited. That was when he got a bit nasty."

"Nasty?"

"Perhaps that's the wrong word. But implying that I'd better think again. What he actually said was that it might be *safer* to deal with his clients, who were a large outfit, rather than relying on buying here and there from farmers who might let you down. He sort of underlined that word, *safer*. The way he said it, I thought he was repeating something that he'd been taught to say. In fact, I got the impression he wasn't a hundred per cent happy about it himself."

"I suppose you'd heard about what happened in Brighton last summer."

They had both of them heard.

There had been the Fooderie and Hamburger Palace which had turned down the approach of FSP. The health authorities had made a lightning raid and discovered a swarm of black beetles in a foodstore which they swore had been kept as clean as a new pin. There had been Gino Ferrari's Fish Restaurant on the front. Coming down to open up one morning Gino had found the dining room almost knee-deep in offal from the Fish Cleaning Station.

"A few dead rats for good measure," said Landless. "It mightn't have been so bad if they could have cleared it up, but someone seems to have taken a picture and sent it to the papers. I saw it myself. Nasty."

"And what happened?"

"Seeing as how they had no further trouble I guess they took the hint and decided to buy everything from World Wide. They were fortunate in a way. Their customers were mostly day trippers and such who wouldn't have heard the stories. They've survived. Same with the Fooderie. The Frenchman wasn't so lucky."

Jonas had heard about Monsieur Laurenceau. He had an upmarket French-style bistro and had built up an exclusive and faithful clientèle. Then had come that disastrous attack of food poisoning. Some of the victims had been very ill indeed. One old lady had nearly died.

"He couldn't take it," said Landless. "It was that old girl nearly croaking that finished him. He packed it up altogether."

"So having got Brighton under control last summer I suppose they're now extending the campaign."

"Here and in Eastbourne."

"Is there anything we can do?" said Maggs. "It's hitting us all."

"Not easy," said Jonas. "What it comes closest to is demanding money with menaces. But they're not asking for money, or not directly. And from what you tell me the menaces are fairly indirect, too. It seems to me that the real answer is to organise. If all the restaurants and all the hotels combined and said 'No', you'd hold them off."

Maggs and Landless looked at each other. Maggs said, "Aneurin Williams," and sighed.

Landless said, "That's right," but he said it without much enthusiasm.

Jonas knew about Aneurin Williams.

He was the proprietor of the Everdene Hotel, one of the largest in Shackleton. He was a Welshman and a reformer. He appeared to have a good deal of time to spare from running his hotel. He devoted it to crusading.

There had been the no-sport-on-Sundays crusade, which had been unpopular. The clean-up-the-cinemas crusade, which had had some support from the parents of young children and the keep-the-traffic-away-from-the-High-Street crusade which had been, as his critics pointed out, not entirely unselfish since the one-way system which he had proposed would have favoured his own hotel at the expense of his rivals. This had been stamped on by the police and had led to a clean-up-the police-force crusade.

"He's not the man to take something like this lying down," said Landless.

"Got busy already, has he?"

"We've had circulars from him, farmers and all. I brought one to show you."

It was stirring stuff. Resist blackmail and intimidation. Englishmen won't stand for bullying. Don't listen to them, give them the toe of your boot.

At the foot there was an invitation (more a summons than an invitation, thought Jonas) to turn up for a mass meeting outside the Town Hall.

"This Saturday," said Jonas. "I take it you'll be going."

"It should be quite a performance. You've got to hand it to him, he's a rousing speaker."

"All Welshmen have got the gift of the gab," said Maggs.

Jonas thought he might go along himself. Aneurin Williams in full spate could be worth listening to. He said, "Okay. You've got your leader. Now all you have to do is stand behind him."

Tea was a sociable gathering, normally held in Jonas's room. Claire poured out. Sabrina came in from her room, protesting regularly that she had no time to waste. If there was any excitement in the offing, Sam came up from the basement to join in the fun. Jonas passed on to them what Maggs and Landless had told him.

"I've looked at the dates of the three incidents," he said, "and I noticed that the trouble at the French restaurant was a fortnight *before* the others. I don't know a lot about food poisoning, but it did seem to me that it would have been very difficult to get hold of the bacillus and introduce it into the food that Madame Laurenceau was cooking. I wondered whether FSP might have seen that the food poisoning was a good starting point for a campaign and built on it."

"If that's right," said Sabrina, "isn't it equally possible that the black beetles really were in the Fooderie store? I don't trust these quick-service places."

"The offal didn't arrive of its own accord in that fish restaurant."

"Might have been a crowd of boys who had a grudge against the proprietor."

"No," said Claire. "It's a regular campaign. Those weren't the only three incidents. The others weren't quite so dramatic, that's all. Customers getting up and shouting the odds about dirty plates, people refusing to eat what was put in front of them and throwing it on the floor. It doesn't take much to give a restaurant a bad name."

"It's happening, all right," agreed Sam. "And I know who's doing it. Louie the Nose and his boys. Mostly they work on the racecourse. Did you hear about that jockey that doubled on them? Broke both his legs and dumped him in the stall with this horse. Then threw stones at the horse till he got really wild and finished the jock off. Crafty, you see. When they found the body they thought he must have gone into the stall and been attacked."

"I don't call it crafty," said Claire. "I call it filthy."

"Well, they're not a nice crowd," agreed Sam mildly.

"What I find it very difficult to believe," said Sabrina, "is that a company like World Wide would employ these sort of tactics. They're a huge international consortium. I believe the ultimate control is either German or American. Surely they're much too big – "

"I thought about that," said Jonas. "They *are* big *and* efficient. They operate on a regional basis. The lot that sells down here would be the South-Eastern Group. Now suppose this group had been doing rather badly in comparison with the other groups in this country. The local regional boss – I've met him and didn't like him much – a man called Claude Schofield, he feels he's for the chop unless he can organise a dramatic turn round. So he gets hold of the top man in FSP – "

"Carl Fredericks," said Claire.

"A boyfriend of yours?" suggested Sabrina.

"Not on your nelly. He's fifty and he's got an expensive stomach and three chins. I think Jonas is right. And I'll tell you why. Claude and Carl are golfing buddies. Suppose one day on the golf course Claude says to Carl, 'Get your FSP reps busy selling my stuff and I'll cut you in for a private commission. Say ten per cent on any increase in sales.'"

"You're right about one thing," said Jonas. "World Wide are the sort of big organisation who wouldn't hesitate to sack a regional boss if his figures were bad."

Claire said, "And that would be particularly unfortunate for Claude, as I heard – only a rumour, mind – that he's been badly dipped lately at the races. If he couldn't pay the bookies, he might find himself being trampled on by a racehorse."

Jonas finished his tea. He said, "It's an unpleasant business. I'm glad we're not directly involved and I hope we shan't be."

On the following morning, which was a Friday, this hope was dashed with the arrival of Aneurin Williams. The first impression was a shock of white hair, bristling white eyebrows and a pair of light blue eyes. The next was an ensnaring Welsh tongue, the voice of an orator from the valleys. When Jonas understood what Mr Williams wanted him to do he said 'No' and went on saying it until he realised that he was making no impression on his visitor.

"It's a simple thing. It just needs a man of your authority, Mr Pickett."

"I don't think – "

"None of the other lawyers in this town are of any use. Not the least use. It requires a man who speaks with authority."

"I'm not sure – "

"All that is necessary is for you to explain the law to Chief Superintendent Whaley."

"Suppose he doesn't believe me?"

"He will believe the law, as expounded by you."

"Just let me get this straight," said Jonas. "The police have forbidden you to hold your meeting tomorrow."

"They have purported so to do."

"And you say they've no right to stop you."

"It's not I who say it. It's the law. I have studied the decided cases. As, no doubt, you also will have done."

"All right, I'll have a word with my partner, who knows a lot more law than I do. If she supports you, I'll speak to Whaley. Not that it'll do a blind bit of good. The police have a lot of latitude in matters like this."

With that, Aneurin Williams had to be content. He would have liked to have gone on talking, but Jonas was firm.

Sabrina, when consulted, said, "He's right. In theory, that is. A public meeting can only be stopped by the authorities if they can show that there's a likelihood of disorder resulting. The normal case is where one lot announce a meeting and their opponents promptly decide to hold a meeting in the next street."

"Fascists and Communists."

"That sort of thing. Of course there's nothing like that here. But the police do have a pretty wide discretion and I can't see the local bench opposing them."

Jonas thought about the local bench and could only agree.

"I suppose I'd better have a word with Whaley. I warned Williams that it would do more harm than good. If I could have fixed it up quietly with Jack Queen, I might have got somewhere."

Chief Superintendent Whaley was large, courageous, thick-skinned and obstinate. Like an articulate rhinoceros, said Claire, who had once danced with him at a tennis club social. His disapproval of Jonas dated back to the early days of Jonas's arrival in Shackleton. He received him and listened to him with formidable politeness.

He said, "I know Claude Schofield. We get all our Christmas supplied from the World Wide stores in Brighton. I've often told him he ought to open a branch here."

"I'm surprised he hasn't," agreed Jonas.

"This other man, Fredericks. I've never heard of him. Who is he?"

"Carl Fredericks runs Food Sales Promotion. It's an advertising agency, with a lot of representatives who go round finding markets for their clients' goods."

"I see. And your idea is that Fredericks is getting a personal rake-off from Schofield and using some of it to pay for muscle to back up his salesmen."

"It's not my idea. It's the idea of a number of hotel and restaurant owners who've had visits from these people."

"And you say they've been threatened."

"No," said Jonas unhappily. "That's just what they're careful not to do. They simply drop hints. It's what happened last year in Brighton that's scaring people here."

"Yes. I had a word with Chief Superintendent Maxted about that. There's been some pressure-selling there, no doubt. He thinks it may have been exaggerated. In any event, Shackleton isn't Brighton. We haven't had any trouble here yet."

"Not yet," said Jonas. He could see that the rhinoceros was heading down a fixed track to a predetermined end and that no arguments were going to stop him.

"What we don't want to do is to stir up trouble here before we've any cause to do so. That puts *us* in the wrong."

"And you think that a public meeting to discuss the matter is going to cause trouble?"

"In the ordinary way, perhaps not. But we've had some experience of Mr Williams. You know him, I expect."

"He's elected himself as my client. That's why I'm here."

"I see." Whaley looked at Jonas thoughtfully. "I've told him we can't have the Saturday afternoon traffic in the High Street disrupted. It's difficult enough to keep the traffic moving as it is. If he insists on holding the meeting in spite of my warning I shall get my men to disperse it. If Williams resists, they'll have orders to bring him in. I hope they won't have to arrest you, too, Mr Pickett."

This was said without a smile.

"I hope so, too," said Jonas. "I'll go along now and tell my client what you've said. If this afternoon's meeting is going to be cancelled, there isn't a lot of time to do it."

Jonas went straight round to the Everdene Hotel. As he went he was cursing Aneurin Williams and cursing him wholeheartedly. The last thing he wanted was a feud with the police. It did neither him nor his clients any good. He hoped, without much confidence, that the Welsh crusader would listen to reason.

He found a worried boy in the front desk at the hotel. The boy said, "Dad's not here. He went out about half an hour ago."

"Have you any idea where he went, or why?"

"He doesn't tell me much. I think it was a telephone call he had. He said it was important."

"Does he know that the police have put a stopper on his meeting?"

"Yes. He knew that. Whaley had been on to him earlier this morning. What he said, as he was going out, was that if everything went as he thought it would, there might be no need for a public meeting after all."

Jonas thought about it. It didn't make a great deal of sense. He said, "I'm going back to my office now. When your father turns up, ask him to give me a ring."

The boy said, "You're going to advise him to play along with the police – I hope."

Jonas gathered that he didn't approve of his father's crusading. Jonas said, "I most certainly am."

He waited patiently, first in his office and then in his flat, until past two o'clock, but the telephone remained silent. It meant missing his lunch, but this troubled him very little. He often ate nothing between breakfast and dinner.

At half past two he wandered down to the Town Hall. There were quite a few people collected round the steps, but Williams was not there and no one seemed to know what to do.

Hamlet without the Prince of Denmark, thought Jonas. Then Whaley appeared, pushing his way through the crowd. He climbed the steps. No need for a loudhailer. His booming voice carried quite clearly.

"I've told your organisers that if they persist in holding this meeting they will be breaking the law. There's no objection to your meeting later, at a more suitable place. But not here and not now."

Jonas wondered what would have happened if Williams had been there. As it was there was no real resistance. People started to drift away. Whaley came down and climbed back into the police car.

*　　*　　*

Shortly after two o'clock on that same afternoon Dr Abrahams, who was the police doctor, had passed through the pier turnstile accompanied by his sons, Pete and Jim. Pete was dancing with excitement. He said, "Hurry, hurry. We don't want to miss the train." They dragged their father through the crowd like two small tugs towing a liner.

"Plenty of time," said the doctor. "The amusement arcade's only just opened."

In spite of Pete and Jim's urging, when they arrived at the ghost train there was already a queue. There were two small girls in the charge of an old lady and a teenaged girl who was trying to control three small boys and a large dog. The rest were unaccompanied children.

The doctor and his sons got the last carriage to themselves. There was a toot, the lights went out and the train plunged into the tunnel.

Dr Abrahams observed the effects with interest. He thought they had been rather skilfully arranged. There were three set-pieces, each one accompanied by appropriate noises-off. The first was the graveyard. It was hung with skeletons which jiggled their arms and legs in time with the tolling of a bell. The children in the carriage ahead of them screamed in joyful unison.

Pete and Jim were silent, but entranced.

Next they arrived at the infernal zoo where there were animals with electric eyes, gaping jaws and a background of banshee howling. The last cavern was, in some ways, the most effective. It was the tomb. In a ghastly green light, to an accompaniment of moaning and sobbing, human heads were displayed projecting through holes in the backcloth: distorted, moronic and leering.

Dr Abrahams was interested to observe that the screaming of the children in the carriages ahead had now a more genuine ring. As their own carriage swung into the third cavern he ceased thinking about this. There was something much more urgent on his mind.

As soon as the train stopped he took out some loose change, gave it to Pete and Jim and said, "I've got something to do. Get along to the slot-machines. I'll join you there."

His sons looked surprised, but scampered off.

The track of the ghost train was circular and operated in both directions so that departures and arrivals could be handled from the same point. The proprietor was getting ready to let in passengers for the return trip when Dr Abrahams stopped him.

He showed him his police card and said, "I'm sorry, but you'll have to shut up shop. I'll telephone the police if you insist, but there's no time to waste."

The effect of this pronouncement on Cyril Aylett was unexpected. There was none of the bluster and protest that Abrahams had anticipated. Instead, he seemed to shrink. It was as though most of the air had been let out of him. He opened his mouth, but no words came out.

"Quick," said Abrahams. "Turn out all the comic effects and switch on some proper lighting. You can do that, can't you?"

Aylett nodded. He pulled out a notice which said 'Closed for Temporary Repairs', led the way inside the turnstile, disregarding the protests of the waiting children, and turned two switches. Then he led the way into the tomb. The glaring overhead light had stripped it of all its mystery. Three of the projecting heads could now be seen as rubber masks. The fourth, though it was painted with the round eyes, white cheeks and fat red lips of a clown, was human.

Dr Abrahams ripped down the backcloth. Aneurin Williams had been lashed to the framework of metal girders with his head projecting through the screen. Abrahams said, "Knife. Or scissors. Don't waste time."

Aylett scuttled away. The doctor worked on the gag which had been fastened into Williams's mouth. He had it out by the time Aylett came back with a knife. The doctor glanced at it, but made no move to take it. He was looking at the gag, a fat wad of cloth, with strings attached. It had been chewed into rags and was wet with blood and saliva.

Aylett said, "Oughtn't we to get him down?"

"Too late," said Abrahams. "He's dead. Been dead some little time. Telephone the police. I'll wait here."

Chief Superintendent Whaley was not easily moved, but for all his stolidity he was shaken. He said, "Your idea, doctor, is that Williams choked himself trying to chew that gag out."

"When a proper autopsy has been made," said Dr Abrahams cautiously, "I think it will show that the actual cause of death was suffocation. Equally, it might have been shock. He wasn't a young man."

"Painting and powdering his face – I suppose they meant it as a joke."

Dr Abrahams said, "A bad joke, that went wrong." He, too, was upset.

"Do you think Aylett was in it?"

Dr Abrahams thought about it. As a professional man he disliked jumping to conclusions. He said, "The way he reacted when I spoke to him demonstrated that he knew there was *something* wrong. When he realised that Williams was dead – well, that was quite a different matter. He nearly passed out."

"The ghost train is his outfit. There was a dead man in it. He can't side-step that. We'll pull him in for questioning."

"I wish you could have pulled him in right away to stop him talking. Too late now."

Whaley grunted agreement. Like all policemen, publicity was something he heartily disliked.

"One thing did occur to me," said Abrahams. "You remember that business at the fish restaurant in Brighton. The people who did it took a photograph and sent it to the press. If the object of this operation was to make Williams look a fool, mightn't they have done the same thing here?"

"You think it's the same people?"

"I'd think so, yes."

"I'll have a word with Maxted about it. He told me he thought the muscle behind the Brighton episodes came from the racecourse. Well, he can attend to that. I'm going to shake down Aylett. He's the man in the middle."

Jonas was saying much the same thing to Sabrina. He enjoyed discussing problems with her because she almost always took the opposite view to his and argued it tenaciously. He called her his favourite No-woman.

He said, "Aylett is the key to this."

"I don't follow that," said Sabrina. "Didn't the boy at the

hotel tell you someone had telephoned his father to arrange a meeting?"

"Correct."

"The idea being that some sort of compromise could be arranged. They'd lay off Shackleton if Williams abandoned his campaign."

"Right again."

"Well, Aylett couldn't do anything like that. He wasn't in a position to make such an offer."

"I didn't suggest it was Aylett who telephoned. Fredericks must have done that. On the other hand, the last thing *he* was going to do was come anywhere near Shackleton. I've no doubt he spent the morning parading round Brighton establishing a series of beautiful alibis for himself. No, no. He'd simply have warned Aylett that Louie's boys were coming and that he was to hide them in the ghost train."

"How would they get into the arcade? It's locked until two o'clock."

"No problem. There's a back entrance, on a lower level of the pier where the public aren't allowed to go. If they dressed as workmen and kept their eyes open, they'd slip in easily enough."

"And what was Aylett supposed to do when Williams turned up?"

"I imagine he'd be hanging round just inside the public entrance to the arcade, out of sight as far as possible. When he saw Williams he'd open it up for him and say, 'Step inside. Mr Fredericks is waiting for you.'"

"Why should he agree to do anything of the sort?"

"I could think of half a dozen reasons. Maybe he owed money. Or Fredericks had scared him by threatening to put the hard boys on to him. He didn't strike me as a very robust character."

"Aren't you forgetting something?" said Sabrina. "The plan wasn't to kill Williams. Just to make him look a fool. As soon as he'd been let out he'd put a finger on Louie's men and they'd be up for criminal assault at least."

"Not necessarily. Remember they were waiting for him *inside* the ghost train. It's pretty dark and they'd probably have put on some sort of mask. All Williams could have said was that he was grabbed from behind and tied up. When they'd finished fixing him up, they could slip out the way they'd come in."

"Or easier still," said Sabrina, "wait till the amusement arcade opened and mix with the crowd." She seemed to be thinking it through, testing it for weaknesses. In the end she said, "You may be right. It could have been done that way. If no one saw Aylett letting Williams in and everyone keeps their heads, the police are going to have the devil's own job proving it."

On Monday morning Landless arrived with copies of the local and national papers. He said, "They're making a meal of it. Lucky they were stopped from publishing the photograph."

"Then there was one?"

"There certainly was. It was sent to the *South Coast Gazette and News*. A friend on the editorial side showed it to me. Naturally they made a copy before they handed it back to the police. Just in case they might ever have a chance of using it, though I don't see how they could."

"Unpleasant, was it?"

"Not just unpleasant. It was – oh, comic and gruesome at the same time and horribly scary."

"Then thank goodness it wasn't published." Jonas had been studying the papers. "The stories are bad enough by themselves."

Landless said, "Someone's got to stop this. What are the police doing?"

"I'm afraid I'm not in their confidence. I imagine they're grilling Aylett."

"That won't get them very far. The people they ought to be grilling are Louie and his boys. Everyone knows it was them who did it."

"Knowing isn't proving."

"Why don't they circulate photographs of these thugs, post them up all over the place, with a notice asking anyone who saw them on or near the pier on Saturday to contact the police?"

"Awkward if it turned out that it wasn't them."

"It's easy to make objections," said Landless, who was

getting angry. "But I can tell you one thing. If the people who did this aren't stamped on, good and hard, and quickly, World Wide are going to have a lot of new customers in Shackleton."

Jonas's mind sometimes moved in a disorderly and illogical way. It was activated by stray thoughts, coincidences and impulses. The mention of photographs had summoned up a mental picture of a squat man with a squint.

When Landless had taken himself off, grumbling, Jonas turned to the classified pages in the local directory under the heading 'Photography'. Some of the entries he was able to dismiss. They were high-class outfits which specialised in studio portraits for weddings and such.

He did not visualise the stout man as belonging to any of them.

In the end he narrowed down the possibilities to three. Instapics, Happy Snaps and Souvenir-pics. He thought he would visit them that evening. By nine o'clock the pier would be shutting down and the photographers would have returned to their shops, bringing the fruits of their day's work with them. Instapics was the nearest. When Jonas went in he saw that he'd made one good guess. The squat man, a Mr Bugden, was behind the counter.

He said, "'Ullo, Mr Pickett. Don't tell me. The grand-children have been after you for that snap you wooden let me take."

"Not exactly," said Jonas. "What I want is information. And since I shall be taking up your time, I'm quite prepared to pay you for it."

Mr Bugden looked at him shrewdly. He said, "Your enquiries wooden relate, by any chance, to the poor old sod they found in the ghost train?"

Jonas nodded.

"Then you can have any information I've got for free and welcome."

"I'm very grateful," said Jonas. "What I was going to ask about was what you might call the tricks of your trade. To start with, I don't suppose you take a photograph every time you click your camera."

"Not always, no. It's a matter of experience. Fr'instance,

people are more likely to buy a snap at the end of their holidays than at the start."

"How do you know when it's the end?"

"When the kids have got brown legs and Dad's nose is peeling."

Jonas laughed.

Mr Bugden said, "Soften as not a happy family like that will buy the snap. If they don't, all right, usually it's just thrown away. A few we do hang on to, such as if you get a shot of someone who's got some publicity value, like it might be the mayor or the top policeman. If there was some story about them, maybe you could make a sale to the local paper."

"And you keep those ones?"

"If they're good pictures, yes."

"Could you show me last Saturday's lot?"

"Sure." He went to a cupboard, selected an envelope and spilled the contents on to the counter. There was a group photograph of the pierrots and pierrettes, who were opening that week at the concert hall, one of a smiling man holding a fish with his wife admiring it ("Won the angling competition") and a solemn one of a clergyman ("Reverend Tobias Harmer from St Michael's, always threatening to close down the pier").

He saw that they all had the date stamped on the back.

"Tell you something else about them. It's not only the date. The sun being out – I can tell you what time of day they were taken. That sort of detail comes in useful sometimes. See that shadow. That's the top of the concert hall roof. Just like a sundial. The pier runs north and south, right? So at one o'clock the shadow's dead central. By four o'clock it's moved off to the east side."

"I see what you mean," said Jonas. He examined the snapshots in front of him. "That man with the fish. The shadow hasn't reached the middle point. Say half past eleven, or twelve?"

"Just about. And the rector was mid-afternoon, I remember. About three o'clock."

"Then the sun was shining all day on Saturday?"

"Every blessed moment. Does it help?"

"It shortens the odds, very slightly," said Jonas. "But it's still a long shot. Could you give your opposite numbers in Happy Snaps and Souvenir-pics a ring and tell them to expect me?"

"Will do. Happy Snaps will be Major Piper. And don't forget to call him Major. He likes it. Souvenir-pics is a Mrs French. They'll both be glad to help when I tell them what you're up to." As Jonas was leaving he added, "I wooden say old Williams was a popular man, but we don't like characters from Brighton throwing their weight around in Shackleton."

Major Piper already had his Saturday snapshots out when Jonas arrived. He said, "I'm afraid they won't be much help to whatever it is you're after."

There were several more of the pierrots' troupe and one of a pudding-faced boy.

"Fell into the sea and was rescued by one of the fishermen. You'd have thought his parents would have wanted a snap, wouldn't you?"

"If he was my son, Major," said Jonas, "I think I'd keep him away from the camera for a year or so. Perhaps he'll be easier on the eye when he's a bit older."

He thanked him and made for his last port of call.

The office of Souvenir-pics was at the far end of the town. His two visits had taken time. It was already dark and a fresh wind was blowing in off the sea. Jonas shivered and turned his collar up. His mind was full of faces. Faces with bloated lips and burst eyes. Faces that worked their jaws and tried to scream, but could make no sound.

There was a light in the shop and Mrs French opened the door to him herself. She said, "Mr Pickett? I've got something I think you might find interesting. When our man noticed Williams he remembered the public meeting and the fuss about it and followed him up to see if he could get a good picture. Which he did."

"It's beautifully clear." Suddenly Jonas found it difficult to speak.

"I thought you might want some copies so I've had six made."

"You're an angel. Let me give you a piece of advice. First thing tomorrow take the original to your bank and ask them to put it in their strongest strongroom."

"You think it's that important?"

"It's not just important," said Jonas softly. "It's dynamite."

When Jonas sat down at his desk on Tuesday morning he reached out, twice, for the telephone and twice drew back his hand. He was aware of the views of Chief Superintendent Whaley. In the present case it was possible that those views were shared by his second-in-command. In the end he said, "Well, he can only snub me." He grabbed the instrument. When he heard Queen's voice at the other end he said, speaking fast, "Look, I wanted to ask you one question. I don't imagine this is a good line to do it on. Could we meet somewhere?"

"A question about what?" Queen's voice was cool.

"About that business on the pier."

The silence that followed was so long that he thought the Superintendent might have gone off to have a word with Whaley. Apparently no, he had been thinking. He said, "I've got to be at the Everdene Hotel at twelve o'clock to take a written statement from young Williams. If you happened to be in the manager's office at the same time – "

"I'll be there at five to twelve," said Jonas. "What I've got to ask won't take more than a few minutes."

When he saw the Superintendent, he noted the signs of strain in his face. His superiors and the press between them must have been giving him a hard ride.

Queen said, "All right. Ask your question and I'll see if I'm allowed to answer it."

"Before I do that," said Jonas, "I'd like to make my own position in the matter clear. Williams was my client. I understand from Mrs Williams that she would like me to go on acting for her and the estate."

Queen had no comment to make.

Jonas went on, "It so happens that I have got hold of something. Whether it's going to help or not, whether it's important or unimportant, turns on a single point. You've been questioning Aylett. Can you tell me, broadly and without going into any detail, what his story is?"

Queen chewed over this in silence. Then he said, "If I answer your question, do you undertake that this something you've discovered comes straight to us? No fooling round, no trying to be clever."

"Just as soon as the information is hard, you shall have it."

"Very well. You said, tell me what Aylett's story is, without details or trimmings. That's easy. There aren't any. It's a flat denial of seeing anyone or doing anything. He thinks two of Louie's men must have got into the arcade by the lower entrance. They must have met Williams and induced him to go in with them. He swears that the first moment he knew anything was wrong was when Dr Abrahams showed him the body. The doctor says that's a lie. It's clear he *did* know something was up. But we can't shake him. He's obstinate and he's frightened. And when you're dealing with a man who's obstinate and frightened, you might as well talk to a deaf monkey."

Jonas could hear the ragged edge of strain in his voice. He said, "If I wanted to telephone you this evening, where would I find you?"

"I've spent the last two nights on a camp bed in my office. I expect I shall be there tonight as well."

When he got back, Jonas sent for Sam and said to him, "I want you to get hold of Aylett. I believe you said you knew him."

"I wouldn't say we was buddies. I met him a few years ago at Portsmouth Fair. Running a coconut shy. The sort where the coconuts are nailed on. What do I say to him?"

"Ask him if he'll come along and have a word with me."

"I'm told he's pretty busy. That ghost train was popular before. Now the queue's a hundred yards long. All the kids in town want to get on it. Gruesome little buggers."

"Do your best," said Jonas. "If he can't come till the arcade shuts, that's all right with me. I don't mind how late he is. I'll wait up for him."

Claire, who was there, said, "I thought your idea was to steer clear of this thing. Now you seem to be getting mixed up in it."

"I'm not doing it for fun," said Jonas crossly. "I'm doing it to help my client, Mrs Williams."

Claire said, "Oh, yeah?" But being a perfect secretary, she said it to herself.

*   *   *

"He'll come," said Sam.

"How did you persuade him?"

"No persuasion needed. When I mentioned your name he seemed quite keen on the idea. He's got to shut down the train and get something to eat. He reckons he'll be here about ten."

"Splendid."

"Matter of fact, I got the idea it suited him better to come after dark. Someone seems to have thrown a scare into him. I told him you'd leave the side door open. The one on the alley. He could slip in that way without showing himself in the street at all. He seemed to like that idea."

Jonas took his evening meal at the South Wind Restaurant. When he had finished, Landless came and sat at his table. He said, "Does the fact that the police have let Aylett go mean that they think he's in the clear?"

"It only means that they haven't got enough evidence yet to charge him with anything."

"Seems the only result of this whole thing is to make the Shackleton ghost train the biggest attraction on the south coast. They'll be running coaches from Seaford and Newhaven next."

"So I've heard," said Jonas shortly. He didn't want to talk about it.

It was nearly eleven o'clock before Aylett arrived. Jonas had been devoting some thought to how he was going to open what was bound to be a tricky conversation. Aylett saved him the trouble.

He said, "As soon as Sam mentioned your name, Mr Pickett, I thought that's just what I want. I want a good solicitor."

Jonas stared at him.

"They've let me go. Just for now. But they'll have me back. I know they will. They'll keep on and on at me trying to make me say – I mean, trying to make me say something different to what I have said. Next time I go, I want you to come with me. That's the law, isn't it? I'm entitled to have a solicitor with me."

Jonas had got his breath back. He said, "There's one thing you've got to understand. No solicitor can act for a client unless that client tells him the truth."

"But that's what I have done, Mr Pickett." His voice was a thin wail. "I've told the police twenty times. I knew nothing about what happened to Mr Williams. Nothing at all. I didn't get there that afternoon until just before the arcade opened up. There was a lot of kids waiting already. All I had to do was switch on the effects and start the train. Honest."

The only illumination in the room was the big green-shaded table lamp. In the bright circle of light which it threw on the desk Jonas placed a photograph. It had been taken at an angle to the main entrance of the arcade and some distance from it. It showed Aylett smiling and holding the gate open for Aneurin Williams. Both of them were side-faced to the camera and there was no disputing their identities.

"I've been told by three experts," said Jonas, "that they can time a photograph like this from the angle of the sun. Some time between noon and half past twelve is the consensus of their opinion."

He said this slowly, in order to give Aylett time to collect his wits and start lying.

"Yes, of course," he said. "That would have been – let me see – about a week ago. Maybe a little more. Mr Williams came to see me about not letting children on to the train without an adult in charge. That was one of his fads, you see."

Jonas said, "I don't think you've examined the photograph quite carefully enough. Look at that placard on the wall of the arcade. You can only see the right-hand half of it. But it's quite clear, isn't it? Jokes and Jollities. That's one of the posters announcing this season's pierrot show. *It was put up last Friday evening.*"

There was a long silence broken finally by Jonas. He said, "When this matter comes to court, as it will, this photograph will be exhibited. The manager of the pierrots will give evidence and so will the photographer. There is no doubt at all" – Jonas's words were falling like stones into a pool of silence – "that this photograph was taken around noon last Saturday. Two hours before Williams was found dead."

Aylett said, "What – " and didn't seem to know how to go on. Then he said, "What can I say?"

"You can tell the truth," said Jonas. "And then I'll see what I can do to get you out of the mess you've got yourself into."

Aylett's resistance broke suddenly and completely. The words came tumbling out. "It was Mr Fredericks. He made me do it. He owns a lot of the concessions on the pier. The ghost train is one of them. If I didn't do what he said I was out of my job, see? And I owed him money already. And he said he'd put Louie's men on to me to collect it. Oh God!"

So both my guesses were right, thought Jonas. He said, "Go on. And talk slowly because I'm going to write it down and you're going to sign it."

"Wrong on both counts," said a voice from the darkness near the inner door. Two creatures had come into the room. A lion and a bear. They must have come in by the side door in the alley. They had slipped into the room with all the stealth and cunning of wild animals.

The lion padded across, swept books and papers off the desk and perched on the space he had cleared. Jonas could see that the mask was well made, fitting round the neck with a stockingette collar. Dark eyes gleamed at him through the slits. The bear had backed Aylett into a corner. He had a husky Midlander's voice. A Merseysider, Jonas guessed. "Wassall this, Cyril?" he said. "Consulting the law. You don't want a lawyer. What you want is a nurse, to smack your bottom when you have naughty thoughts." As he said this he brought one arm across and caught Aylett a swipe on one side of the head which slammed him against the wall. As he threw up his hands to guard his face the bear kicked him in the stomach. Aylett folded forward on to his knees, retching.

Jonas half rose in his chair. The lion said, "Siddown, Granpa, and behave yourself and doan get ideas." He grabbed the telephone, jerked it off its cord and slammed the instrument back on to the desk.

The bear was standing over Aylett. He had grabbed his hair in one hand and bent his head back so that Aylett was forced to look up at him. He said, "Did my ears deceive me, Cyril, or did I hear you say something about making a statement? You wouldn't do a thing like that, would you?"

Aylett managed to shake his head.

"That's what I thought, because you know what happens to people who talk out of turn, don't you?" When Aylett said nothing he slapped him across the face. There were rings on two of his fingers and they tore long gashes in his cheek.

"Stop it," said Jonas.

The bear swung round on him. He said, "That's a funny thing to say, isn't it, Leo?"

"Very funny," said the lion.

"He's telling us to stop it, when we haven't even started. When we've finished with Cyril, we'll think up something special for you. Teach you to keep your nose out of other people's business."

The overhead light came on. Sam was standing in the doorway. He said, "What's this? Circus time?"

It was clear that the bear recognised him. He said, "You keep out of this," but a lot of the confidence had gone out of his voice.

"That's no way to talk to an old friend," said Sam. "Colley, innit? I thought it was. Used to be a bit of a boxer in your youth, I seem to remember. Let's see some style." He formed up to the bear as though he was facing him in the ring, then lashed out with his right foot, catching him on the knee. Jonas heard the kneecap crack. The bear let out a scream, went down on the floor and lay there nursing his knee and cursing.

Sam took no more notice of him. He turned his attention to the lion, who had removed himself from the corner of the desk and was standing beside it, clearly uncertain what to do next.

"You a boxer, too?" said Sam. "Or just a fighter?" He sidled up to him, presenting his left shoulder. The lion lashed out with one foot. Sam stepped aside, caught the lion's foot in both hands and twisted it. The lion managed to grab the desk with one hand and started to hop. He had his back to Jonas who picked up the telephone and brought it down hard on the lion's head. The lion went down without a sound.

"Really, Mr Pickett," said Sam. "That's no way to treat Post Office property."

Jonas said, "Thank you, Sam." He was surprised to find he could speak at all. "You'd better get the police. Use the phone in Claire's room."

"I rang 'em before I came in," said Sam. "I think that's them coming now."

*   *   *

"I take it," said Queen, "that you'll be preferring charges."

"Certainly. And in case there's any doubt about who said what, I might mention that I already had the recorder switched on to get Aylett's statement. The whole scene's on tape."

"The court should enjoy it," said Queen grimly. He turned to Aylett. "Do I gather you've got something to tell us? If so, go ahead. You've got your lawyer here."

Aylett looked at Jonas who said, "The whole story. It's your only chance."

When he had finished, Queen said, "You'd better get that face of yours attended to. The car will take you round to the station. We'll have the statement typed out and you can sign it."

When they were alone, he said, "Nice work, squire. Did you know those beauties would come after him?"

Jonas said, "No. That was luck." He added, "Shake the tree and you'll find that all the fruit will fall off."

It was three months later before Jonas had the chance to spend another morning on the pier. It had been a busy three months, but satisfactory. As soon as Fredericks had seen all the guns pointing at him he had lost no time in involving Claude Schofield, who had turned on Louie the Nose. It had been a reign of terror in reverse, thought Jonas. Everyone trying to shift the blame on others and only involving themselves more deeply.

At Lewes Crown Court sentences had been dealt out by Mr Justice Roche to all concerned which had satisfied even Chief Superintendent Whaley. Aylett, who had been given an indemnity, was the main witness for the Crown. Defence counsel had given him a shellacking, but there was no shaking his story.

Very satisfactory. Even Whaley had been moved to say that he thought Mr Pickett had done a public service. A temporary truce, thought Jonas.

It was the end of the season and the pier was nearly empty. He walked back to the arcade, purchased a fivepenny disc from the attendant and went over to the corner where the old slot-machines stood.

"Real works of art, they are," said the attendant. "They don't make 'em like this any more. They ought to be in a museum, really."

Jonas inserted the disc. The tricoteuses waved their needles, the aristocrat bowed his head, the blade of the guillotine descended. The blade was blunt, but repeated applications must have weakened the aristocrat's neck and on this occasion his head fell right off and rolled amongst the old ladies.

"End of the Reign of Terror," said Jonas.

"Not a bit of it," said the attendant. "It's happened before. We sew his head on again."

This seemed to Jonas so funny somehow that he started to laugh.

5

THE ADMIRAL

"For eleven months in the year," said Admiral Fairlie to Jonas, who was his solicitor and friend, "Shackleton is as nice a spot as you could find on the south coast. Plenty of young families on the new estate. The fathers have their businesses at Saltmouth or Poole, but they prefer to live here because it's quiet."

"And the rates and rents are lower."

"Maybe. Good folk, anyway, who work hard and give no trouble. Then there are the old brigade. People like me, who came here to retire. It's not so up-market as Eastbourne, but there's plenty to do."

"One repertory theatre, one cinema, a bingo hall and a dance-hall. And if everything else fails, you can spend your money in the slot-machines in the amusement arcade on the pier."

"Right," said the Admiral. "For eleven months no complaints. Then we come to August, which ought to be the best month in the year. And find that August is" – he paused to pick his words carefully – "a shambles, an inferno, a nightmare."

"Bailey's Circus and Funfair."

"Which isn't a circus at all. Just a roundabout, complete with steam organ, which makes so much noise that no one can hear themselves speak for a quarter of a mile downwind of it and the rest a shanty town of side-shows, run by a crowd of swindling didicoys, whose brats spend their days shop-lifting and their evenings making piddling nuisances of themselves round the streets."

Jonas thought about it. His sympathy was with the Admiral. The circus did not worry him personally. Being his own master he usually arranged to take his holiday in August and departed for Switzerland, a country he preferred when it was empty of skiers and full of wild flowers. But not everyone was as well placed as he was. He knew that a lot of the older people did suffer.

"Couldn't the council do something?"

"In the old days, when I was on it, and a few of my friends with me, we would have done. I promise you. Now it's different. The council's split. People like Colonel Rattray and Saul Melford, they'd be happy to clear Bailey right out. But they're outvoted by the commercial lobby. People like Forbes and Greenaway. What they say is, it brings a big crowd into the town, and that means money through the shops and cafés. After all, it's only a month! Why not let everyone have a bit of fun? Besides, they say, it's never been proved that the circus people are the ones who commit these crimes. Which is partly true. Even with the shop-lifting, because the circus brats lead the town children on, only they're cleverer at it. So it's the townees who get caught."

"What about the house-breaking?"

"No proof."

"Difficult," said Jonas. "As long as they abide by the terms of their licence from the council I can't see any legal way of turning them out. All I can suggest is that you and your friends keep your eyes open. Get one or two cases of crime and you might make the council listen. The police will support you. They hate the circus. Have a word with Superintendent Queen."

"Jack Queen's a good man," agreed the Admiral. "But he can't do much on his own."

"There is one other way," said Jonas. "Why not get back on to the council? You'd have no difficulty. Lots of people would be glad to vote for you. You and one or two other people who think like you."

"Ten years ago I might have done," said the Admiral sadly. "I'm an old man now." He paused. "Here's a better idea. Why don't you stand for the council?"

"Good grief," said Jonas. "Didn't I tell you that I came to Shackleton for peace and quiet?"

*　　*　　*

The Admiral's house stood below the eastern end of the front where the concrete of the Esplanade stopped and the chalk and turf of the East Head began. It was a square building set on a ledge in the hillside. From its flat roof he could, as from his quarter deck, oversee the town. Bailey's Circus was in plain view and although it was nearly a mile away the blare of the steam organ came clearly to his ears.

He had a telescope, with a mounting on the roof, through which he used to inspect the shipping in the Channel. Swinging it inland he picked out the details of the fairground. The parked caravans, where the stall-holders and their families lived; the stalls which sold a hundred useless trinkets, the roundabout dominating the centre.

"Like an Eastern market," said the Admiral. "Smelly, noisy and alive."

He went down to put on the kettle for his tea. For the most part he looked after himself. Mrs Matcham, the daughter of one of his old petty officers, came each morning to clean the house, cook his lunch, and lay out a cold supper. Breakfast and tea he managed for himself.

"He's no trouble at all," said Mrs Matcham. "It's my belief he could do it all himself if he chose. But I think he enjoys a gossip. It stands to reason. He's lonely."

After tea the Admiral armed himself with a walking stick and made his way down into the town, stopping from time to time to talk to his numerous friends, and to pass on the advice Jonas had given him. All promised to do what they could, but were not hopeful. "Like rats, those gypsies," said Colonel Rattray. "You know they're there, and you know they're up to no good, but you can't catch 'em at it."

Following Nelson's precept the Admiral decided to close with the enemy. He walked down to the Lammas. When he got there he found to his surprise that he had to pay to go in.

"Novel idea," he said to the man on the gate, "making us pay for the privilege of being skinned."

The gateman (could it be Mr Bailey himself?) smiled and said, "You see that, sir?" It was a new perimeter fence, stout mesh, topped by two strands of barbed wire. "We had to do it. No choice. First two or three years we were wide open. A lot of riff-raff got in and made trouble. Now we can keep things under control. Better hang on to your ticket. You may have to show it when you go out again."

"I expect you know your business," said the Admiral. He paid twenty pence and went in.

He found every known device to tempt money from the pockets of the unwary. There were gambling machines of all sorts. Machines in which race-cars circled the track and space-craft circled the moon. There were stalls where you could throw at dart boards and stalls where you could shoot rifles at targets, or at ping-pong balls bouncing on jets of water. It seemed to the Admiral to be harmless and rather childish.

He came finally to the roll-a-disc stall and stopped by it to examine the technique of what was clearly a popular pastime.

For ten pence you purchased eight metal discs, roughly the size of an old-fashioned penny. These you rolled down a slotted piece of wood on to a board, which was divided into spaces, each of them a little, but not much, larger than the disc itself. If you succeeded in landing your disc fairly in a square, not touching any of its edges, you received back five, ten or twenty pence according to the number marked on the square.

The Admiral, who had been something of a mathematician in his youth, had just calculated that the chances against landing a disc of that size clearly inside a smallish square were roughly thirty to one when he became aware that a disturbance was taking place on the far side of the stall. A young man with a very red face was saying, "You scooped up my disc with the others but it was in a square marked 'ten'. Why aren't I getting paid for it, eh?"

"Touching the line, I'm afraid, sir," said the man in charge of the stall.

The Admiral switched his attention to him. Thick-set, black-haired, brown-faced, sure of himself.

"It bloody wasn't touching any bloody line. It was smack in the middle."

The stall-holder jerked a thumb at the notice which hung above the table. "In any doubt or dispute the decision of the proprietor is final."

"It's a bloody swindle," said the young man.

"Other people waiting to play."

"If they want to be swindled."

"Come away, Jack," said the girl who was with him. "It's not worth arguing." She pulled him by the arm. He went reluctantly. His place in front of the board was immediately filled. There seemed to be no lack of people willing to lose their money playing against odds that would have shamed the authorities at Monte Carlo.

The Admiral edged away and made for the roundabout. He was thankful that he was a little deaf. The great whirling machine was slowing to a halt. Some of the riders dismounted and there was a rush of children to take their places. The smaller ones climbed into the cars, the miniature stagecoaches and the railway carriages. The older ones jumped on to the painted and gilded horses, tigers and birds which made up the glamorous menagerie of the roundabout. When all were seated there were still a few places left. The man in charge, casting an eye around, spotted the Admiral.

"Come along, sir," he said, "only ten pence. Show the youngsters how to do it."

The vacant mount seemed to be asking for a rider. He was a magnificent red, black and gold cock, crowing defiance out of a lifted beak.

"Why not?" said the Admiral. He climbed aboard and swung himself into place.

The owner, slightly alarmed at the success of his salesmanship said, "You will hold on tight, won't you, sir?"

"I was riding before you were in long trousers," said the Admiral. "Let her rip."

It was a curiously enjoyable sensation. He treated himself to two more rides. The pair of horses in front of him were occupied by two boys, dressed identically in jeans and blue sweat-shirts. A cut above the other children, he thought. They had both looked back once at the Admiral, mounted on his fiery rooster, and then at each other, but neither of them had smiled. Serious types, evidently.

His ride finished, the Admiral climbed down, feeling a bit stiff, and decided to walk it off by circling the encampment and inspecting everything. Some of the stalls were interesting but most of them were gimcrack. He bought a china ashtray in the shape of an oyster shell for Mrs Matcham.

It was getting on for suppertime by now and the crowd was

diminishing. No doubt it would thicken up later. One of the many complaints which the police had against the fair was that it was allowed to function until midnight. This meant that drinkers, who had been turned out of the pubs at eleven, often made for the fairground for a final fling.

An inferno, it must be, thought the Admiral.

His perambulation had brought him to the far end of the compound. It was at that moment that he heard the sound of running feet. It was the boys he had seen on the roundabout and they were going fast.

The first one threw himself at the wire-mesh fence, wriggled under the bottom strand of the barbed wire and landed on the other side. The second was not so lucky. The barbed wire caught in the belt of his jeans and held him firm.

The Admiral could now see his pursuer. It was the roll-a-disc stall-holder. He was red in the face and he had a hedge stake in his hand, a dangerous-looking weapon.

Seeing the boys at his mercy he checked for a moment, took careful aim, and brought the stake down hard on the curved bottom. The boy made no sound, but jerked like a gaffed fish. The stake descended again.

The Admiral said, "That's enough. If you hit him again with a weapon like that you'll do some damage."

"I'll hit him as much as I want, the fucking little bastard."

"No, you won't," said the Admiral.

There was a note in his voice which made the man hesitate.

"Because I happen to have some influence with the Watch Committee. If you hit the boy once more, I can promise you that you won't see Shackleton again. More likely you'll see the inside of a police station."

The boys had taken advantage of the interruption. The first boy, turning back, had managed to free number two from the barbed wire. He wriggled clear, and both of them took to their heels.

"Right," said the man sourly. "Now he's got away with it."

"Got away with what?"

"Got away with not paying. They get in through holes in the fence. They can't go out of the gate because they'd be asked to show their tickets. So they try to get out the way they got in. I saw the little buggers sneaking off and I guessed what they were up to."

"Then by letting them get away with it I have lost the fair forty pence. I'll pay for them." He produced the money.

"It isn't the money, it's the principle," said the man. None the less he pocketed the coins. "They get away with it. Others copy them."

"No doubt," said the Admiral. He took the stick from the man and examined it. "That's much too heavy to hit a boy with. An inch or two higher up and you could easily have broken his back."

"Next time maybe I will," said the man.

"A real brute," said the Admiral, when he met Jonas in the town on the following afternoon. "If I hadn't stopped him I really think he might have killed that boy. Maimed him anyway."

"You realise that if he had," said Jonas, "you would probably have been able to clear them all out."

"Thank God I'm not a cold-blooded solicitor," said the Admiral indignantly. "Did you really think I was going to stand by . . . "

"I didn't think it for a moment. I hope I'd have done the same. Did you hear what happened last night?"

"I heard a lot of shouting."

"There was a stand-up fight. Some of the men from the engineering works and the circus people. Quite a few casualties, Queen told me. Including one of his own men."

"The Watch Committee aren't going to like that."

"One good thing came of it. They've agreed to shut the place at eleven o'clock. Which ought to keep things a bit quieter."

"I can tell you something else that will quieten them," said the Admiral. "It's going to rain. And rain hard. Not today, perhaps, but certainly tomorrow."

"By the way, I hope you enjoyed your ride."

"Oh, you heard about that, did you?"

"Talk of the town."

As he walked back to his office, Jonas was thinking about the Admiral. He had heard about his ride on the roundabout from Mrs Rattray who had come to see him about one of her periodical rows with the vicar. "He can get away with it," she said. "Everyone likes him. He ought to be made Mayor. Permanently."

Jonas agreed. He had looked up the old man's record, starting when he was a young sub-lieutenant in the First World War.

When he got to his office he telephoned Superintendent Queen, who said, "You heard about it, did you? One more show like that and even the old women on our council might do something."

"I've had an idea," said Jonas. He passed on what the Admiral had told him. "Why don't you find out the name of that stall-keeper and pass it up to Records?"

"You mean he might have some form," said Queen thoughtfully. "It's an idea."

During the late afternoon, when some of the heat was out of the day, the Admiral liked to take a walk up the cliff path in the direction of Hove. It was not a good path and few people ventured up it even in summer. It was intersected by steep clefts, each of which involved a slither in and a scramble out. It was at the bottom of one of these that he checked. He smelled something. No question about it. It was the smell of cooking and it came from the far end of the cleft where it turned a sharp corner.

The Admiral advanced cautiously, picking his way over the boulders. The cleft turned twice, getting narrower at each turn, until it ended in a sort of cave. A fire of driftwood was burning brightly in the mouth of the cave. Suspended over the fire from a tripod of iron rods was a large new-looking saucepan. One of the ingredients in it, if the Admiral was able to trust his nose, was onions.

Two figures moved at the back of the cave. The Admiral felt no surprise when he recognised them. He had felt that he would run into the boys again somewhere. As they came out into the light he could see that they were twins. Not identical twins. One was darker and had a more sharply cut face. The other was fairer and rounder, but the resemblance was marked. He guessed they were about eleven or twelve.

The dark one said, "That's a bit of luck, sir, meeting you. I didn't know who you were but I certainly thought I ought to thank you. I didn't feel like stopping."

"I don't blame you," said the Admiral. "We'd better introduce ourselves properly. My name's Fairlie."

The boy indicated his twin and said with old-fashioned gravity, "David Bourdon. I'm Colin."

"Borden? Like Lizzie?"

The boys looked blank.

"Lizzie Borden had an axe," said the Admiral, "hit her mother forty whacks."

"She sounds quite a girl," said Colin, "but no relation that I know of. We spell ours B-O-U-R-D-O-N."

The name meant something to the Admiral, but he couldn't place it. He said, "Have you come to live in Shackleton?"

"Just visits. We're here for the summer holidays. A lady looks after us. She's called Mrs Garibaldi. She's a widow."

"We did wonder at first," said David slowly, "if her father might have been the man who liberated Italy."

"I think," said the Admiral, "that it's unlikely – " Then he saw that they were laughing at him. He said, "If she's looking after you I guess she has her hands full."

"We don't give her any trouble," said Colin. "She gets us our breakfast and a meal when we get back in the evening. We've been given money to buy our lunches and teas."

"So instead of buying them you cook your own and save the money. What is it, by the way, apart from onions?"

"It's a young rabbit. We snare them up on the downs. Once we baked a hedgehog in clay. It tasted most peculiar." He took a spoon and stirred the contents of the pot. "It's nearly done. There's enough for three."

"It's kind of you," said the Admiral hastily, "but I've just had my tea. Do I gather your parents have dumped you down here for the holidays?"

"We haven't exactly been dumped," said Colin. "Dad's very busy. And Mummy – isn't."

Oddly enough the Admiral understood exactly what Colin meant. But he did not feel they knew each other well enough for him to pursue it at the moment.

He said, "Having saved the money intended for your daily

sustenance, you spend it at the funfair. Saving even more by not troubling to pay your entrance fee."

"Only dopes pay," said David. "Why, the very first day we were here the kids showed us half a dozen ways of getting in. And out again. The trouble was we were in too much of a hurry to look for the right spot, with that bloke after us. We've had trouble with him before."

"You certainly had trouble that time."

"Wham-bam," said David. "You ought to see the marks. They're black and blue and turning yellow at the edges already."

"It was ten times worse than any whacking at school," said Colin. "I thought he was going to break me in two. If you hadn't been there, I believe he would have done."

"When you say you've had trouble with him before?"

"Oh, he was cheating with that roll-a-disc thing and we told him what we thought of him. He couldn't get out at us that time because he was stuck in the middle. He was pretty angry."

"They all cheat," said David.

"How in particular?"

"Well there's the shooting gallery," said Colin. "That's a thing a lot of people go for. It's a complete swizz. To start with, the rifles are sighted all wrong. The one I had shot high and to the right. I found that out by doing a group. Then I aimed low and left and I thought I'd done a jolly good target. When the man brought it back he said, 'Hard luck, try again.' Then he explained that shots only counted if they went right into the bull. Right in. You didn't score by cutting the edge of it. That's nonsense."

"You've done a lot of target shooting?"

"He's jolly good," said David. "He's in the school eight and last term – "

"Mr Fairlie doesn't want to know about that," said Colin severely. "Give the rabbit a stir. The darts are just as bad. If you do happen to get one in the fifty they've a way of shaking the back-board so that it falls off. They said, 'Throw a little harder, son, then maybe it'll stick in,' and grinned all over their silly faces."

The Admiral, who had been examining the sky, said, "I can

tell you one thing. You're not going to be very comfortable here tomorrow."

"Why's that?"

"You've had the best of the weather. We're in for a good old south coast dowsing. You can always tell, when those mare's-tail clouds start driving up the Channel on the wind. It doesn't last long, but it's a shower-bath when it arrives. Would you like to come and have tea with me? I can't promise you hedgehog or rabbit, but there could be poached eggs."

The boys looked at each other. Colin, who was clearly the one who took the lead, said, "We'd like to do that, sir. Could you tell us where . . . "

"It's the first house as you come down this path towards the town. You can't miss it. Let's say half past four."

At ten o'clock next day the rain clouds drove in solidly, bank upon bank, from the south-west. In a matter of minutes the seaward face of Shackleton was changed. The beach parties fled, the stall-holders put up their shutters, the ice-cream vendors pedalled away, coloured umbrellas came down, deck-chairs were stacked, pleasure boats were stripped of their cushions and oars and turned keel uppermost.

The Admiral saw it from his upstairs window and chuckled. It would not last long, but it was a welcome catharsis. Like hosing-down after coaling.

His visitors arrived punctually at half past four in dripping blue raincoats with their hair plastered down on their heads. They seemed to be in excellent spirits. During tea they devoted themselves to the business of eating. The Admiral did most of the talking. He explained to them what the authorities thought about the fair, the chances of getting rid of it, and the difficulties in the way of doing so.

His audience seemed to be listening but were so busy with poached eggs and anchovy toast that it was difficult to be sure.

When almost everything in sight had been eaten and Mrs Matcham had cleared away the plates and cups, the Admiral's guests showed no inclination to leave. They removed themselves heavily from the table and sank down on to the sofa.

Colin said, "We know now. You're not a mister."

"True."

"You're an Admiral."

"Long retired."

"You fought in the war against the Kaiser."

"One of my neighbours has been talking."

"Not a neighbour. Dad rings us up every evening to see how we're getting on. We asked him about you."

"It was a terrifically long call," said David. "It must have cost pounds."

"I expect the Admiralty paid," said Colin.

"Good Lord," said the Admiral, "I have been stupid. The penny's only just dropped. Your father's Sir David Bourdon, the First Sea Lord."

"That's right," said David.

"A month ago he jolly nearly wasn't," said Colin.

The Admiral knew now why the name had rung a bell. It had been in all the papers. Not the details, but the outlines of the story as ferreted out by the defence correspondents. The government had proposed to add to the apparent strength of a diminished navy by reconditioning two obsolete aircraft carriers. The First Lord had insisted that they spend their money – admittedly a much larger sum of money and one which had been earmarked for welfare projects – on the latest types of nuclear submarine. He had not only insisted. He had made it clear that he was prepared to put his own head on the block. The government had given way.

He remembered something else. A few years ago, Lady Bourdon had been killed in a flying accident. He had guessed then that was what Colin had meant when he said, "Mummy isn't."

David said, "One thing Dad told us about. Is it right about what you did in the war? Q-ships and all that?"

"Yes."

"He said you'd tell us about it."

"It's all in the books."

"We haven't read the books."

"I suppose most books nowadays are about the last war. Or the next war."

"Or the war in the stars."

"I think science fiction's boring," said Colin. "I like reading about real wars. Things that actually happened."

"All right," said the Admiral. "It was like this. We fitted out a few merchant ships to look like real old tramps. Mostly they flew Dutch or Norwegian flags. It made no difference. In 1917 the U-boats were sinking everything they set eyes on. We had guns on board, quick-firers and even heavier stuff but it was all hidden."

"How?" said Colin.

"The usual cover was a collapsible deck-house, made of canvas. You pulled a rope and it all fell apart. But you had to convince the submarine that you were abandoning ship. That was called a panic-party. Dutch skippers did sometimes take their wives along with them. So one of the men would dress up as an old Dutch frau and come on deck with the men and wring her hands and bellow. There was a lot of competition for that part."

"I bet," said David.

"Then everyone, or apparently everyone, climbed down into the boats. The submarine would have surfaced by this time and be watching. The idea was that they didn't like taking neutral lives. Bad for world opinion. They simply wanted to sink the ships, because the more tonnage they destroyed the better. As soon as the boats were clear of the ship, they got ready to put a torpedo through her."

"And then," said Colin, "whoosh. Down came the phoney deck-house. Bang-bang-bang. Goodbye submarine. What a super idea. How you must have laughed."

"Right at the beginning," said the Admiral, "almost the first time out, before the Germans got suspicious, it was even funnier than that. The submarine came right alongside. I think the commander wanted to assure the Dutch captain personally that no harm was intended to him or his crew. They would all be allowed to get safely away in their boats before the ship was sunk. Whilst they were parleying his wife came on deck screaming and crying with a baby in her arms. She rushed over to the rail and tossed the baby clean down the conning tower of the U-boat."

The boys stared at him wide-eyed.

"The baby was a bomb with a very short time-fuse," said the Admiral. "But those were early days. Afterwards the U-boats got a lot more cautious and stood well away and then it wasn't always such fun."

He told them about other engagements, in some of which he himself had been involved. Outside the rain poured down in a steady stream. The Admiral said, "Heavens, it's past six. Mrs Garibaldi will think you've been drowned."

The boys got up reluctantly from the sofa.

The Admiral said, "Look. If you're bored, or it's too wet or cold outside for sitting around, you can use this place. If I'm not here the back door key's under a tile in the outhouse. I'll show you where."

When they were going they both said "Thank you," politely and marched off into the rain.

I hope I didn't bore them, thought the Admiral. They certainly hadn't bored him. He realised more strongly than ever before what he had lost by having no grandchildren of his own. Both his sons had been killed in the last war. His only daughter had married an ambitious politician who had been too busy in all-night sittings in the House to waste his time presenting her with children.

There was refreshment in children. Even his most cynical married friends admitted it. Children might be a nuisance when they were small and a problem in their teens, but there was a period between six and twelve when they were an unmixed delight. They had a sort of innocence. They might do wrong out of thoughtlessness but they would not plan it. Nor would they think wrong of anyone, until he had proved himself a brute.

The boys he had been talking to had something more. Some of the spirit of their mother who, the Admiral recollected, had been French; and more than a little of the toughness and initiative which had taken their father to the top of his profession. These were the sort of youngsters into whose hands the governance of the country would fall when the last of the present generation had passed on.

It was going to be a perilously difficult world as, one after another, the old bastions went down: religion, family life, the rule of law. Stormy seas which were going to need clear heads to chart the course and strong hands on the tiller.

The Admiral woke with a start from a daydream which had

nearly turned into a nightmare. He stumped off to see what Mrs Matcham had put out for his supper.

All next day, which was a Thursday, the rain bucketed down. On Thursday night the wind swung round to the south, and by lunchtime on Friday the sun was shining strongly as though to make up for its previous lapse. The holidaymakers, especially the ones who were due to go home that weekend, crowded back on to the beaches; the housewives made a concerted rush for the shops to lay in stores for the weekend.

On the Saturday morning, after breakfast, the Admiral walked down to pass on to Jonas the latest news from the council. He said, "They had a meeting yesterday afternoon. It was a close thing. They couldn't bring themselves to turn out the whole show, which was what Rattray proposed. Someone pointed out that if they did, they'd have to refund at least part of the licence fee which had been paid, and all the money men looked glum. The furthest they would go was to say they'd consider the matter again next year."

At this moment the telephone rang. Jonas listened for a moment, said, "Yes, he's here with me," and to the Admiral, "It's Queen. He wants to talk to you."

The talk was one-sided. The Admiral said nothing but "I see" and "Yes". As he replaced the receiver he said, "It's trouble, at the council offices. He wants me to come along and pour a little oil on troubled waters."

"What's up? A riot?"

"Something of the sort. Are you coming?"

"Try and stop me," said Jonas.

The streets were empty, but they could hear the swelling noise ahead of them.

"It's the families from the new estate. It seems their wives went shopping yesterday afternoon and a lot of them left their doors on the latch. A silly thing to do, but they'd never had any trouble before and didn't bother about locking up. When they got back they found someone had been through the unlocked houses and taken a lot of stuff. And they reckon they know where the thief came from. They're really worked up about it. Had a meeting when the men got home last night and decided that if no one would deal with the circus they'd attend to it themselves."

"Attend to it?"

"Bust it up."

"Mob law. Can't have that. What are they doing?"

"They marched down to the council office and demanded to see the town clerk."

"Little Mr Timms. He'll be scared stiff."

"He was. But he managed to get the front door shut and telephoned the police."

"So what are the crowd doing now?"

"Milling round in the street and shouting. They'll be breaking windows soon. Queen got in the back way; with two or three members of the Watch Committee he'd collected en route. They're in the Council Chamber, in a state of siege."

They had reached the main street by now. It was jam-packed with people, and the blast of horns from blocked motorists was adding to the general pandemonium. Jonas had had some experience of mobs. He thought this one sounded angry, but not really dangerous yet. But the first broken window would fire the fuse. The leaders were milling round the main door. A big red-haired policeman stood stolidly outside it. A lot of the people were not really involved. They had come along to see the fun. Jonas and the Admiral pushed through them without much difficulty and reached the front of the building. Positioning himself on the top step, the Admiral bellowed in his quarter-deck voice, "Listen to me a moment. Stop shouting and listen."

Jonas thought he was the only person who could have made them listen. The hubbub died down a bit.

"There's no point in trying to fight the police or break down the door. What you need is a deputation. You've got a grievance. Right. They'll have to listen to you. Half a dozen of you."

"Preston and Collinson," suggested Jonas quickly. They both happened to be his clients.

"And Mrs Garibaldi," said the Admiral. "You'll come? Right. We need three more volunteers."

The idea of a deputation was gaining ground. The Admiral

said to the policeman, "Let this lot in, Davey, quick, then shut the door behind us."

They found Queen in the front hall with two more policemen. The Admiral explained his plan. Queen said, "Good idea. I'll take you all up."

In the Council Chamber three members of the Watch Committee were forming a protective phalanx round poor Mr Timms, who looked as though he was about to burst into tears.

"Why don't we all sit down," said Queen, "then we can talk things out."

The Admiral said, "I hope one thing's clear. We can't have violence. It won't do you any sort of good."

"It won't do them circus bastards any good either," said Mr Baker, a large and aggressive engineer. But it seemed that he was in a minority. Tempers were cooling.

"What we've got to do," said Queen, "is get the fullest and most accurate description of the things that have been taken. Mr Timms will write it all down. Suppose you start, Mrs Garibaldi."

Mrs Garibaldi had lost a silver teapot, which had been given to her by her late husband on the twenty-fifth anniversary of their wedding and a pair of small silver candlesticks. She described them in loving detail. Her next-door neighbour, Mrs Preston, had lost two athletic cups won by her son at school. None of the losses seemed very serious but Jonas knew exactly how the people felt about them. It was not the value of the goods, but the fact of the intrusion. To have alien fingers dabbling among their private possessions was a form of rape.

When the list was complete the Superintendent said, "You've most of you been to the funfair and you've seen the people who run it and I expect you'd recognise them if you saw them again. Now think hard. Did you see any of them near your houses yesterday afternoon?"

There was a general shaking of heads.

"It's like this," said Mrs Preston. "As soon as the sun came out we all went down to the town to do our weekend shopping and the kids made straight for the beach."

"Most of the afternoon," agreed Mrs Garibaldi, "I don't suppose there wasn't anyone around in the estate at all."

"Did any of you meet anyone on the road, going out or coming back?"

Heads were shaken again.

"You see how difficult that makes it for us. But what we can do and will do, is to circulate the descriptions you've given us as widely as possible. The tea pot and the cups had engraving on them. They won't be easy to pass – "

There was more discussion, but the steam was out of the meeting. Looking out of the window at the end of the hall Jonas could see that most of the crowd had drifted away, and the police had the traffic moving again.

Jonas congratulated Queen on his handling of the affair.

Queen said, "I did think it was going to be nasty, but they're reasonable folk really. Incidentally, I've got on to that stall-keeper. His name's Golding. He's got a wife who's as big a brute as he is by all account. And has got a bit of form."

"Theft?"

"Assault with intent to injure. He nearly killed a man in a pub at Sidmouth. Some argument about money. He collected three months for that, and would have got more, only it was partly the other man's fault."

"I knew he was an ugly customer," said the Admiral, who had been listening to this.

The twins, who had been watching the Admiral's house, had seen him leave when he went to visit Jonas. They waited for a few minutes and then made their way round to the back, found the door key under the tile and entered quickly. They knew that Mrs Matcham had the day off on Saturday.

"No hurry," said Colin, "we've bags of time."

David said, "It's all right if he does come back. He said we could come here whenever we wanted, didn't he?"

Colin looked at his twin thoughtfully. Then he said, "Yes, that's right. Let's go in."

They made their way upstairs. When not in use the telescope lived in a cupboard in the attic. They took it out, carried it on to the flat roof and fixed it on the permanent housing which stood there.

"Be jolly careful," said Colin. "If you look at the sun through it, it could blind you."

"Stale," said David.

They positioned the telescope so that it was focused on the funfair. Then they fetched two stools from the attic, sat down behind the telescope and took it in turns to watch. The one who wasn't watching had a notebook and a pencil.

Colin said, "If he comes back, remember that we're bird-watching. Write some birds' names in the book."

"What birds?"

"Any birds," said Colin impatiently, and resumed his inspection of the funfair. He was concentrating on the side where the stall-holders' caravans were parked and their families lived.

If the Admiral had been watching them he would have seen no reason to doubt their toughness and initiative. He might have qualified his thoughts about their innocence.

Half an hour later David said, "Got it. It's the blue one, quite a bit separate from the others. It's got a box of geraniums on the window ledge."

"You're sure?"

"Certain. I saw him go in and come out again. And his wife came out. That's the one all right."

Colin said "Good." They packed up the telescope, put it back in the cupboard, returned the stools to the attic, and departed as unobtrusively as they had come.

That afternoon, having nothing better to do, the Admiral again made his way down to the fairground to see if he could pick up anything which might help the wobblers on the council to make up their minds. Nine-tenths of the way there, he thought. One more good push.

Being Saturday, the place was crowded and there was a small queue filtering through the entrance. Immediately in front of him was a girl pushing a pram with a baby in it. Rather a slatternly-looking girl with a lot of make-up on her face. The baby was invisible under a pile of bedclothes. Poor mite must be suffocating, thought the Admiral, and wondered if he should say something about it, but decided that a mother, even as young as that one, probably knew what was best for her own baby.

There were quite a few policemen about, he noticed. The

stall-holders looked a bit edgy, but the crowd seemed reasonably good-tempered. Golding was busy at his roll-a-disc stall which had the usual crowd round it. The Admiral watched for a bit and thought that he seemed more generous in his paying-out than he had been before. Maybe he had sensed the hostility of his customers. A clever brute, thought the Admiral. In a long and active life he had met many brutes, but few of them had been clever.

A woman arrived, pushing her way through the crowd round the stall, carrying a thermos of some hot drink. She ducked under the board and took charge of the game whilst her husband refreshed himself. A big woman, with a rasping voice, she had no difficulty in keeping the game going. A fitting mate for the brute, thought the Admiral.

It was at that moment that he had a shock. He happened to be looking back at his own house, clearly in sight, perched halfway up the cliff. And as he was looking he saw a flash of light. Someone on the roof was using a mirror, slanting it into the strong sun and then turning it away again. A primitive but effective form of heliograph. The message was clear too. The Admiral had not forgotten his morse code.

"Okay," said the mirror and then again, "okay – okay – okay."

"What on earth," said the Admiral. "This wants looking into."

He made quickly for the exit. It took him some time to get through the crowd which was coming in. The stout man in the singlet (surely it was Mr Bailey) recognised him and waved to him genially.

"Going already, Admiral," he said. "Not spent all your money, have you?"

"Not quite," said the Admiral shortly. He noticed another dissatisfied customer just ahead of him. The girl with the pram was leaving too.

Back at his house the mystery deepened. The key was under the tile. There was no sign of breaking in. There was no sort of disturbance and if someone had been up on the roof they had left no mark. The telescope, which was one of the most valuable things in the house, was safely stowed in the attic cupboard. The Admiral made his way down through the house, checking as he went. His orderly habits enabled him to say, with certainty, that nothing was missing.

Could the whole thing have been his imagination?

He was prepared to believe that a flash of sunlight might have deceived him but regular flashes spelling out a message? Was he becoming like one of those people who saw unidentified flying objects? There had been a story in the papers about a market-gardener at Wrexham who had not only seen one, hovering above his garden, but had read a message, flashed from one of its portholes. Oddly enough that had been in morse code too.

The Admiral shook his head angrily. He might be over eighty, but he wasn't cracked. Not yet. Anyway, there was nothing to be done about it. The police had plenty on their hands. He could hardly bother them with a non-burglary.

It was twelve o'clock on the following day and the Admiral, who had been attending morning service at St Michael's Church, was surprised to find a police car outside his gate. It was Superintendent Queen, and he looked happy.

"We've nicked 'em," he said. "Had a tip-off on the telephone yesterday afternoon. Went round and found all the stuff stolen from the estate, in a sack, hidden under that man Golding's caravan. The owners have identified every bit of it. We've had an emergency meeting of the Watch Committee. No opposition this time. A unanimous recommendation. No licence for Mr Bailey next year. I fancy we've seen the last of him."

"What did Golding say about it?"

"Said it was a frame-up, naturally. But couldn't suggest who did the framing. It'll take more than a bit of fast talking to get him out of this one."

"Excellent," said the Admiral. A suspicion of the truth was forming in his mind. Too faint as yet to make consecutive sense. Certainly too faint to be expressed to the Superintendent.

As he consumed his solitary Sunday luncheon the picture sharpened and gained definition. Small items were added to other small items, until what had started as suspicion approached certainty.

He was clearing away the dishes when there was a knock on the door. It was the two boys.

Colin, taking the lead as usual, said, "We've come to say goodbye. Our holiday's over. We've been ordered to go back and cheer up Dad."

"I'm sure you will," said the Admiral.

"It's been a super holiday," said David. "We'll be coming back next year, I hope."

"One thing you won't find here, I'm certain, is Bailey's Circus."

The boys looked at each other. The faintest flicker of a smile crossed David's face. Colin was impassive.

The Admiral said, "And when did you learn the morse code?"

There was a moment of complete silence. Then both boys burst out laughing.

David said, "I told you he'd cotton on to it." And to the Admiral, "How did you spot it? Were you able to read the flashes?"

"I've been reading morse code since I was a midshipman. Was it you with the pram?"

"It was," said David, "and I nearly had a fit when I saw you behind me in the queue. I was glad we'd put the make-up on pretty thick."

"And in the pram, I take it, you had the stuff you'd lifted from Mrs Garibaldi and the others."

"That bit wasn't much fun," said Colin. "We knew the houses were empty, because we knew who lived in them and we'd seen them go out. But all the time we were thinking, suppose someone's been left behind. There was actually a dog in one, but luckily it was one we'd made friends with."

"I was scared stiff," said David. "We just nipped in, picked up the first things we could lay our hands on and nipped out again."

"I see," said the Admiral. The boys looked at him anxiously.

"And the second part of your plan, which you also carried out successfully, was to leave the stuff under Golding's caravan."

"That bit was easy. It was right away in a corner by itself. We'd spotted it with your telescope."

"And you gave us the whole idea," said Colin. "That Dutch skipper's wife and the baby."

"So I'm responsible, am I?" said the Admiral.

They guessed from his tone of voice that he wasn't going to make trouble and smiled at him engagingly.

He said to David, "I'd no idea you were such an accomplished performer."

"Oh, he's a first-class actress," said Colin.

After they had gone, something in the tone of the last remark lingered in the Admiral's mind and stirred a memory. He pulled down his copy of *Who's Who* and turned to the entry under 'Bourdon, Sir David'.

First there was a summarised account of his career in the Royal Navy. Then, in the terse shorthand of that compilation: "M 1960 Félicité, née St Honorée (killed in air crash 1983). Two children: one s, one d."

"I suppose I should have guessed," said the Admiral as he shut up the heavy scarlet volume. He wondered if he should tell Jonas the end of the story. He would very much have liked to do so, but decided against it. Jonas was a solicitor, and might have some compunction about a brute going to prison for something he hadn't done.

The Admiral had none at all.

6

WE'VE COME TO REPORT
A MURDER, SIR

"For the last few months," said Dan Cullingford, "I've been wondering about myself. And when you start wondering about yourself that keeps you awake at night and when you don't sleep properly that makes you feel worse than ever."

"A great deal of illness is psychosomatic," agreed Jonas. "You look fit enough." His visitor had clear blue eyes and the face, more red than brown, of a man who lived much of his life in the open air.

"I've no reason not to be. I still take a lot of exercise. Now that I've only got the one full-time assistant we have to share the games between us. On Wednesday I played an hour of football with the boys and felt perfectly all right whilst I was doing it. It was when I sat down afterwards that I began to wonder."

"How old are you?"

"I'm the wrong side of fifty."

Jonas, who was the wrong side of sixty, thought of saying that he took a minimum of exercise and managed to get along all right, but realised that this would be little consolation to Dan Cullingford. Instead he said, "I suppose you've had a proper check-up?"

"I saw Dr Brassie yesterday."

"What did he say?"

"The sort of thing doctors always say when they don't really know the answer. He said he thought it was possible I had what he called a tired heart. For a real check-up I should have to go into hospital for a day or two."

"He said that, did he?" said Jonas thoughtfully. He knew that Dr Brassie was not an alarmist. "What did you say?"

"That I might be able to manage it at the end of term. That's only eight weeks away. However, I didn't really come to talk about my health. That was only incidental. I wanted you to advise me about remaking my will."

"There's an existing will, then?"

"I've brought it along." He fished a legal-looking envelope out of his pocket. "I made it when I got married. Hadn't bothered until then."

Jonas looked first at the envelope. It had the name Porter and Merriman on it. Cullingford saw him looking at it and said, "It was Ambrose Porter who did it for me. After he died I never had anything more to do with the firm. I mean – it's all right to come to you, isn't it?"

Jonas, who like all solicitors, was cautious about appropriating clients from other firms said, "Yes, of course. If Ambrose Porter was the one you really went to and you haven't consulted them for ten years."

"I'm glad about that. His son's all right as a person, I mean. But he seemed a bit lacking in experience."

Jonas was aware that old men disliked consulting young solicitors. He was reading the will. It was a simple document under which Daniel Stanley Cullingford, schoolmaster, left everything to his wife, Laura, and appointed her sole executrix.

Cullingford said, "The real thing I'm worried about is what might happen to the school if I popped off suddenly. I've got an excellent number two, a man called Tim Delavigne. He'd be happy to keep Clifton House going, but only if he could run the show himself."

"Understandable."

"And as a matter of fact, it would work rather well, because there's a spot of romance in the air."

It took a prep schoolmaster, thought Jonas, to refer to impending matrimony as a spot of romance. He said, "Who is she?"

"Pamela Ricketts. She looks after gym, painting and music."

"All of them?"

"The iron law of economics. The days are past when you could employ specialists in every department. However, she's competent enough in music and art and a qualified PE instructor. She did two years at Bedford."

"PE?"

"In your day," said Cullingford patiently, "it was called physical training. Now it's physical education. A subtle difference."

"I learn a new fact every day," said Jonas. "Well, I can see that she'd make an admirable schoolmaster's wife. Tell me exactly what it is you want me to do."

Cullingford thought about this for some time. Then he said, "What I'm going to tell you is absolutely confidential."

"Of course."

"If I left my will as it is now, as soon as I was dead I think Laura would shut the school and sell the property. You know where it is. Between the Lewes road and the factory estate. If she could get planning permission for development – and I don't see why she shouldn't – well, she'd get a great deal of money for it."

"I see," said Jonas. "Yes. You want to put it out of her power to sell the property, and you want Delavigne to have control of the actual running of the school."

"I don't want to cut her out altogether, you understand – it's just that I don't want her to be in a position to interfere with Tim."

Or with Mrs Delavigne-to-be, thought Jonas. He could see considerable complications if the two ladies didn't get on together. He said, "I'll draft something for you to look at. It'll have to be a trust of some sort, and that means you'll need two trustees. Have you got two reliable friends who'd take the job on?"

"Major Appleby would do it, I'm sure."

"The headmaster of St Oswald's? Yes, I know him. A very sound man."

"The other one might be Leo Sambrooke. You may have seen his name in the High Street. A firm of estate agents. Sambrooke and Dodds. His boy's at the school now."

"Sounds just the man for the job. Ask him if he's prepared to act." He was examining his desk diary. "In fact I see that

Appleby is coming here this afternoon. He wants me to explain the new Finance Act to him. I could tell him what you want him to do, if you like."

"Please," said Cullingford. "And I'll tackle Sambrooke."

Jonas thought that he looked a bit more cheerful than when he came in.

"Clifton House is a good school," said Major Appleby, "and Dan Cullingford is a first-class teacher." He and Jonas had just spent an hour trying to understand the latest piece of gobbledy-gook put out by the Inland Revenue. "I'd hate to see another outfit go under. I think I told you that when I came here after the war there were eight schools. Now just three, Tanner's place, my own place – and Dan Cullingford's. Tanner and I aren't in competition with Dan. When he saw the other schools folding up he read the signs correctly. He started to phase out all his boarders and take day boys instead. That was about six years ago. Clifton House is entirely a day school now."

"And there are enough of them to go round?"

"Certainly. In fact he's got a waiting list. There are a lot of professional and business families in Shackleton who don't like the idea of sending their sons to state schools, but can't quite face boarding school fees. Or who want to put off paying them as long as possible. And incidentally, I think Dan's got a very good number two in Delavigne."

"I'm glad you think that," said Jonas, "because it will make it easier to explain what he has in mind."

He spoke for ten minutes. He was used to expounding legal technicalities to non-legal people, and when he had finished Major Appleby nodded his head.

"In words of one syllable," he said, "Dan wants to make sure that his wife can't flog the lot as soon as he's in his grave."

"Correct," said Jonas. "And I do congratulate you. I've often heard people start by saying 'in words of one syllable' but I've never known anyone actually pull it off."

Appleby laughed and said, "Of course, one can see that she'd have every inducement to do it if she could. Tanner and I have both had that estate agent, Derek Price, of Price and Westbury, nibbling round. He's dead keen to get hold of building land, and would give a lot for the Clifton House playing fields. We both sent him off with a flea in his ear. To tell you the truth, I can't stand the chap."

"Thirtyish, fatter than he should be at that age, smooth dresser, drives a BMW?"

"That's the fellow. Chases girls as well as building land, so I'm told. One question: you realise that I'm a bit older than Dan. What happens if I die first?"

"Then we appoint someone else. But I don't think it's likely to happen."

Appleby looked at Jonas shrewdly. He said, "You don't think Dan's a very good life?"

"I happened to be talking to Dr Brassie. Knowing that I'm Cullingford's solicitor I suppose he felt able to be frank. What he said was, as long as Cullingford would exercise a little common sense and stop playing violent games of football on cold afternoons there's no reason he shouldn't go on happily for years."

"I see," said Appleby. "That's the form, is it? Well, thanks for telling me."

That was the second week in October. Dan Cullingford died on All Saints Day, which fell on a Monday that year. He had been giving some sort of demonstration in the gym and had fallen dead. When Dr Makepeace, the coroner, heard what Dr Brassie had to say he agreed that there was no need for an inquest. The burial service at St Michael's was conducted by the Reverend Tobias Harmer and the address was given by the Bishop of Lewes, who also conducted the committal. The sun was shining, but it gave out little heat and Jonas, his coat collar turned up to his ears, felt a shiver run through him as the coffin was lowered into the ground. He had not known Cullingford long, but long enough to become fond of him.

The church had been jam-packed, and most of the congregation had come out to the churchyard to witness the final rites. Laura was there, in a black two-piece suit over a cream-coloured shirt and was veiled. The school staff and the boys of Clifton House were all in attendance. Two of the boys stood in front of the bishop at the head of the grave when he spoke the words of committal. One of them, a stocky, freckled boy, he knew was Superintendent Queen's son. The other, a tall thin boy in spectacles, was not known to him. Both looked appropriately solemn.

Claire, who had come with Jonas, said, "I do hate that sort of thing. It's barbarous. Give me a quiet private cremation every time."

"I don't know," said Jonas mildly. "A lot of people enjoy funerals. And it doesn't make any difference to the party chiefly concerned."

"Not to him," agreed Claire, "but I bet the leading lady was enjoying it all behind that tootsie little veil. She'll be round to see you in a day or two."

"Surely she'll wait for a bit. A decent interval, anyway."

"Would you care to bet on it?" said Claire. "I'll make it an even fiver that she turns up before the end of the week."

The telephone call came that Thursday, when Claire was in Jonas's room taking dictation. She lifted the receiver, listened impassively, and said, in her most secretarial voice, "It's Mrs Cullingford, sir. She wants to know if she can come and have a word with you."

"Monday morning?" suggested Jonas hopefully.

"You're in Eastbourne on Monday and Tuesday on that planning enquiry." Claire had the desk diary open. "You've nothing on before midday tomorrow."

"All right." Jonas sighed, took a five pound note out of his wallet and passed it across the desk. "Tell her eleven o'clock."

When Laura arrived she was wearing the same black suit but she had brightened it up with a fuchsia-coloured scarf at the throat and Jonas concluded that her sorrow for the loss of her husband was likely to be short-lived. He knew quite well what she had come to talk about, and after five minutes of sparring she came to the point.

She said, "My husband showed me the will he had made. I meant to bring it along with me, but it seems to have disappeared. He told me he was coming to see you. Did he show it to you perhaps?"

"He showed it to me," said Jonas slowly. "That was the first time he came to see me. When he came here again – that was a week later – to sign his new will, he tore the old one up.

Anyway, it was no longer effective, because the new will totally revoked the old one. But I always think it's a mistake to have too many wills hanging about. It can easily lead to confusion."

He had dragged this statement out to give Laura time to react. He saw the flush rising in her cheeks and the tightening of her mouth.

She said, "He never told me he was making a new will."

"No?"

"Wasn't that rather unusual?"

"Not really. I expect he planned to tell you about it later. There was no reason to worry you about it whilst he was alive and well."

"Worry me. Why should it have worried me?"

Her feelings were very near the surface now.

"I've had copies made for you and the two executors. Perhaps you'd better read it."

Laura picked up the document that Jonas had put on the desk in front of her, but seemed unwilling to pick it up. She said, "Two executors? What are you talking about? I'm his executor. The sole executor. He told me so."

"That was in the old will. The executors in his new will are Major Appleby and Leopold Sambrooke."

"Do they know about this?"

"They know about it and have agreed to act." Seeing that Laura was making no attempt to read the document Jonas said, "You might find some of the legal terms confusing. Shall I explain it to you?"

Laura said, "Yes." Her mouth was scarcely open, and the word came out like a hiss.

"Well, to start with, he leaves you all his personal chattels. That's to say, everything he possessed outside the school."

"Which was nothing. He had nothing except the school."

"I wouldn't say that. Everyone has something. Furniture, books, pictures, shares, money in the bank."

"No shares. And an overdraft in the bank."

"All right," said Jonas, who was finding Laura hard to take. "He may not have had much, but what he did have is yours."

"The school. Tell me about the school."

"He left the school and the grounds to his executors."

"What!" Not a hiss, this time. A scream. "He left the school to old Appleby and Sambrooke. Why? What had they done to deserve it?"

"Hold your horses. He didn't leave it to them beneficially. They hold it on trust."

"Trust?"

"The will tells them what to do with it. As long as the school carries on, the profits – that's to say, the income it produces – goes in equal shares to you and Mr Delavigne. If they sell it, and they've got the power to do that, then again, what they get is split equally between the two of you."

"Can I make them sell it?"

"No one can make them sell it. It's a matter for them. Anyway, it's clear that your husband wanted the school to go on as long as it could. I think that's obvious from the fact that it's the executors who have the right to appoint the headmaster."

Laura sat in silence for an appreciable time. She was chewing over the bitter dish that had been served to her. He could see her mouth moving. Violent forces were working on her. He thought, she's so far off-balance that she might do or say anything.

When she spoke the undercurrent of bile almost choked the words. She said, "You've got it all nicely worked out between you, haven't you? But you're not going to get away with it. I can promise you that. I'll have that will set aside."

"Yes?"

"Yes, yes, yes, yes, yes. I'll go and see a real solicitor. One who doesn't conspire behind people's backs. We'll see what the Law Society has to say about you, Mr Tricky Pickett."

Jonas rang the bell on his desk, and Claire came in. She said, "Did you want me?"

"You'd better be here. If this lady proposes to slander me again, it would be as well to have a witness present."

Laura left without another word.

Tim Delavigne was standing in the headmaster's study looking out of the window. Dan's sudden death had shaken the school from top to bottom, but the ship was slowly climbing back on to course again. All the parents had been sympathetic.

None of them had wanted to take their boys away. With any luck, he thought, he and Pamela should be able to cope.

A car came storming up the drive. Laura jumped out and slammed the door behind her.

Tim's feelings towards Laura at that moment were ambivalent. He was sorry for her. The loss of her husband must, surely, have been a blow. When he had made some such comment to Pamela she had said nothing. She had neither agreed not disagreed. In fact, she had been very odd about the whole thing.

Whilst he was thinking, in a puzzled male way, about women and their unfathomable natures, Laura came in. This time she did not slam the door. She left it open, stalked across to Dan's desk, and sat down behind it.

She said, "I wonder if you'd very much mind asking me before you make free of my study."

Tim stared at her.

"Until something else is legally and officially decided, I take it that I am in charge here."

"Yes. I mean – I suppose so. Actually I thought – "

"Yes, Mr Delavigne. What did you think?"

"I thought it had been arranged that I should take over."

"Arranged? Arranged by who?"

"Well, by Dan's executors."

"I see. So you're in the plot as well, are you? Well, let me tell you this, Mr Delavigne, that I've been having a word with *my* lawyer. Not *your* lawyer, Grandfather Pickett, but a young Cedric Porter who knows something about the law, and has a few manners into the bargain. And I showed him a copy of the will, and he said that until the executors had had a meeting and made an appointment, I was in charge. Well?"

"I expect he's right," said Tim. He was seeing a side of Laura that he had never suspected before and wanted only to get out of the room.

"Then perhaps you would be good enough to send Miss Ricketts to see me."

He found Pamela in the Art Room and said, "Laura's in Dan's study. She wants to see you – and look – I'm afraid she's rather upset. Hardly responsible for what she says. So watch out."

"I'm not afraid of Mrs Cullingford," said Pamela coolly. "She can't kill *me*."

"What are you talking about?"

"I'll tell you later. Mustn't keep Madame waiting."

Tim sat down at one of the desks and stared at a well-executed painting of three apples on a plate. He was normally courageous enough, but there was something frightening about mental imbalance.

It was five minutes before Pamela reappeared. There was a faint flush across her cheekbones, but otherwise she seemed unruffled.

She said, "Well, you see, she didn't kill me."

"What did she want you for? What did she say?"

"She sacked me. I've got to be out by Sunday night."

"Sacked you? She can't do that."

"She seems to think she can."

"What for?"

"I wasn't quite clear about that. Either for impertinence or incompetence. Or maybe for both."

"This is mad. What are we going to do?"

"I think we must have a word with Mr Pickett."

"I'll telephone him right away."

Jonas listened carefully to what Tim had to say. He then asked to speak to Pamela, who was the more coherent of the two.

He said, "I can certainly act for you, now that Mrs Cullingford has gone elsewhere. You said it was Cedric Porter he'd seen? He's quite a sensible chap. Better than his old father. I think I'll have a word with him. Which means I shan't be able to see you until later tonight. Could you both get away after supper?"

"We'll do that," said Tim. In fact the thought of supper with Laura had deprived him of any appetite.

Jonas caught Cedric Porter on the point of slipping away for a round of golf. He said, "If you don't get stuck in too many bunkers you should be back in the clubhouse by seven o'clock. There's a small room behind the bar that no one ever uses. Shall we meet there?"

He thought that Cedric Porter sounded relieved at the idea of a meeting.

* * *

"This is off the record?" said Porter.

"Certainly," said Jonas. "Anything said is off the record and totally deniable."

"To tell you the truth, I'm glad to have the chance of discussing it in a friendly way, because it really is a very awkward situation."

"Awkward for everyone," agreed Jonas.

"I've seen the will. I'm assuming that as soon as the executors can meet they'll use their powers to appoint Delavigne headmaster."

"Yes. You can assume that. Unfortunately Major Appleby has pushed off with a party of senior boys on some sort of expedition. He won't be back until late on Monday night so the earliest he and Sambrooke can meet is Tuesday morning. And, I'd agree with you that until they meet, Mrs Cullingford retains a sort of residual authority."

"Yes," said Porter unhappily. "But I did point out to her that anything she does can be reversed as soon as Delavigne takes over."

"What did she say to that?"

"Frankly, I'm not sure she was really listening. I hope she took it in and doesn't do anything stupid. After all, she can't do a lot in three days."

"So far, she's only sacked Miss Ricketts."

"She's done what?" In his agitation Porter dropped the golf ball he had been fiddling with and it rolled away under the seat.

Jonas retrieved it and handed it back to him. He said, "If I was a psychiatrist I'd diagnose her trouble as acute persecution mania. The six people who are persecuting her are her late husband, myself, Delavigne, Miss Ricketts, Major Appleby and Leopold Sambrooke. Dan is out of her reach, but if she could wipe out the other five, she'd do it cheerfully."

"You don't mean –"

"Maybe I was exaggerating. No – I don't think she's reached the homicidal stage, but it wouldn't take much to push her over the edge."

Cedric Porter said, "I trust you're wrong," but he didn't sound very hopeful. "All I can suggest is that we ought to keep in touch, unofficially, until we can see what's going to happen."

"I agree," said Jonas grimly.

When he got back to the office Tim and Pamela were waiting for him. Sam was doing his best to entertain them but without a lot of success. Tim said, "We both cut supper. Couldn't stand the thought of it."

"All right," said Jonas. "Bring me up to date."

"There's not a great deal to report. Laura has spent most of the time in Dan's study, with the door locked. Heaven knows what she's up to. She did a lot of telephoning. I think she was trying to get hold of young Porter and was very put out when she discovered he wasn't in the office."

"In a way," said Jonas, "what she's doing is explicable. Grabbing Dan's office for herself and sitting in his chair. She's asserting the position she thinks she ought by rights to have had. What's out of character, Miss Ricketts, is sacking you. She must know that she can't make that stick. As soon as Tim's appointed, which will be on Tuesday at the latest, he reappoints you. At least I imagine so."

"At once, if not sooner," agreed Tim.

Pamela said, "The real reason she's trying to get me out of the place is that I was in the gym when her husband died. I didn't actually see what happened because I was busy with some juniors at the other end of the room. I heard a crash and ran up. He must have been trying to climb one of the ropes and fell from nearly the top of it. It wasn't the fall that killed him, Dr Brassie says, it was the effort of climbing. Actually, if you know how to do it, climbing a rope is as easy as walking upstairs. But I don't think he did know."

"Then why did he try to do it?"

"Laura was there. She's made a point lately of coming into my gym classes and more than once she's seemed to be making fun of Dan because he couldn't do everything the boys did. Last week, I remember, they were going over the vaulting horse and she said, 'Even tiny boys can do it. You ought to be setting them an example,' which he did, easily enough. But clearing a vaulting horse is not the same as climbing a twenty-foot rope."

"Did you actually hear her suggesting that he climb it?"

"No. But she may have thought I did."

"Are you suggesting that she killed her husband?"

In the face of this direct question Pamela hesitated. "It's an awful thing to suggest, but yes, I think she had the possibility in mind."

"Why? To run the school herself?"

"Not to run it. To sell it."

Jonas thought of what Dan had said to him in that room less than a month ago. He said, "I suppose you realise that there's nothing in all this that adds up to anything like proof. No one could begin to base a charge on it."

"I didn't imagine you could," said Pamela. "Once she's out of the way I'll be happy to forget all about her."

She looked at Tim, who smiled his agreement.

"I'm not sure that you *can* get rid of her."

"But – "

"When Tim becomes headmaster he can stop her from interfering with the school. But that doesn't mean he can turn her out of the house. The law is very protective of widows and their rights in the matrimonial home."

"Let her stay on?" said Tim. "It would be an impossible position for all of us, quite impossible. It just would not work."

"Has it occurred to you that there may be some method in Laura Cullingford's madness? She'll have been told what her legal rights are. If she really can make it impossible for you to carry on, you'd have to sell the place. Which is exactly what she wants."

Tim and Pamela looked at each other. The idea had obviously never struck them.

"I may be quite wrong," said Jonas. "Anyway, there's no point in crossing that bridge till we come to it. The next few days are going to be critical. We'd better keep in touch."

After they had gone Jonas sat for a long time in his office. In forty years of legal practice he could hardly remember a more difficult situation, or one with more unpleasant possibilities. Suppose what Pamela had suggested was true. Suppose Laura had planned to kill her husband. If so, she had done it in such a way that the law could not touch her.

"Thou shalt not kill," he quoted to himself, "but needst not strive officiously to keep alive."

And what was Laura going to do now? With a woman of her temperament it was impossible to guess, except that it would certainly be unexpected and possibly violent.

The street outside was very quiet. Faintly he heard the clock in the market square striking the hour. Ten o'clock. He'd no idea it was so late. He switched out the light in the office and went upstairs to his flat. Tomorrow was Saturday. Nothing much could happen before Tuesday, after Appleby had got back. That should at least give them a quiet weekend.

He was still thinking this when the telephone in his bedroom rang at seven o'clock on the following morning.

"Sorry to wake you up," said Superintendent Queen.

"I am awake. I'm just putting on my shoes."

"Good. Well the fact is, Mr Pickett, that I think I ought to warn you that you'll be getting your first clients at eight o'clock."

"Who?"

"One of 'em's my son James. T'other's a friend of his at the school, Vincent Sambrooke."

"At Clifton House?"

"Right. They're the two senior boys. In fact they're leaving at the end of the term. They've both got places at Brighton College."

"Were they the two boys I saw at the funeral standing in front of the bishop?"

"Right. And what I wanted to say is that they're both sensible kids. Much more grown up than I was at their age."

"Children grow up faster now," agreed Jonas. "What do they want to talk about?"

"Jimmy wouldn't tell me."

"Why?"

He heard the Inspector chuckle. "He told me he'd heard me say that if people knew their rights they'd always have a word with their solicitors *before* saying anything to the police."

Jonas said, "Good heavens. I hope whatever trouble they're in it's not serious."

"I got the impression," said Queen, "that it wasn't them that was in trouble."

*　　*　　*

The boys arrived promptly at eight o'clock, and sat down in the two chairs which Jonas had placed opposite his desk. James looked at Vincent who was clearly to be the spokesman.

He said, "We've come to report a murder, sir."

"Of whom, by whom?"

Vincent faced this without flinching. He said, "Of Mr Cullingford, by his wife."

There was a long pause while Jonas made up his mind what to say. Laugh at them? Impossible. Get angry with them? Equally impossible. In the end he simply said, "I suppose you realise that what you're saying is extremely serious?"

Vincent had taken off his glasses to clean them on his handkerchief. Having replaced them he looked quite steadily at Jonas and said, "Yes, sir. We know it's serious, but it's true. We were in the gym, quite close to where it happened. We both heard Mrs Cullingford say, 'Go on, Dan, be a big man. Show the boys how to do it.' We didn't think he wanted to, but she kept at him. She said, 'Shall I get Pamela – that's Miss Ricketts – to show you how to do it?' That seemed to annoy him, so he took off his coat and started up. Then – but you know about that, sir."

"Yes," said Jonas. "I know about that. If what you're implying is true – and I say if, because I can see no certainty in it at all – can you think of any reason why she should do such a thing?"

"Oh, we know that, sir."

Jonas stared at him.

"If we didn't know that, we wouldn't have come along. It was what young Russell told us yesterday evening that made us certain we were right. He'd seen Mrs Cullingford in Mr Price's BMW. It was parked up a lane near his house, but he could see them quite clearly through the hedge."

"Did he say what they were doing?"

For the first time Vincent seemed to have lost a little of his remarkable poise. He said, "What he said, sir, was that they were snogging."

"And what did he mean by that?"

"He's only eleven," said Vincent apologetically. "I don't think he knows a lot about that sort of thing. I mean it was getting dark, and he couldn't see much. What I expect he meant was heavy petting."

Jonas was wondering what a judge and counsel would make of this sort of evidence. He said, "If it was dark, mightn't Russell have been wrong about the car?"

"Oh no, sir," said Jimmy, speaking for the first time. "He may not know much about sex but he knows *all* about cars. He says it was a red four-door six-cylinder BMW 520i with one of those black spoilers. Price is the only man in these parts who's got one of those."

"I see," said Jonas. This sounded a little more like hard evidence. "What about the people in the car? Of course he'd know Mrs Cullingford, but how did he know the man was Price?"

"He said they'd bought their new house through Price and Westbury. He'd seen Price talking to his father more than once."

Vincent, who had recovered his poise, said, "Jimmy and I talked it out. We knew Mr Price had been shopping round for building land. At one time he asked my father to come in with him on a deal. Dad wasn't keen, because, he told me, he didn't trust Price. But if Mr Cullingford was out of the way, he could pick up Mrs Cullingford *and* the land. It seemed quite obvious."

By this time Jonas had decided on the line he must take. He said coldly, "Things may seem obvious in a sort of detective story way, but we're dealing here with real life. There could be all sorts of explanations of what you've told me. Meanwhile, I'll give you some advice. I imagine you came to me for advice?"

The two boys nodded.

"Then you are to say nothing to anyone until I let you. If you do, you may cause untold harm. You haven't spoken to your fathers?"

Two heads were shaken.

"Good. Then keep your mouths buttoned. You'd better hurry, or you'll be late for school."

As the boys were leaving the office Vincent said, "Did you see that, Jimmy?"

"No. What?"

"In the BMW. Mr Price."

"Did he see us?"

"Yes, I think he did. Ten to one he'll sneak to Mrs Cullingford."

James thought about this as they trotted along. They couldn't stop to talk about it. They were going to have their work cut out to get to school in time.

"Don't see she can do much about it," said James. "It isn't as though we'd done anything wrong."

They were a minute late, but scudded up the drive and slipped into their places as the short service which started the day's routine was about to begin.

On Saturdays there were two periods of work followed by a half-hour break at eleven and one more work hour before lunch. Since no games had been arranged for the afternoon, once lunch was over everyone was free to go home.

It was during the break that the message came round. Everyone was to be in the big school room at half past eleven.

"Does everyone mean us?" said the visiting master who taught mathematics.

"Apparently not," said Tim. "Just the boys."

The master said, "Good show." He himself had no further class to take and was planning to catch the eleven forty to London. "What's it all about anyway?"

"No idea. Orders from the head lady."

The boys shuffled into the schoolroom and sat down. Laura mounted the platform where the master's desk stood and stared down at them. She was breathing heavily, as though she had been running. There was a white patch along each cheekbone.

She said, "Sambrooke and Queen, come out here."

The two boys came and stood in front of the desk.

"You were both late for prayers this morning."

"I thought we were just in time, Mrs Cullingford," said Jimmy.

"There's no such thing as being just in time. Either you're in time or you're late."

"Yes, Mrs Cullingford."

"What made you late?"

So Price *has* sneaked, thought Jimmy. Now for it. He said, "I had a message from my father for Mr Pickett."

"A message? Why couldn't your father have delivered it himself?"

"I don't know, Mrs Cullingford."

Laura, who had been standing, now stepped off the platform and stood beside Jimmy. She said, through her teeth, "I think you're lying."

"I'm not lying, Mrs Cullingford. You can ask my father. He knew I was going there."

"I've no doubt he'll support any lies you choose to tell. But you're not going to get away with it."

She swung her right arm, hand open, and hit him in the face. She was a powerful woman, and the blow was so unexpected that Jimmy toppled over sideways, clutched at one of the legs of the desk, and pulled it down on top of himself. It came with a splintering crash, spilling books, rulers and an open inkpot from which a black lake spread slowly on to the planks.

Laura took no further notice of him. She moved across to Vincent who guessed what was coming and whipped his glasses off. Her open hand hit him on the side of the face. Since he was ready for it he did not fall down but stood staring at her blankly. She hit him again, and then again.

The rest of the school stood watching her in horrified silence.

It was just after half past two that same afternoon when Superintendent Queen and Leopold Sambrooke arrived together at Jonas's office. They were both very angry. They told Jonas what had happened, supplementing each other, and adding to each other's fury.

"Vincent's got a badly split lip, and the doctor thinks he may have a cracked cheekbone."

"Jimmy's had to have six stitches in a long tear in his scalp. That was when the desk fell on him."

"They're both pretty shocked, I can tell you."

"They weren't the only people who were shocked. A lot of

the smaller boys were so scared they wouldn't even stay for school lunch. They scuttled straight off."

"There are no two ways about it," said Sambrooke. "That woman ought to be in a home, under proper restraint."

"And what we want to know," said Queen, "is what we can do about it. Because we're not letting her get away with it."

"That's right," said Sambrooke. "What's the position? The legal position?"

"Well," said Jonas. "Mrs Cullingford was standing in, temporarily, as headmaster. The law about schoolmasters isn't entirely clear, but it's generally accepted that they have the right to give their pupils moderate punishment."

"Moderate," said Sambrooke viciously. "A fractured cheekbone and a broken head for being one minute late for school."

"Only it seems that wasn't their real offence," said Queen.

"What was it, then?"

"Coming to visit you."

"I see," said Jonas. "Yes, I thought I saw that BMW parked outside. Price must have seen them leaving."

"Look here," said Sambrooke. "What we want – "

Jonas held up one hand. "I know what you want," he said. "And please don't misunderstand me. Of course what Mrs Cullingford did couldn't be justified under any code of law. It was sheer spiteful rage. A totally unwarranted attack, in front of a hundred witnesses. No court would tolerate it. But the real point is this. If a case were brought which court would be hearing it?"

The two angry men stared at him. Queen seemed to have some idea what he was getting at.

Jonas said, "If Mrs Cullingford had not been in a position of authority – I mean, if she had just come up to a strange boy in the street and had done what she did to your boys – the right course would have been a simple charge of criminal assault. First offence. She would probably have been bound over. You follow me?"

Queen said, "Yes." Sambrooke was too angry to speak.

"But where someone exceeds – grossly exceeds – an imagined right, the proper course is a civil action, which would certainly result in her being forced to pay costs and heavy damages."

"Let's hit her where it hurts most," agreed Queen.

"Quite so. The trouble is that a civil action takes time. Certainly months, maybe years."

"That's impossible," said Sambrooke. "She can't be left in that school for another day. She's not safe."

Queen, who knew Jonas better than Sambrooke, said, "You've got some idea, haven't you, Mr Pickett?"

"Yes," said Jonas. "I'm not sure whether it's a good one or a bad one."

He spoke for some minutes.

"It's going to mean a lot of hard work for you," he said. "And you'll have to move quickly. You've only got this afternoon and tomorrow."

"You can do a lot in a day and a half if you give your mind to it," said Queen. "One thing, we shan't have to waste much time over explanations."

Sambrooke said, "Might be a good idea to get the press in on it. Sammy Clayton's father is sub-editor of the *South Coast Gazette and News*. It publishes bi-weekly, on Tuesdays and Fridays."

"Tuesday," said Jonas thoughtfully. "Yes, that should be about right."

At the school that morning Tim, who had heard the crash of the desk going over, had hurried into the room. He had almost been knocked over by Laura sweeping out. He silenced the shrill babble of explanations and said to one of the visiting masters who had come in with him, "Can you look after everyone for half an hour, Alex? Keep them all in here. I'm going to get these two boys home."

When he got back to the school Alex said, "Am I glad to see you! I had to lock the door to keep half of them from running away."

Tim said, "Does anybody *not* want to stop for lunch?"

A dozen hands went up. Mostly boys who lived within walking distance of the school. He said, "All right, off you go."

Lunch was a mad-house, with everyone talking so excitedly that they could hardly find time to eat. "A pity," said Pamela. "Cook always makes a special effort for Saturday lunch."

Laura did not put in an appearance.

When it was over the boys dispersed, some on foot, some on bicycles. A few more were collected by their parents. Tim could see them beginning to talk before the car doors were even shut, the words coming out like bubbles in a cartoon, "Mummy, do you know what Mrs Cullingford . . . ?"

When the last of them had gone Pamela said, "What are you planning to do?"

"I'll tell you what I'm *not* going to do," said Tim, "and that is hang about here waiting for the storm to break. I thought we might run over to Brighton. We'll have dinner there and get back late."

"So you're running away?"

"Right," said Tim. He had a word with Annie, the more sensible of the two housemaids who lived in. He said, "I expect there'll be a lot of messages, people asking particularly to talk to me. Could you just make a note of the calls, and say I'll ring back first thing tomorrow. Leave the notes in the letter-rack in the staffroom."

Annie looked doubtful, but promised to do her best. After that they spent a peaceful afternoon, sitting in the sun on Brighton Pier and resolutely refusing to discuss school matters. They had a good meal and a glass of wine at the Albion Hotel, and thus fortified drove back to Clifton House. There was a chink of light from the window in the headmaster's study, but otherwise the building was in darkness. They went in by the back door and Tim made his way to the staff room.

There was a single sheet of paper in the letter rack.

It was in Annie's schoolgirl handwriting. It said: "Ten p.m. No messages so far."

They stared at each other in disbelief.

Over Sunday the mystery deepened. The telephone was silent; no one came to the house. Laura confined herself to her own quarters. Tim and Pamela went for a walk over the downs behind Shackleton, had a combined tea and supper in a village pub, and once again got home after dark. Still no messages.

"The trouble's going to start when the boys get here tomorrow," said Tim. "I don't mean Jimmy and Vincent. They may still be under doctor's orders. It's the other boys. They'll have had time to tell their parents all about it."

"And the story," said Pamela, "will have lost nothing in the telling."

The members of the visiting staff who were involved in Monday's programme turned up in good time and joined Tim and Pamela in the main classroom. Laura did not normally attend prayers. The service, a brief and interdenominational one, had been conducted since Dan Cullingford's death by Tim. The science master played the piano, badly. Everyone was ready. There was only one thing missing. There were no boys.

After ten minutes it became clear that this was not a question of lateness. It was mass desertion.

Tim was not sure whether he was worried or relieved. On the whole, relief predominated. Whatever happened now, this was going to bring things to a head. He wondered who had organised it.

He sent the visiting staff home and went straight to have it out with Laura. From her vantage point in the study she must have been able to observe what was happening.

She said, "Is this something to do with you?"

"Certainly not."

"Then what – ?"

"The fact is," said Tim brutally, "that you've frightened the boys so badly that their parents won't let them come to school. I don't blame them. What you did was cruel and totally uncalled for."

For a moment he thought that Laura was going to explode but the spirit was out of her. She said plaintively, "What are we going to do? What *can* we do?"

"The first thing," said Tim, who was looking out of the window, "is to deal with the press. Isn't that Giles Clayton, from the *Gazette*? His son's in the school. No doubt that's why he's first in the field. I expect there'll be others. Are you going to talk to them?"

"No," said Laura wildly, "I can't. I wouldn't know what to say. You must do it. After all, by tomorrow you'll probably be headmaster."

"If there's any school for me to be headmaster of."

"What are you going to tell them?"

"The truth," said Tim, and went out.

In fact Giles Clayton was their only visitor. He listened to what Tim had to tell him, and said, "Yes, that's more or less what Sammy told me. It's pretty bad for the school, isn't it? I could tone it down a bit, perhaps."

Tim had already made his mind up about this. He said, "Don't tone it down at all. Tell the whole story."

The *South Down News* and the *South Coast Times*, both of which were weeklies, telephoned later that afternoon. Their interest in the story was diminished by the fact that the *Gazette* was ahead of them. In any event, by the time they came out on Friday the story would be public property.

Laura's nerve did not finally break until Tuesday morning. The story was on the front page of the *Gazette* under a full-size headline: "The Schoolboys Who Daren't Go To School". Thinking about it had been bad. Reading the story of it in cold print was intolerable. It led her to take a step which, if she had been in full control of herself, she would have known to be unwise. She telephoned Derek Price at his office.

At first there seemed to be some difficulty about putting her through. Finally she lost her temper with his secretary and said, "If he doesn't ring me back in five minutes I'm coming round in person."

Almost as soon as she had put down the receiver the telephone rang. Price sounded cool. He said, "From what I've seen in this morning's paper, it looks as though you're in trouble."

Laura said, "We've got to talk about this. Now. This morning."

Price said, "It wouldn't be very sensible to meet in public. People might start to imagine things." Laura said nothing, but he had no difficulty in visualising the state she was in. Like an unexploded bomb, he thought. "I'll tell you what," he said. "I'll drive out to the school. The back entrance. Meet you there. Then we can drive up on to the downs, and talk this over."

Half an hour later they were parked in a lay-by from which they could look down on Shackleton, its roofs shining under the clear November sun.

Laura said, "We planned to get married as soon as we could

after Dan's death. As soon as public opinion would stand for it, was what you said. Well, after what's happened I'm past worrying about public opinion. I've got to get away from here, and I'm not going alone. If we got a special licence we could be married in a month."

When Derek said nothing she added, "Couldn't we?"

He said, "I'm very fond of you. And I don't want to sound mercenary, but things are a bit different now."

"Different?"

"Well, when we made the arrangement, I understood that after Dan's death the school would be yours. Now it seems you've only got a half share of what it fetches when it's sold."

He looked at her out of the corner of his eye to see how she was taking this. She seemed to be taking it surprisingly well.

She said, "Cedric Porter told me about that. There are institutions who buy these things. It's called a settled reversion. It could be sold now for quite a reasonable sum."

"I expect that's right," said Price. "But there's something else. The buzz is that the fathers of both the boys you hit are planning to sue you. When you'd paid damages and costs there mightn't be much left of what you got for your share in the school."

"I see," said Laura. "Well, that's that, isn't it? Perhaps you'd be kind enough to drive me back to the school."

Derek stole another glance at her face. She seemed to be taking it all very calmly. If he had been shrewder, he would have looked at her hands. Those traitors were clasping and unclasping themselves.

Halfway down the steep hill into Shackleton she leaned across, grabbed the wheel and twisted it.

"I'm not sure what she meant to do," said Major Appleby. "Perhaps she was trying to kill them both. If that was her idea, it didn't work. She hit a telegraph pole, and turned the car over. Price got off comparatively lightly. Broke an arm and three ribs. She cracked her skull, and will be in hospital for months."

It was a fortnight after the accident, and the Major had called on Jonas for a further discussion on income tax.

Jonas said, "R. and L. Sykes have already had instructions. Price is going the whole hog. Not just damages. He wants a charge of attempted murder. She'll wriggle out of that. She'll say it was an accident. Her word against his."

"Whether she wriggles out of it or not," said the Major, "it's quite clear she can't come back to the school."

"How are they doing there?"

"They're fine. I took our football team down to play them yesterday and we got walloped. Sambrooke and Queen scored two goals each."

7

HOLY WRIT

In his youth Jonas Pickett had been a keen golfer. When he qualified as a solicitor he had abandoned the game as a distraction from the more important matter of making a living. Now he had been lured back on to the course.

"An old roué returning to the sins of his youth," said Claire uncharitably.

On that Sunday afternoon he had a game arranged with Ronald Sykes, now the senior partner in R. and L. Sykes. It was a fine April afternoon, with no threat of rain and he had decided to walk to the golf club. He was crossing the market square when he noticed the crowd at the far side and could hear people shouting. He had lived long enough in Shackleton to guess what was happening. Well, it was not his trouble. Let them sort it out for themselves.

The town had once boasted three cinemas. Now only one remained open. One had turned itself into a dance-hall; the other had taken to bingo. Claire, who kept him informed of all local gossip, had said, "I hear they've got permission to open on Sunday afternoons. It was a close thing in the committee. A good deal of opposition from local fuddy-duddies."

"Absurd," said Jonas. "I play golf on Sunday. Why shouldn't they play bingo?"

Claire had said, "Tell that to the Reverend Tobias Harmer."

The rector of St Michael's was, in truth, a notable character. Physically notable, being over six foot high, with snowy white hair, piercing eyes and a nose like the beak of a bird of prey; and a notable menace to all in charge of local arrangements. Assisted by other earnest reformers he had striven to

147

clean up Shackleton. He was now engaged in demonstrating a one-man opposition to Sunday bingo.

He had taken his stand, Jonas saw, on the top step in front of the doorway of the hall and was underlining his arguments with flourishes of a stick.

"You will find it written in the Commandments of our Lord that you keep holy the Sabbath day. Six days shalt thou labour and do all that thou hast to do, but the seventh is the Sabbath of the Lord, thy God. In it thou shalt do no manner of work – "

"Bingo isn't work," called an objector from the back of the crowd.

"A jesuitical argument, my friend. *You* may be amusing yourselves, but what about the people who are running the place?"

He swung round and a small man who had poked his head through the half-opened door hastily withdrew it.

"It is in the sweat of *their* brows that you are pursuing your godless pleasures. Pray keep your distance, madam."

The crowd was divided. The people at the back looked on the whole thing as a welcome distraction on a dull Sunday afternoon. The front rank were hopeful bingo players. They were angry.

Someone behind him said, "If he hits anyone with that stick I shall have to take him in."

He turned and saw Detective Superintendent Queen.

"Wouldn't want to arrest a man of the cloth. Couldn't you have a word with him?"

"For God's sake, Jack. He's not my client."

"You could have a try."

"I've got a date at the golf club."

"Public order's more important than golf."

Jonas considered this for a moment. He saw that one of the ladies, a Mrs McClachan, a leading light in the Women's Institute, was edging up to the rector. Strife was imminent.

"I'll try," he said and pushed his way through the crowd.

He had reached the top step before the rector focused his grey eyes on him and said, "Who the blazes are you, sir?"

"I'm a lawyer."

"Woe to ye, ye lawyers. Luke eleven, forty-six."

"And because I'm a lawyer I believe in the law. Every word of it, you must remember, has an exact and important meaning."

The rector had allowed Jonas to get so near that he was inside the sweep of his stick and in no immediate danger. He leaned closer and continued speaking quietly, but firmly.

Surprisingly, the rector allowed him to finish. Even more surprisingly he smiled, swung round and said, "It would appear, ladies, that I was wrong about one point. A small point, but an important one." He bowed to Mrs McClachan. "Enjoy your childish game, ladies. I'll not stand in your way."

The crowd parted and allowed him through. The rear ranks seemed disappointed at this tame conclusion. Noticing this, the rector said, "Have patience, friends. The matter is not disposed of. Only postponed," and he stalked off down the street swinging his weapon like a quarter-staff.

"How the blazes did you manage that?" said Queen.

"I told him he was misquoting his own authorities. The seventh day is the Sabbath. But it is the Jewish Sabbath. That's not Sunday, it's Saturday."

"Well, blow me down," said Queen. "I'm most obliged, I'm sure. If he comes back next Saturday we'll have a few of our men here. And someone on the door a bit tougher than that rabbit Henshawe." He saw Jonas looking at his watch. "If you're late for your game I'll give you a lift. My car's just round the corner."

Jonas was in time for the tee-off. He played less successfully than usual. His mind was on other things. Later, in the bar, where a garbled account of what had happened in the market square seemed to have reached the club, Sykes said, "Is that right you managed to make Harmer see reason?"

"Sort of," said Jonas.

"It's more than I've ever been able to do."

"Do I gather he's your client?"

"He was. I guess he'll be yours now."

"I'm not looking for clients," said Jonas. "All the same, he sounds quite a character. Let's go over to the table in the corner. I'd like to hear more about him."

"If he does consult you," said Sykes, "you needn't be afraid you're poaching on my preserves. Harmer's the bad penny. He gets passed round from hand to hand. He started with Porter and Merriman, who normally conduct church business. But that didn't survive the cleansing of the temple."

"What are you talking about?"

"Well, you see, the trouble is there's no church hall at St Michael's, so functions had to take place *in* the church. They had a stall, just inside the door, which sold postcards and books and religious stuff and every so often they'd have a more ambitious affair, a sort of jumble sale, cakes and jam and sweets and cups of undrinkable coffee. The usual sort of thing. The Women's Institute ran it. The mistake they made was not telling Harmer what they were up to. It was early days. I suppose they thought he'd be as broadminded as his predecessor."

"Natural, perhaps. But foolish. What did he say?"

"He didn't say anything. He just threw everything out into the churchyard."

"Everything? Cakes and jam?"

"The lot. All among the tombstones."

"It must have made a terrible mess."

"It made a terrible row. Cedric Porter edged out of it by refusing to keep Harmer as a client. So he went to Smardon and Clover. I suppose young Clover thought he could handle him. Well, he couldn't. So he came on to me. I've had him for nearly two years. Certainly kept us lively. There was no saying what he'd be up to next."

"Is he mad?"

Sykes considered this question seriously. Then he said, "No. In any legal meaning of the word he's unquestionably sane. The trouble is that he operates strictly by his own rules. Take that time he bought a second-hand car. When the moment came to renew the licence he was quite prepared to pay the road fund tax."

"Render unto Caesar the things that are Caesar's."

"Exactly. But he refused to insure it. The Bible says, 'Take no thought for the morrow.' Insurance was taking thought for the morrow. Therefore it was forbidden."

"So what did he do?"

"Sold the car and bought a bicycle."

While Sykes pushed his way over to the bar to get them a second drink, Jonas thought about it. If the rector did decide to consult him – and he had a feeling that he might – would he take him on? He would be a difficult client, but he had spent his professional life dealing with difficult clients. The truth of the matter was that he was beginning to get very slightly bored. The firm had plenty of clients, but most of the ones who came to him personally were friends like Admiral Fairlie and Major Appleby. Very often, he suspected, they came for a chat as much as for a consultation. The real legal work was done by Sabrina.

The letter arrived three days later. It was formal and perfectly sensible. The rector wrote to say that he had a small planning problem and wondered whether Mr Pickett could help him. He had informed his existing solicitor, Mr Sykes, who had raised no objection to his transferring this particular piece of business.

Jonas rang up Sykes who laughed and said, "Over to you and the best of luck." The opposition came, on different grounds, from Sabrina and Claire.

"There's no point wasting time over him," said Sabrina. "He'll be away before long."

"What makes you say that?" said Jonas. The discussion was taking place over the coffee that was a mid-morning ritual in the office.

"Congregation drifting off."

"Don't forget Lavinia Semple," said Claire.

Jonas knew about Miss Semple. He had often seen her, an untidy bundle wrapped in black, being trundled along the front in a bath-chair.

"Ronnie Sykes acts for her," said Sabrina. "He was telling me she makes a new will every month. She's the only daughter of Semple's Jams and Jellies. Rolling in money. Now *she'd* be a client worth having."

Jonas said, "We're not discussing whether I take on Miss Semple. The question was whether I should agree to act for the rector."

"You can't do it," said Claire flatly. "The man's unbalanced."

Sabrina disagreed. "He's a very interesting man. And quite an accomplished musician."

Claire snorted and said, "I suppose if you'd lived at the time of Nero you'd have called *him* an interesting man. A splendid performer on the violin, too, I believe."

"The comparison is inapt. Nero was an evil man. Whatever else you may accuse the rector of you could hardly call him evil."

She enjoyed arguing with Claire, who sometimes lost her temper. Mrs Mountjoy never lost hers.

Claire shifted her ground. She said, "The one I'm sorry for is David. It can't be any sort of life for him, alone in that gloomy house all day."

When they first arrived in Shackleton she and Sabrina had both lodged at the rectory for some months.

"And who is David?" said Jonas.

"He's the rector's son. Didn't you know he was married?"

"I confess I thought of him as a prototypical bachelor. Do I gather his wife has left him?"

"Certainly not," said Mrs Mountjoy, with a sidelong look at Claire. "I'm told they were a devoted couple. His wife died when David was born."

"All right, Sabrina," said Claire. "He may have been a rational creature eight years ago. All I'm saying is that he's not normal now."

Jonas said, "If the boy's eight, how come he spends all the day at home?"

"He doesn't," said Mrs Mountjoy. "That was one of Claire's figures of speech. He's a day boy at Clifton House."

"Only after a bitter fight with the education authorities," said Claire. "The rector maintained he could educate him better than any hired usher."

"Which he probably could have done," agreed Mrs Mountjoy.

"All right," said Jonas patiently. "David's at school all day. What about the evenings? There must be someone who looks after the house."

Claire said, "There's a couple who come in when they're wanted. She cooks and cleans and he does the garden. But they are always out of the house by dusk, I noticed."

"I suppose," said Sabrina, "that they thought the rector turned into a werewolf at night."

"Stop it, you two," said Jonas. "I want facts, not debating points. Aren't there any other members of the family?"

"There's a sister," said Claire. "A Mrs Baxter. The widow of Myron Baxter."

"The famous ornithologist?"

"Could be. She certainly seemed to know a lot about birds. When we were there she was around for most of August. She used to take David for long walks."

"A woman of real intellect," said Sabrina. "She was up at Lady Margaret Hall a little before my time and we had a number of friends in common."

"There you are," said Claire. "Between her and the rector they could have given David a first-class education."

"And if he'd never mixed with any other boys he'd have turned out a first-class freak."

"Time," said Jonas. "Back to work."

"I read the other day," said Claire, "that the great Lord Coleridge was educated entirely by his father. He could read Latin fluently when he was six, and speak it."

"And look what a bore he was when he got on to the bench," said Sabrina. She usually contrived to get the last word.

"You have to understand," said the rector, settling himself in the chair opposite Jonas's desk, "that St Michael's is almost entirely unendowed. The man who set it up supplied the funds to build the church and left his own rather unsuitable house as the rectory. Also some land. The money that was over was enough to provide a modest stipend for the incumbent, but it left no reserve for repairs. And the need for them is becoming urgent. I decided that the logical answer was to sell part of the land to a builder. I was told that, with planning permission, we could get as much as thirty thousand pounds an acre."

"Easily that," said Jonas.

"So I applied for planning permission for the four acres that front the Lewes road. It was refused. I was told that my only remedy was to ask for a public enquiry. That has been agreed – reluctantly."

"You conducted these negotiations yourself?"

"There was no need to trouble Mr Sykes. I was fully cognisant of the facts."

"But now you want me to act for you?"

"It seemed to me, from the brief conversation we had in the market square" – a smile twitched the corner of the rector's mouth – "that you were the possessor of a subtle mind."

"I don't know about that," said Jonas. "But it's true that I've had some experience of planning appeals. Have you got a date yet?"

"Certainly. Next Monday."

"A week from now! We can hardly be ready by then."

"Is much preparation needed? I have brought with me the town clerk's letters. They are not lengthy. What else do you need?"

"We shall need witnesses, if we can get them. Local people, prepared to support your application. A week doesn't give us much time."

The rector said, "In six days the Lord made the heaven and the earth and all that in them is." Interpreting Jonas's expression he added, "Don't worry. I'm no William Jennings Bryan. I accept that the book of Genesis is a fairy story. But understand this, please. The Bible, the whole of it, the Old Testament as well as the New, has orders for us, if we can interpret them. I don't call them messages. I call them orders. Commands which are not always easy to understand. But when we do understand them" – the rector's eyes were fixed on Jonas with almost hypnotic force – "we have no option. We are soldiers. We obey the orders of our commander."

Jonas's immediate reaction was, 'I wish I'd had my tape recorder switched on.' He was being presented with an understanding of the rector's mind, which might be of critical importance in their future dealings. He objected, however, to being hypnotised and broke the spell by standing up. He said,

"We've got a lot to do, so let's get on with it. Perhaps you could start by making enquiries from your neighbours to see if they might be prepared to help you."

They found Mrs Baxter in the outer office, chatting to Claire.

"Where's David?" said the rector. There was an unexpected note of anxiety in his voice. "I don't like him to go out in the street alone."

"It's all right," said Mrs Baxter. "He's talking to the lady in the other room."

David was sitting beside Sabrina, examining a sketch that she had drawn.

"The wing feathers don't quite go like that. They go up at the end and they stick out more."

Sabrina amended the drawing with a few rapid strokes.

"Yes, that's more like it."

"Come on, David," said the rector. "These people have got work to do."

"He was showing me the difference between a kestrel and a sparrow-hawk," said Sabrina. "Very interesting."

When they were alone, Claire said to Jonas, "It's a pity Mrs Baxter doesn't live with them permanently. She could keep some sort of eye on her brother."

"You've got a bee in your bonnet about that man," said Jonas.

"Then I wish it'd get out and sting you," said Claire tartly. "You don't seem able to grasp the fact that he's dangerous."

"Dangerous? Aren't you exaggerating? Eccentric certainly."

"Listen," said Claire, with more than usual earnestness. "People tell me things that perhaps they don't tell you. You know how he's been trying to get the amusement park on the pier shut on Sundays. Well, the first time he tried to do it by arguing with the man who ran it. When this chap wouldn't see his point of view – possibly made some stupid crack – the rector knocked him off the end of the pier into the sea and stalked away without as much as looking round to see if he could swim. Fortunately he could. Otherwise he could easily have been drowned."

"So what happened?"

"Oh, it was hushed up somehow."

Jonas thought about this. Then he said, "Well, I should have been all right. I'm a good swimmer."

Claire said nothing. But later, to Mrs Mountjoy, she said, "He's impossible. He's behaving like a small boy. He regards the whole thing as a 'dare'. Other lawyers couldn't handle the rector, but he can. He doesn't realise he's playing with fire. Couldn't you say something to him?"

"If he wouldn't listen to you," said Sabrina, "I'm certain he wouldn't listen to me."

The morning hearing of the public enquiry was over. The rector had behaved with perfect propriety. Since he had not been able to find anyone willing to give evidence for him he had had to act as his own witness.

The Inspector had a bad cold, which he relieved from time to time with a pastille. The opposition was represented by the town clerk, Mr Timms, and Mr McClachan, a member of the Planning Committee. Jonas had felt, from the start, that he was batting on a sticky wicket. He pointed out the desperate need of the church for funds and the equally desperate need of Shackleton for more houses. He touched on the suitability of the site and glossed over the fact that it was in the Green Belt, an area in which development is normally prohibited.

When he saw McClachan making a note he guessed what it was about. This was the most serious weakness in their case. When he had said all he could, and some of it twice over, the rector gave his evidence and the town clerk rose to cross-examine him. It was clear from his manner and from the way he phrased his questions, that he was hoping to provoke an outburst. The rector foiled him by answering as shortly as possible; sometimes simply by 'yes' or 'no'.

In the end it was the town clerk who lost his temper. He snapped out, "Is it true, sir, that since you have been rector of St Michael's there has been a falling-off in attendance at the church?"

"A small decrease, yes."

"If it's only small, how do you account for the fact, which

appears from your own accounts, that the collections this year are fifty per cent less than last year?"

The rector considered the matter. "I think," he said gently, "that the actual figure is forty-two per cent."

"If this decline continues, is it not likely that in the near future the church will be closed altogether?"

The Inspector, who had been showing signs of restlessness, said, "I fail to see the relevance of this line of enquiry, Mr Timms." And to the rector, "There is no need for you to answer that question."

"I have no objection to answering it," said the rector. "What will happen in the future is neither in your hands nor in mine. It is in the hands of God."

His voice was still calm, but it was as cold as naked steel. It punctured the town clerk who said, "I have no more questions," and sat down.

"In that case," said the Inspector, helping himself to another pastille, "it will be a convenient moment to adjourn."

During the lunch break Jonas congratulated the rector on his restraint. He looked surprised. "I could hardly go wrong," he said. "The instruction given to us in St Matthew's gospel is explicit. If a man smite you on one cheek, turn to him the other."

"It certainly worked in this case."

"What is your honest opinion? Have we any chance of winning?"

"I think the Inspector is sympathetic to the needs of your church. Whether we can win depends on how well their witness has done his homework."

Unfortunately it soon became clear that McClachan had prepared his case very thoroughly indeed. He was a qualified surveyor, with an intimate knowledge of Shackleton. He was able to identify six other sites which were ripe for development. Two of them were nearer to the centre of Shackleton than the rector's field and were outside the Green Belt.

"In short," said the town clerk, "although, at some future date, it might be appropriate to consider this site for development, your view is that, at the moment, it would be premature?"

"In my view, totally premature."

And that's one back for your wife's cakes and jams, thought Jonas.

When Mr Timms sat down there was a long moment of silence. Jonas knew that it was unusual for an Inspector to say anything after the parties had finished. But he sometimes helped them by indicating how his mind was working.

He said, "Mr Pickett, you will appreciate the force of what the last witness has told us. I should like to say, however, that I am not unmindful of the needs of the church. Had this application been for some purpose connected with the church, a residence for a curate, perhaps, or a church hall, then my views on the matter would certainly be different."

While the Inspector was speaking Jonas had become aware of a change in the rector. He was no longer sitting quietly, but was tapping with one foot on the ground and his face was mottled. Now he was scribbling on a piece of paper. He pushed it towards Jonas who read, written in emphatic capital letters, 'CAN I SAY SOMETHING?'.

Jonas seized his own pen and wrote underneath it, 'Only if you no longer wish me to act for you.'

The Inspector observed that something was happening. He turned courteously towards the rector and said, "Have you anything you would care to add?"

In the silence which ensued Jonas was aware of the struggle that was going on. The outcome depended on the strength of such influence as he had been able to establish over his difficult client. Finally, with a sound like the gasp of someone coming up from deep water, the rector said, "No, sir."

"I think we'd better go back to my office," said Jonas. "I'll take you in my car."

When they got there, Jonas said, "I had a feeling that you were going to be rude to the Inspector. Perhaps you could explain why."

The rector, who had recovered his composure, said, "Tell me, Mr Pickett, what would your opinion be of a parent who held out a sweet to his child and when the child stretched out his hand to take it, threw it into the fire? It is my dearest wish to build a church hall. It would solve many of my problems. The sale of those four acres of land, coupled with planning permission, would produce one hundred and twenty thousand pounds, or thereabouts. And that happens to be almost exactly the amount which a builder has quoted to me for the job. So what is the Inspector saying? That he would guarantee that I would get permission to put up my hall. That is the sweet. But equally that he could guarantee that I could *not* raise the money by building houses. So – ”

The rector held out one hand and opened the long thin fingers, as though he was dropping something.

At that moment the telephone rang.

“I must apologise,” said Jonas. “When my secretary and Sam Conybeare are both out, calls get put straight through to me. I’d better deal with it.”

It was Ronald Sykes. He said, “I think you know I act for Lavinia Semple – ”

“Yes, I know it,” said Jonas. “And I’ve got a client with me, so if you don’t mind – ”

“I think you ought to hear this. She died last night.”

“I’m very sorry. But – ”

“And she’s left everything to the rector.”

Jonas swung round to look at the rector, who had clearly heard what Sykes had said. He seemed unsurprised.

“Were you expecting this?”

“Miss Semple is one of the most faithful of my flock. She came to see me after morning service two weeks ago. She indicated what was in her mind. I besought her to do nothing hurriedly. I had no idea, of course, that she was to be gathered so soon.”

The telephone said, “Are you still there?”

“Sorry,” said Jonas. “The fact is, I have the rector with me.”

“Oh, I see.” The reserve in Sykes’s voice sounded a warning.

Jonas said, “Perhaps we ought to have a word about this.”

“I agree,” said Sykes. “And as soon as possible. I’d come to you, but I’m rather tied up at the moment. Could you possibly come round to my office?” He did not add, ‘Without the rector,’ but the implication was clear.

* * *

Sykes said, "One of Miss Semple's few remaining pleasures was the making and altering of her will. Normally, she told me what she wanted to do and I drew up the document. This time, as you can see, she tried her own hand at it."

Jonas looked at the paper on the desk. It was an old woman's writing, spidery, but absolutely clear.

"She's copied the legal wording from the last one I made for her. And it's been properly witnessed and dated. My brother and I are executors. We wouldn't anticipate any difficulty in getting probate."

"Then," said Jonas, "what's the trouble?" He knew that something was worrying Sykes. He had heard it on the telephone and he heard it again now.

"Well, you see, it's a big estate. There's property in London and the Home Counties. She couldn't dispose of that. It's entailed and goes to a cousin. What she's left the rector is her free estate: money and shares."

"Yes, I follow that." He picked up the will and studied it. A notion of what was upsetting his colleague crossed his mind. "It's the last five words, I suppose."

"If I had drafted the will I certainly shouldn't have put them in."

To my old friend Tobias Harmer D.D., Rector of St Michael's Church Shackleton I bequeath all my unentailed property as I explained to him.

The difficulty was becoming clearer.

"You mean," said Jonas, "that without those last five words it would be a gift to the rector personally. With them, there's a trust tacked on."

"There's certainly a suggestion that she told him what she expected him to do with the money."

"So it could have been meant as a gift to the church and not to him."

The two lawyers looked at each other. The cat was out of the bag now, claws and all.

Jonas said, "What *is* the rate of tax?"

"As I told you, it's a very large estate. It might be as high as seventy-five per cent."

"Which would be avoided if this was a gift to the church."

"Exactly."

"But payable if it was a personal gift to the rector."

"Yes."

"In that case," said Jonas, "the vital question is, what *did* she say to the rector after morning service two weeks ago?"

With a layman it would have taken Jonas three times as long to explain the point. The rector's theologically trained brain grasped the implications at once.

He said, "I see. Yes. So what is it you want me to do?"

"I want you to remember, if you can, the exact words Miss Semple used when she promised you this legacy."

"Why is what she said important? I thought it was only what the will said that mattered."

"Correct. But there's one exception. If a will is worded so that it can mean two different things, outside evidence *is* allowed, to show which was meant. Particularly in the case of home-made wills, which tend to be vague."

"How much money is involved?"

"Sykes could only give me a rough estimate. Certainly not less than a hundred thousand pounds. More likely a hundred and fifty thousand."

The rector thought about this for some time. His face was expressionless, but his fingers were opening and closing on the arms of the chair. Finally he said, "Very well, I can tell you what Miss Semple said. Not perhaps the precise words, but the sense of them. She said, 'You will understand that this money is for the church.'"

"Splendid," said Jonas. "That seems quite clear. I will draw up a statutory declaration."

"Explain, please."

"Oh, it's a solemn declaration which you swear to in front of another solicitor. I'm sure Ronald Sykes will be happy to oblige us. As soon as I've drafted it we'll go round and see him."

"And if I am prepared to make this declaration, the whole of the money comes to the church. If I am unable to make it, three-quarters of it may go to the government."

"In a nutshell," said Jonas.

*   *   *

161

"Just a formality really," said Sykes, with professional cheerfulness. "Initial the first page. That's right. Then sign the document at the foot of page two. Excellent. Now you take the Testament in your right hand and we'll both stand up. Ready?"

It was a copy of the New Testament bound in black buckram and limp with much handling. His clients normally grabbed the book and gabbled the required words. The rector was the first person he had known to handle it with proper reverence.

Sykes said, "Please repeat after me, 'I solemnly and sincerely declare that this is my name and handwriting.'"

The rector repeated the words.

"'And that the contents of this my declaration are true.'"

Jonas, who had come with the rector, had a sudden urge to interrupt. To shout out 'stop'. He knew this was irrational and absurd. He had administered the oath to hundreds of his clients without he or them giving it another thought. The difference here, he realised, was that the rector understood the meaning and implication of what he was doing. He was pledging his word to his God that he was telling the truth.

After a pause, which seemed to go on for ever, but may only have lasted a few seconds, the rector repeated, "And that the contents of this my declaration are true."

"That will cost you one pound," said Sykes.

Jonas had the fee ready and passed it across the table. They left the office and walked away down the street together. They had nothing to say to each other. Back in the office Jonas found Claire waiting for him. She said, "You're looking very serious."

Jonas said, "Am I?" with unusual brusqueness and disappeared into his own room, leaving Claire staring after him.

Three days later, towards the end of the afternoon, Mrs Baxter arrived unannounced at the office. Claire could see that she was badly upset about something. Maybe it was the same thing that was worrying Jonas. He had been in a very odd mood lately. She said, "I'm afraid Mr Pickett's out. If we'd known you were coming –"

"I'm glad. I'll find it easier to explain to you. Mr Sykes and Mr Pickett have done something terrible to my brother."

Claire didn't pretend not to understand her. She said, "You mean that statutory declaration?"

"I don't know what it was, but whatever they made him do it's destroying him. I was planning to go home yesterday, but for David's sake I had to stay. I daren't leave him alone."

Claire said, "Do you think your brother's mad?"

The brutality of the question shook her, as Claire had intended it to do. "Mad? I don't know. But I can tell you this. He hasn't slept for the last two nights. His bedroom's next to mine. Last night I could hear him pacing, backwards and forwards, hour after hour. That was bad enough, but it was worse when he stopped, quite suddenly. Absolute silence. I began to be afraid."

Claire said, in the same matter-of-fact voice, "You were afraid he'd killed himself?"

"Yes, I was. And I couldn't possibly go to sleep without knowing. So I opened the door quietly and looked in. He was on his knees by his bed. I went back to my room and managed to get a little sleep. This morning he's hardly spoken to me. Just 'thank you' when I got him his breakfast. I'm scared silly, Miss Easterbrook, and I'm not ashamed to admit it. Isn't there something we could do?"

"What about his doctor?"

"He hasn't got a regular one. And – well – I know he's got great confidence in Mr Pickett. If you could only persuade him how bad things are, I'm sure he'd think of something."

"I'll try," said Claire reluctantly. "But don't bank on it. When his mind's made up he's the most obstinate man I've ever known."

As was his custom on a fine afternoon, Jonas had been for a stroll along the front and he came back refreshed and happy; a happiness which disappeared as soon as he had grasped what Claire was trying to tell him.

"Really," he said, in the querulous voice of someone who was arguing with himself. "All we asked him to do was to tell the truth and even if he was lying, he was doing it for the sake of his church, not for himself."

"Which will be a great comfort to everyone when he cuts his throat."

"If he's decided to kill himself, there's nothing you or I or anyone can do. Short of putting him in a strait-jacket."

"You don't often admit yourself beaten," said Claire. "You can usually think of a way out."

This was clever of Claire. It was an appeal to Jonas's professional pride. The result was that he stopped justifying himself and started thinking. He said, "I suppose it would help if we could take the pressure off him. I'll have a word with Sykes. If he hasn't put that declaration in yet, I could ask him to hold it up. Then, if the rector agrees, we could tear it up and forget about it. It will cost him a lot of money."

"It might save his life," said Claire.

"I'll go round to the rectory as soon as I can get away tomorrow morning."

It was nearly eleven o'clock next morning before he could leave the office. Sam had some stuff to pick up on the Lewes road, so he took him in the car with him. When they turned in at the long laurel-shadowed drive and drew up in front of the rectory there was no sign of life. Three rows of windows stared down at them like blind eyes. No birds were singing.

"Gloomy sort of place," said Sam. "Wouldn't care to live here myself."

"Something's happened," said Jonas. The silence was so overpowering that he had to stop himself from speaking in a whisper. "I wish I'd come round sooner."

"Better go in and find out, hadn't you?"

"I suppose so." It was an effort to move.

"Like me to come along?"

Jonas took a grip of himself. "No," he said. "Stay here. But turn the car round."

He jumped out, walked briskly up the front steps and jerked the old-fashioned bell-pull. He could hear the bell jangling. But no sound of life.

He tried the front door. It was unlocked. He opened it and stepped through into the hall. As the last echoes of the bell died away he heard something else. In the room at the far end of the passage someone was sobbing.

*   *   *

David was worried. His father had been his friend and his confidant for as many years as he could remember. Now something had happened to upset him. He could observe the physical signs, but without understanding what lay behind them. The fingers which moved as though he was playing on a silent piano; the curiously distant look in the grey eyes; the livid wounds that had opened under them.

His aunt, too, had been behaving oddly. She seemed unwilling to leave her brother alone for more than five minutes, but would come bustling in with plans and suggestions, most of them stupid in David's opinion. At breakfast that morning, whilst she had been there, almost nothing had been said. When she left the room, animation had returned.

His father had started to talk, entertainingly and informatively, about birds. About the cuckoo, who had just opened his spring solo; about the vanguard of the house-martins who were ejecting the sparrows from the nests they had appropriated in the absence of their owners during the winter. Better still, he had proposed an expedition.

"We'll take sandwiches and make a day of it. I thought we might go up Scarr Down. A boy told me there was a colony of chaffinches building there."

"Right up to the top of the Down? You mean the Druids' Stone?"

"Is that what they call it?" For a moment the animation had gone and the old bleak look was back in his father's eyes. With rare tact for a boy of eight David broke off what he had been going to say; the gruesome but exciting things other boys had told him about the Druids' Stone. Instead he said, "Shall I cut the sandwiches?"

"I cut them before breakfast. They're in my knapsack."

"Shall I tell Aunt B what we're going to do?"

"No, I'll tell her. You get your windcheater. You'll need it up on the tops. Wait for me in the drive."

If David had shut the front door, as his father had intended, he would have heard nothing. He rather wished he had shut it, because what he did hear was unusual and upsetting. First it was the talk in the kitchen. It seemed to go on for a long time. Then, something he had never heard before, his father was shouting. Loudly and angrily. Between the shouts he could hear his aunt's high-pitched protests. Then a door slammed and his father came striding back down the hall. He had his knapsack over one shoulder and a stick in his hand.

David said, "What was Aunt B going on about?"

"She thought the climb to Scarr Down would be too much for you."

"That's nonsense. I've been twice as far as that."

"So I told her, Davy. Come on, then."

As they went David slipped his small hand into the large one swinging beside him and father and son went down the drive hand in hand.

When Jonas reached the kitchen and looked inside he realised that Mrs Baxter was on the verge of a hysterical breakdown. As soon as she saw him she started talking, but nothing that came out made much sense.

He heard what sounded like 'atonement', then something about the Druids' Stone, which was a monument he had once visited. Then, suddenly, out of the froth and jumble of words came two names that did mean something to him, 'Abraham' and 'Isaac'. When he heard them, all alarm bells started ringing together. He stepped forward, swung his arm and smacked Mrs Baxter's face with his open hand.

The sobs were cut off and she looked up as though she was seeing him for the first time.

"Are you telling me," said Jonas, "that your brother has taken David up to Scarr Down?"

"Yes."

"How long ago?"

"About half an hour."

He said, "And you let them go? After he'd as good as told you what he meant to do?"

Mrs Baxter raised a tear-streaked face. "How could I stop him? He's insane – "

But Jonas was no longer there.

Sam had turned the car and when he saw Jonas come running down the steps he started to move over. Jonas said, "Stay where you are. You're a better driver than me. We shall have to move fast."

"Where to, skipper?"

"Scarr Down. Head for the golf club. There's a side road just before you get there."

By this time they were in the road that circled the industrial estate. A van pulled out ahead of them. Jonas said, "Pass it."

"Ho!" said Sam. "Necks for sale, is it?" He squeezed past the van, swinging in with inches to spare in front of an indignant car coming the other way. "If there's one thing I don't like it's drivers what sound their horns at you just because they're scared."

"Concentrate on driving," said Jonas. He was studying the map. "The turning's about two hundred yards ahead. Just past that white cottage. Got it? Right. Don't dawdle."

It was a country lane, clearly too narrow for cars to pass at speed. If they met anything head on they would both go to glory. Sam uttered a short prayer.

"Next turning to the right."

This was a track, deeply rutted in places by the farm carts which had used it. The car bounced and juddered. Jonas realised that he could never have controlled it. His foot would have been on and off the accelerator and they would have been stalling and starting. As the track started to climb there was a quagmire left by the recent rain. If they had not been going at a fair speed they would have been helplessly bogged. As it was they had just enough momentum to reach the firm ground beyond and skidded out, sideways. Sam wrenched the car back on to the track. For a stretch, though the track was going steeply uphill, it offered no obstacles.

Sam found a moment to grab a handkerchief out of his pocket and wipe away some of the sweat that was pouring down his forehead.

They could see the top of the Down now and the single stone standing up against the sky.

The footpath to the Druids' Stone ran, straight and uncompromising, up the shoulder of the Down. The man and the boy tackled it steadily, pausing from time to time to look back. As they climbed, their line of sight cleared the trees and houses and the sea came into view, lead and silver under the April sky. They seemed to have the world to themselves.

Rabbits thumped on the turf and bolted back to their burrows as they approached. Above them a hawk swung in the sky. He was not interested in the two humans toiling up the path. He was watching the rabbits.

"Nearly there," said the rector.

Neither of them had spoken much. David was saving his breath for the climb. His father's thoughts were far away; beyond the hills, across the sea, in a country of his own making.

In an open circle of turf at the top were two stones, one flat, the other upright at the end of it. David said, "The boy who told you chaffinches built in a place like this must have been crazy."

The rector sat on the edge of the flat stone, slipping the knapsack off his shoulders and putting it down carefully beside him. He said, "I brought you here to tell you something, Davy. Come and sit here."

David came over and squatted beside him.

"You know how much I love you. You know that you are more precious to me than anything in the whole world."

Most boys would have been embarrassed. David had lived alone with his father so long that nothing he said or did had the power to surprise or worry him. Instead he turned his attention to the important question of what his father had brought for their picnic. He fiddled open the clasp of the knapsack and looked inside.

The rector had put out a hand to stop him, but realising that it was too late he sat quite still.

David started to laugh. "Silly Daddy," he said. "Do you know what you've done? You've brought the knife and forgotten the bread." He loved knives. This was a beauty, with a black handle, a copper tang and a shining blade. His father took it from him gently and laid it down on the stone beside him.

"What were you going to tell me?" said David.

"We're going on a journey."

"You and me?"

"Yes. I shall be with you."

"Are we going far?"

"Very far." The words seemed to be choking him.

"And is that car coming to fetch us?"

The rector leaped up. Standing, he could hear the sound of the car which had been masked by the slope of the hill and could see the dust of its passage.

It was heading straight for them.

The rector said, in a loud voice, "Blessed be the Lord who has taken this burden from me. Run, David, quickly. See who is coming."

David moved off obediently. He was worried because his father was behaving so oddly, but he was not frightened. He recognised Jonas and said, "Hello, Mr Pickett. I'd no idea you could get a car up as far as this. It must have been some drive."

"It was," said Sam grimly.

Jonas jumped out and walked across the clearing. At the far side it fell away into a small cliff. He peered over the edge, swung round and came back. He said, "David, I'm afraid your father's fallen and hurt himself. You must go back quickly with Sam to fetch help."

For a moment the boy hesitated. Then he said, "You'll stay with him, sir?"

"Yes," said Jonas. "I'll stay with him." And to Sam, "Bring Jack Queen if you can find him."

When the car had bumped off down the track he went back to the far side of the clearing, parted the bushes and looked over. Then he made his way cautiously down to where the rector lay. The knife had been driven upwards, under his ribs and into his heart. Both his hands were still clasped round the handle.

That evening, after everything had been done that had to be done – after Mrs Baxter had taken charge of David and Inspector Queen had taken charge of the body – Jonas was sitting in his office with Sam and the office whisky bottle. He had poured out a second glass for both of them. He was thinking that one thing he would have to do was apologise to Claire for ignoring her repeated warnings. Tomorrow would do for that.

"Are you telling me," said Sam, "that he was going to kill that nipper?"

"Yes."

"For the Lord's sake, why?"

"Because he had sinned. And the only expiation he could make was to sacrifice his most precious possession. I've no doubt he intended to kill himself immediately afterwards."

"And our arrival stopped him knocking off the kid?"

"I don't think it was quite like that. I think he took our arrival as a sign that he had been spared from making the sacrifice. What counted, you see, was his willingness to do it."

"Was that what happened in the story you were telling me about Abraham and Isaac?"

"It's some time since I read it," said Jonas. "But I seem to remember that in that case it was an angel who appeared at the last moment."

"Angels, is it?" said Sam. "That's a new one." He finished his drink thoughtfully.

8

THE BIRD OF DAWNING

On the morning of Tuesday, July 14th, Fred, the jobbing gardener, arrived at old Dr Rainey's front gate at nine o'clock precisely. One of the things people liked about Fred and which made them willing to pay him four pounds an hour for an eight-hour day was that he really did work for eight hours. And, as a result, he never lacked employment. His Mondays and Tuesdays belonged to Dr Rainey; Wednesdays and Thursdays to Mr and Mrs McClachan; and Fridays and Saturdays to Sabrina Mountjoy, who had taken him over when she bought Captain Horrocks's house and glad to do so. Being a partner in Jonas Pickett's legal practice was, she maintained, a full-time job.

Fred hobbled round the house and down to his private kingdom, which was the potting shed at the bottom of the garden. His limp was the result of war service. Apart from this, despite his seventy years, his frugal habits and open air life had preserved his health and strength marvellously.

"Looks more like fifty than seventy," Mrs McClachan often remarked to her husband. "And strong as a horse." Her husband, who was in fact fifty and looked more like sixty, agreed with her resentfully. He played a lot of golf, but it seemed to do nothing for his waistline.

Fred set to work without delay. There was a lot to do in a vegetable garden at that time of year. The asparagus was finished and the runner beans were to come, but the French beans, the peas and the Jerusalem artichokes were all flourishing and the new potatoes, carrots and little globe turnips were in course of being dug up and stored for the winter.

171

For the moment, however, they would have to wait. There was a more important job in hand. There was a south-facing bed under the brick wall at the foot of the garden. He had promised the doctor that he would try to grow tomato plants there, but the earth would need careful cleaning first.

He took down the spade and fork that were hanging in the shed among the rows of flower pots, trays of dried bulbs, sacks of compost and silver sand, tins of weedkiller and twists of bast. He rubbed them over with a piece of sacking. This was a ritual gesture. Like all his tools they were spotless. Then he attacked the new bed, trenching it deeply and methodically depositing the roots and other growths which he extracted on the bonfire he had lit the day before and which was still smouldering nicely.

At eleven o'clock he suspended work, left fork and spade sticking in the earth and made his way up to the back of the house. This was the accepted first break. The procedure varied. Mrs McClachan would make him a cup of tea. Sabrina Mountjoy left the back door open and a tin of instant coffee with milk and sugar on the table. Dr Rainey, if he was in the house, would make the coffee for both of them, using real beans. He was finicky about the kitchen, did a lot of his own cooking and, by all accounts, did it very well.

The kitchen door was locked. Fred rapped once or twice on the kitchen window, without producing any reaction, then made his way round to the front of the house. The front door was fast, too. Fred stood for a few seconds, scratching his head. Then he touched the button of the bell and heard it sounding inside the house. He had never used the front door. Previously his entry had always been through the kitchen.

After waiting for a long minute he pressed the button again, keeping it pressed. When this produced no result he went back, down the path and out into the road. There was a telephone booth at the corner.

The Sergeant on duty at Shackleton police station listened impatiently to Fred's rambling comments and put the call through to Superintendent Queen. Fred then had to say it all over again, but here he found a more attentive listener.

Queen remembered that there was something in Station Orders about Dr Rainey. There had been instructions that the man whose beat passed the doctor's house should keep an eye open for possible intruders. This particular item dated from before Queen's arrival. No reason was given for it. He told Fred to get back to work and went along the passage to the office of Chief Superintendent Whaley, head of the Shackleton force.

Whaley said, "Yes. I remember that going into orders. In fact, I fancy I put it in myself. It was about four years ago when we heard about the precautions the doctor was taking. He'd had a very sophisticated alarm system put into his house. We knew about it, because it was linked to this station."

"The normal sort of system?"

"No. This was security *and* alarm. A firm in Brighton did the job. Lockfast, or some such name. If the doctor's died in the house, you'll need their help to get inside."

Nearly an hour later, after doing some telephoning, Queen was standing outside Dr Rainey's front door. There were two men with him. Mr Cowdray from Lockfast Home Protection Services and Mr Terriss from the Shackleton office of the SE Electricity Board.

"It was a lovely job," said Mr Cowdray, "if I say it myself. Builder's work and all. First we had to replace most of the windows."

Queen had noticed this. It was a low, two-storey house and the windows on both floors were the same. Steel frames with small square openings.

"They're all locked, on the same circuit as the doors. You could break a pane of glass and put your hand through, but that wouldn't get you much further, as you couldn't open the window. If you tried to force the window lock you'd get a nasty electric shock and nothing much else."

"So how do we get in?" said Mr Terriss.

"You let us in. By turning off the electricity. There's a control box in the road outside that services this house, along with the other three houses on that side of the road. We won't need it off for more than a minute."

Mr Terriss agreed that this was feasible. He had brought the necessary equipment in his car. Having opened the control box he worked for some time inside it. When he stood up and raised one hand Mr Cowdray, who had a key ready, slid it into the lock and opened the door. They stepped into the hall, which was dimly lit and silent as a church on a weekday.

"Dr Rainey!" said Queen. He had intended to shout, but the atmosphere was so oppressive that it came out as a strangled croak. He called again, louder, but without any real expectation now of being answered.

On the left of the hall was the sitting room. Queen opened the door and looked in. It was empty. Behind that and opening out of it, the doctor's study. Also empty. On the other side of the passage the dining room. Here they found Dr Rainey, sitting in the chair at the head of the table. His head had fallen forward on to his hands.

Queen raised the head gently. It was clear that Dr Rainey was dead. Queen, who had seen many dead men, was startled by the look on his face. It was as though he had seen death coming and had hated it more than he had feared it.

Whilst the police surgeon and the photographers and finger-print men were doing their work ("Treat it as a murder until we're sure it wasn't," said Whaley) Queen was talking to Mr Cowdray. He said, "I understand this was a security *and* an alarm system. How does it work?"

"Very simple. Very effective. That's the control." He pointed to a small box of grey painted steel in the cupboard under the stairs. There was a single keyhole in the front of it. "If you're going out, turn the key once. That sets a normal alarm, which rings in your police station if anyone tampers with the doors or windows whilst you're away. Okay?"

Queen nodded. Several of the larger houses had that arrangement. It was a standing source of irritation, as careless householders forgot that the alarm had been activated and set it off by mistake; but he could never remember an alarm from Dr Rainey.

"Last thing at night, you turn the key twice, which is what's been done here. That locks the doors and all the windows electrically. Then you can go to bed and sleep sound. Only drawback, you can't have your bedroom window open. The doctor had an air-conditioner he used in summer."

Queen thought about it. He said, "I take it the electrical locking only operates if all the windows and doors are shut. Suppose you'd left one open, by mistake?"

"The machine would tell you. It'd go on bleeping until you shut it."

"Then what you're saying," said Queen thoughtfully, "is that once this thing was functioning, no one could get in from outside."

"Only by cutting off the electricity and, as you saw, that needed special equipment."

Queen put all this in his report, which Chief Superintendent Whaley read, together with Dr Smallhorn's conclusions which were that Dr Rainey had died of renal failure. "That's not uncommon with an elderly person," the report said. 'The liver and kidneys get tired and stop functioning. As a matter of fact, I suspected that something like that might happen when he came to see me last month."

"That's that, then," said Whaley.

So the death of Dr Rainey was certified as being due to natural causes, the coroner was not troubled and the funeral was conducted a week later in St Michael's Church by the new young incumbent.

It was a quiet affair. Many of Dr Rainey's patients had predeceased him. Some of the town notables thought it respectful to attend. Amongst them were Jock Lovibond, the chairman of the Borough Council, and Jonas Pickett, who had a special reason for being there. After the interment he had a word with Lovibond.

"I'm having a copy of his will made for you," he said. "In a sense, you're his residuary legatee."

"How could I be? I hardly knew the man."

"It comes to you ex officio. Having no near relatives he decided to leave his whole estate to the chairman of the Borough Council to be expended on such charitable and useful objects for the locality as he might select. When I've paid the debts – there weren't many – and the funeral expenses and duties, there should be around fifty thousand pounds left."

"Which I can spend on anything for the borough that I like?"

"You'll have to be careful that it's charitable. However, charity covers quite a wide field. Education, religion, the relief of poverty."

"I call it very handsome. I think we ought to put up some sort of memorial tablet in the church, don't you?"

"I think that would be most appropriate," said Jonas.

Every police station keeps, among its many other records, a book known as the Occurrences Book. Into it go reports of anything out of the way which a policeman may have observed on his patrol. It is not an exciting work. Flights of fancy are discouraged. It deals with facts. "At 3 a.m. this morning Major X left his house driving his Ford Corsair." No doubt there were half a dozen good reasons for Major X's early departure. A long journey to the Midlands? Sensible to use the roads when they were empty. An early plane to catch at Heathrow? Ninety-nine times out of a hundred the entry led to nothing. On the hundredth occasion it proved to be the one essential item of information needed to tie up a case.

All senior officers studied the book from time to time. Superintendent Queen was doing so about a fortnight after Dr Rainey's funeral. He was looking for scraps of information which might enable them to identify a persistent peeping Tom who had been upsetting the local people. Such people might not be breaking the law, but their activities, as he knew, could lead to all sorts of trouble. It was whilst he was turning the pages that he came across the entry. "July 14th, 6 a.m. PC Trotter, returning past the front of No 8 Princes Road, had observed a man moving off down the little lane at the side of the house." Since the man did not appear to be doing anything illegal, PC Trotter had not pursued him. He had simply made a note in the Occurrences Book. Princes Road was a high-cost development of eight well-spaced houses, four on each side of the road. No 8 was the end house on the north side. It was Dr Rainey's house.

Queen noted the significance of the date and place and sent for PC Trotter. It was clear that the constable had attached very little importance to the incident. As soon as he had come off duty he had gone to bed and by the time he had returned to the station in the afternoon the unexciting death of Dr Rainey was already fading into past history. Now it seemed that the top brass was interested and he had to prod his memory.

He said, "He was too far away to pick up any detail. I'm

sure it was a man, not a woman. Chances are I wouldn't have noticed anything at all if it hadn't been for the bird."

"Bird?" Mysterious female? Sex angle?

No. Trotter was not using the word to describe an attractive young lady. He meant the feathered sort.

"At least, I thought it might be a bird. Then I thought, no, it couldn't be. It was what you might call mechanical."

"Like a cuckoo clock?"

"That sort of thing. Except it wasn't going 'cuckoo'. It was more sort of chirruping. High-pitched chirruping."

"And it seemed to come from No 8?"

"Thereabouts. It didn't go on all that long. It had stopped by the time I got up there, see."

"How far away were you when you first heard it?"

"I was almost at the corner."

"Then it can't have gone on for more than a few seconds."

"That's right." Trotter was beginning to be sorry he'd ever mentioned it. If the bird story got out he was going to have his leg pulled, that was for sure.

"You did know, I take it, that there was a standing instruction to patrolling officers to keep an eye on that particular house?"

Trotter had to admit that he had not known this, or if he had known it he'd forgotten it. Since that particular entry was four years old, Queen found it difficult to blame him much. He dismissed him with a stern admonition to re-read and memorise *all* standing orders.

When Trotter had departed, he sat for some time thinking about his subordinate. If he had been writing a confidential report on Trotter he would have described him as sound. Not clever, not imaginative, but totally reliable. And there *was* a possible explanation of what he had heard: a high-pitched mechanical chirrup. If the explanation was true it led to consequences so dark and difficult that he hesitated to think them through. He decided that the first thing was to have a word with the Chief Superintendent.

Whaley heard him out, grunted and said, "What do you propose to do about it?"

"I think, sir, the best way to settle it would be to carry out an experiment."

He explained what he had in mind. "The house has just been put up for sale. We could get the keys from the agents and station a reliable man – Sergeant Fox, I suggest – inside the house to do what was necessary."

"It will have to be done when there's a minimum of noise outside."

"I thought 6 a.m. would be the logical time. Then we should get an exact repeat."

"Would you like me to be there too?"

"Very much," said Queen, slightly surprised.

"I only hope it isn't pouring with rain."

Happily it was a fine, still August morning when Whaley, Queen and Constable Trotter met at the corner of Princes Road. Trotter seemed a little overawed by the company. He had no idea what was expected of him.

Queen, who had his eye on his watch, said, "Place yourself at the end of the road and when I tell you to start, walk at your normal pace down the road."

A reconstruction of the crime, wondered Trotter. It seemed a bit pointless.

"Start," said Queen.

Trotter said, "Christ!" and turned pale. He knew that the house was empty. And now he heard, coming from it, exactly the sound he had heard before. Was the spirit of Dr Rainey haunting his old residence?

The noise stopped.

"Keep going," shouted Queen urgently.

Trotter paced forward, hardly daring to contemplate what was going to happen next. He reached the end of the little lane that ran between the doctor's house and the next one. His astonishment escalated when he observed a figure disappearing down the path. He was about to pursue it when Queen stopped him.

"All right!" he said.

"All right," said Whaley grimly. And to a still shaken Trotter, "I take it you can confirm that that was the noise you heard?"

"I certainly can, sir," said Trotter. "But who – ?"

"The man you saw was Sergeant Fox. He was helping us.

I've warned him. And I'm warning you. Not a word about this to anyone. You understand?"

"Yes, sir."

He understood nothing. But that was a direct order and could be obeyed.

Later that morning Queen and Whaley faced each other in Whaley's office. Neither of them looked happy.

Whaley said, "Experiment successful. What does it mean?"

"It can only mean one thing, sir. There was another man inside the house. When the electric lock is on, a door or a window can be opened *from the inside*. Whilst it's open, the apparatus gives a warning bleep. That was the noise Trotter heard."

"And once the door was shut again, the noise would stop?"

"Exactly. The man would slam it shut behind him and nip off, down the garden path and into the lane. The timing was right for that, too."

They thought about it and the more they thought the less they liked it.

"By the way," said Queen, "I meant to ask you. That order about keeping an eye on the doctor's house. What was the reason for it?"

"I seem to remember that he'd had some sort of threat. He took it seriously enough to fortify his house, so we took it a bit seriously, too."

Queen said, "If someone did kill him, it must have been by poison. Yet Dr Smallhorn seemed satisfied that death was due to natural causes."

"Dr Smallhorn's an old woman," said Whaley. "He'd give any diagnosis that saved him trouble. I didn't question it at the time, because there seemed no reason to do so. Now, I wouldn't rely on it any more than when he said my daughter was suffering from heat rash and it turned out to be measles."

"So," said Queen, "there's only one way to settle it."

"Right. An exhumation order. I don't like it, but I can't see any way round it."

"We shall need the agreement of the next of kin, which means going to Jonas Pickett."

Whaley said, "Yes." He did not say it with great enthusiasm. There had been passages in his earlier dealings with that lawyer which he remembered with distaste. However, time had smoothed things over and there had been at least one occasion on which Jonas had proved decidedly helpful to the police.

"All right," he said. "He's by way of being a friend of yours, isn't he? You have a word with him."

"I'm Dr Rainey's sole executor," said Jonas. "I didn't like the idea, but he insisted. As soon as I've got the estate wound up, I shall hand over to Jock Lovibond. He'll have to appoint trustees to help him with the charitable part."

"But, for the moment," said Queen, "you're in charge of everything?"

"Correct."

"And you've got all his papers?"

"I've got what there was. There wasn't a lot."

"I wondered if they might have given us a lead about his next of kin."

Queen, who had considerable confidence in Jonas's professional reticence, had explained what they had in mind.

"It's often been my job to go through the papers of a dead person," said Jonas, "but I can't remember any case in which they were so uninformative. He seems to have destroyed his professional records when he retired. Sensible thing for a doctor to do, perhaps. Then there are the sort of household records you'd expect. But there isn't a single paper that's more than four years old. No birth certificate. And – this really is odd – no passport."

"Might it be at the bank?"

"The bank has the deeds of this house and some share certificates. No personal papers at all. And when he left his previous solicitors, a Portsmouth firm, and came to me – that was shortly after I got here – he seems to have removed his papers from them and destroyed the lot."

Queen said, "It looks as though something happened four years ago that scared him. It was then that he asked for police protection and fortified his house."

"I think that's right," said Jonas. "He got a jolt of some sort."

"But it doesn't help us much."

"There's one point in his papers which might give us a lead. I explained to him that his will could only be proved in this country if we could establish that his domicile was England. Fortunately he was able to make a clear statement about that, as you'll see."

He pushed a copy of the will across to Queen, who read: " 'I, Claud Rainey, doctor of medicine, declare that I am a domiciled and naturalised Englishman.' "

"The point is that this declaration does suggest two lines of enquiry. As he's a doctor there must be some record of his qualification. The BMA would be the people to ask. I think you'd have to do that. They wouldn't open up to me. On the other hand I have got an old friend in the Home Office. He might be able to tell me about the naturalisation. Also, perhaps, it would help if I had a word with the gardener. He works on Fridays and Saturdays for my partner, so it'd be easy to keep it informal. He'd be more unbuttoned with me than with you."

The truth of the matter was that Jonas enjoyed an enquiry of this sort. Queen was well aware of this. He respected Jonas's ability and the sources of information that a long professional life had made available to him. He was delighted to have his help.

"I'll dig out the papers," said Michael Doneval, "and see what I can turn up."

Although he was now number two in the Aliens' Department at the Home Office, Michael, who had once been Jonas's articled clerk, still tended to call him 'sir'.

"If it wouldn't be too much trouble," said Jonas.

"The amount of trouble will depend on when he came over. In the years immediately after the war, I'm told, there was a sort of tidal wave of immigrants. Mostly professional men. Not as many as went to America, of course. But more than enough to keep this department busy. Especially since we weren't back to peacetime staffing levels."

"Difficult to see why a lot of professional men should have wanted to uproot themselves *after* the war was over."

"I imagine," said Doneval drily, "that they'd seen what the Germans were capable of and thought it might be the Russians next. And we must still have been feeling sorry for the people in the occupied countries, because, from what I can see in the records, we were letting them in pretty easily just then. All they had to do was to produce one respectable citizen from their own country to act as a reference. Give them a clean sheet as far as crime or over-enthusiastic co-operation with the Germans were concerned."

"A referee," said Jonas thoughtfully. "If he should happen to be still alive that would indeed be helpful. We might get the whole story."

"Why don't we talk about it over lunch?" said Doneval. "I'll see if I can get a table at the Travellers."

Over lunch their talk wandered from the stupidity of the English cricket selectors to reminiscences of Doneval's brief flirtation with the law.

"I was sorry you didn't stick to a solicitor's practice," said Jonas. "You'd have made a great success of it. Even when you were a youngster I noticed you had a wonderful knack of side-tracking any conversation that looked like getting difficult for you."

"That's useful in the Home Office, too," said Doneval. "You know, sir, one thing you told me is really significant. You say that he didn't appear to have a passport."

"No trace of one."

"Do you think it's possible that he was afraid to apply? There are special rules when the applicant has been natural-ised. The Passport Office has to have certain facts from his pre-naturalisation days. Country of origin, his original name, if it's been changed and so on. Everything that you've told me seems to suggest that he was anxious to bury his past."

Jonas, who was cutting himself a slice of the club's famous Stilton cheese, said nothing until he had completed this important operation. Then he said, "Yes, that seems to be the picture that's emerging."

"If you want a word with Fred," Sabrina had said, "you'd better go up to my place about eleven tomorrow. You'll find him in the kitchen, making himself a cup of coffee. Make one for you, too, if you ask him nicely. He's a remarkable person."

Jonas had previously classed Fred as the sort of man you

would pass in a crowd without noticing him at all, but when he viewed him across Sabrina's kitchen table he changed his mind. He *was* remarkable. He had a face like a clenched fist. There was strength in the nose and chin and the line of the thin lips was uncompromising. His voice was surprising too. It was totally classless and unemphatic. He might have been anyone, done anything, been anywhere. The face was giving nothing away.

Not a man to take liberties with, Jonas decided. He said, "Dr Rainey was my client. I've been asked by the police to see if I can trace his family and his next of kin. We wondered if you could help. You must have known him better than most people."

"I worked for him for two years. He never said anything about his family. Or about himself. When we did talk it was mostly about gardening or cooking."

"I'm told he was a keen cook. Do you happen to know what he was planning to have for dinner that Monday night?"

"It would have been a mutton stew. He was cutting up the meat when I came for my coffee at eleven. He called it by a French name. Navvy something."

"And all the vegetables came out of the garden."

"All except the tomatoes. He had some he'd bought from the shop. He didn't fancy shop vegetables. That's why I was going to grow some tomatoes for him. They can be tricky. You need a south wall and a lot of luck."

"But you'd managed all the other vegetables he was using that evening?"

"Right." Fred ticked them off on his thick, brown fingers. "Potatoes, onions, peas, mushrooms, globe turnips, artichokes."

"It sounds delicious. Tell me, when you spoke to him that morning, did he seem to be in his usual spirits?"

"He was never a very happy man, I'd judge."

"Oh. What makes you say that?"

"The way he behaved. As if he was afraid that someone was after him. He'd ask if any stranger had been enquiring for him particularly."

"Can you remember any who had?"

Fred scratched the grizzled hair at the back of his neck while he thought about this. He said, "Only the usual sort of people that I can remember. Trying to sell him double glazing or insurance or things like that. He'd have no truck with them."

"Did you see him when you went up to the house in the evening to collect your money?"

"I didn't see him. He'd left the money on the kitchen table. I could hear him moving about in the house, though."

"You're sure it was him?"

"Who else would it have been? The meat was in a pan on the fire. He'd need to keep an eye on it, wouldn't he?"

"That would have been five o'clock?"

"I work till five. Then I have to clean up. It would have been a quarter or twenty past."

Jonas finished his coffee and got up. There seemed to be no more that Fred could, or would, tell him. He debated whether he ought to offer him a tip, but decided against it. There was something about Fred which made the idea inappropriate.

When he told Sabrina she said, "He might have taken it, because he's a polite person. But he wouldn't have needed it."

"Has he got a lot of money?"

"Do you know his cottage in Friary Lane? A very agreeable little property. He bought it when he came here four years ago. It's been valued at eighty thousand pounds and there's no mortgage on it."

"How do you know all this?"

"He's selling it and he's asked me to act for him."

"A tip would certainly have been inappropriate," agreed Jonas. "Have you any idea where his money came from? He can hardly have made it by gardening."

"From something he said I gathered that he had a cottage at his last place. Probably bought it for twenty thousand pounds and sold it for forty thousand pounds. Once you get on the property market ladder you can't go wrong."

"I suppose not," said Jonas. "You're a cook, Sabrina. If you were planning a dish, based on mutton, but involving also — see if I can remember — potatoes, tomatoes, onions, peas, mushrooms, turnips and artichokes, how long would it take to cook?"

Sabrina was almost licking her lips. "What you're describing," she said, "is that most delicious French dish, a navarin of mutton."

"That's right. It was a French word, navvy something," he said.

"You start by browning the meat in butter. Then you add the spices, with a cupful of flour to make a roux. Then – "

"I'm not intending to cook it," said Jonas. "I just wanted to know when it would be ready to eat. You can take it that the procedure had already started by a quarter past five."

Sabrina was making some intricate calculations, murmuring to herself words like 'bubble', 'stir in' and 'simmer'. It was a witch's incantation. Then she said, "It'd be ready by half past seven. And eaten by eight. Once it was on the table he wouldn't want to waste a moment. One thing I don't follow, though. You say that when Fred was describing this dish to you he said, 'a French word, navvy something'."

"Yes."

"But that's impossible. He spoke excellent colloquial French. Much better than me and I used to think I was a dab at it."

"How do you know?"

"I heard him. One of those French onion-sellers had come to the door. I don't think he knew I was in the front room, doing some work. I could hear them chatting."

"And Fred was keeping his end up?"

"He wasn't just talking French. He was talking like a Frenchman. And was the onion-seller lapping it up!"

"It doesn't make sense," said Jonas. He thought about Fred. "Did he say where he was going when he left here? Or why he was leaving?"

"Not where he was going. I asked him that, in case he was thinking of buying a house. But he told me why he was going. He said that what had happened had upset him."

"He didn't look to me," said Jonas, "like the sort of man it would be easy to upset."

Next day, Queen called on him. The Superintendent listened to what Jonas had to tell him. He said, "I haven't got a lot to tell you myself. The BMA looked up their records. Claud Rainey was a Belgian. He came over here at the end of the war,

did his training at Bart's and qualified in 1951. Then he came
down here and practised until his retirement eight years ago.
A perfectly straight record. They did say one thing, though. It
seems that he had already got a long way on with his medical
training in Belgium. That being so, there was a concession
which would have short-circuited his training here. Only, of
course, he had to provide proper details. Apparently he was
unable, or unwilling, to do so; which meant that he had to
start again at the beginning."

"He certainly seems to have been shy about his past life,"
said Jonas. "And I don't see how we're going to dig it up."

The answer to this was on his desk three days later.

As I expect you will already have discovered [wrote
Michael Doneval], Claud Rainey, otherwise René
Claude, was a Belgian. He came over here in July 1945,
with a number of other European immigrants. His
'sponsor' was a Bruxellois dentist called Hervé Maxente.
As I told you when we met, the office was understaffed
and overworked at the time, but that shouldn't have
excused us from spotting that when Maxente came over
here three months later and changed his name to Max
Humbolt *his* 'sponsor' was René Claude! Which means,
of course, that they could both have been bad hats,
sponsoring each other. Humbolt, who set up his practice
at Alfriston in Sussex, died four years ago. Now that
Rainey's dead too there doesn't seem much anyone can
do about their Siamese twins' act.

"A double dead-end," said Queen when Jonas showed him the
letter.

"Maybe," said Jonas, "but have you noticed one point?
Humbolt died four years ago. Four years ago Rainey barri-
caded his house and started worrying about strangers who
might be enquiring for him."

"Could be a coincidence."

"I don't think it was a coincidence. I think that Rainey took
his compatriot's death as a warning. I'll go further, I think
that the mysterious man who left his house at six o'clock that
morning was the stranger he'd been warned against."

Queen turned it over in his mind. He was a practical policeman. He distrusted theories, particularly when they seemed to lead nowhere. He said, "So what are you going to do about it?"

"If the office can spare me for a couple of days, I'm going to Alfriston."

Jonas secured a room at the Star Hotel, which has a seventeenth-century background of smugglers and secret passages, but excellent twentieth-century accommodation. He did not have to pursue his enquiries very far. The newsagent, from whom he bought his morning *Times*, had been one of dentist Humbolt's patients.

"And a right good dentist too. We couldn't understand why he stuck to a small place like 'Friston. Could have made three times the money in Brighton or Eastbourne. Glad he did, though. Died four or five years ago. Had that big house at the bottom of Hindover Hill. Brigadier Arkinwright has it now."

The Brigadier had been trying to mow his lawn, but had given up the attempt. "Grass still too wet," he said. "Come inside. We shall be more comfortable there."

Jonas explained, with certain omissions, what he was after. The Brigadier, who must, he thought, have been at least seventy and long retired, listened politely, if inattentively, to an enquiry which did not concern him.

He said, "I never actually met Humbolt. He had no family, you see. So when he died his house was immediately put on the market. I saw it advertised and snapped it up."

"Oh dear," said Jonas. "Another dead-end. If he'd left a widow she might have been able to help me. It isn't Humbolt I'm after, though. It's a man who was a compatriot and a close friend of his. He, too, has died without any visible family connections."

"Tiresome," said the Brigadier. "But I don't really know that I can help much."

"Tell me, was there an inquest?"

"Yes, they had to have an inquest. Humbolt had been in pretty good health, you see. And hadn't troubled the doctor for years. So his death was a bit of a mystery. But it turned out to be a coronary. There was a piece in the local paper about it."

The Brigadier, who was clearly the sort of man who kept his records under control, went to his desk and fetched out a yellowing clipping. "Keep it if you like."

Jonas thanked him and tucked it away in his wallet.

As they walked out of the front door the Brigadier said, "Only one thing wrong with this house. Too much garden."

"You keep it very nicely," said Jonas.

"As well as I can, but it's a back-breaking job for a man of my age. I was sorry I couldn't secure the gardener along with the house. Charlie must have been a wonderful worker despite his game leg. He only came for two days a week, but everything was in apple-pie order when I took it over."

Jonas said, "I suppose he wouldn't still be around?"

"No. He sold his cottage when Humbolt died and moved off. I did see him once before he left. Odd thing was I was sure I'd seen him before somewhere. Unusual sort of face. He was a popular local character. Someone may know where he's gone."

The newsagent, who was evidently the clearing house for all local gossip, said, "Yes, we all knew Charlie. He worked two days a week for Mr Humbolt, two days for Mrs Lamprey and two for the Clarks. I expect they'll have kept in touch."

"I don't suppose," said Jonas, almost holding his breath, "that you happen to have a photograph of him." As he spoke he was busy trying to construct a plausible reason for his request.

To the newsagent, fortunately, it seemed a perfectly natural thing to want. He thought for a moment and then said, "He took first prize for his roses the year before he left. Very popular victory. There was a photograph of the Mayor of Seaford presenting him with the cup. I haven't got a copy myself, but the *Seaford and Newhaven Gazette* could find it for you, I don't doubt."

The *Seaford and Newhaven Gazette* turned the relevant number up for him. Having two copies they were happy to sell one to Jonas. He cut out the photograph and tucked it away in his wallet alongside the account of the inquest.

He was aware that his trip to Alfriston had not solved the mystery of Dr Rainey's death. It had added another mystery to it.

*　　*　　*

Superintendent Queen examined the cuttings deliberately. It was impossible to tell from his face whether he was surprised or annoyed. Both, perhaps, Jonas thought. But he could see the implications clearly enough.

"No doubt about it," he said. "Charlie, who worked for Mr Humbolt, is the same man as Fred. The photograph's conclusive."

"Quite conclusive."

"But where does it take us?" He was re-reading the account of the inquest. "This wasn't a hasty guess by an old bumbler like Smallhorn. The autopsy was conducted by Andrew Friend."

"Very sound man," agreed Jonas.

"And look what he says. 'I understand that the deceased regularly smoked twenty or thirty cigarettes a day. This alone could have brought on the occlusion of the coronary artery which was the direct cause of death.'"

"I've been thinking about that," said Jonas. "Suppose that Humbolt's death *was* natural. We know that he and Rainey had some connection with each other. Something disreputable, perhaps, which had happened in Belgium and which made them both bolt like rabbits as soon as the war was over. Rainey hears about Humbolt's death. He doesn't believe it was natural. So he starts to take elaborate precautions. Then Charlie – or Fred as he now calls himself – arrives. Good jobbing gardeners are so scarce that he must have been confident he'd land a job with Rainey sooner or later. In fact it took him two years to do it. He didn't mind waiting. He's struck me as being a very patient man."

"And you're suggesting that it was Fred who poisoned the doctor."

"Who else? Most of the ingredients of his last meal were under his control."

"And that he was the man Trotter saw leaving the house at six in the morning?"

"That seems logical."

"There's nothing logical about it," said Queen irritably. "To start with, how did he get back into the house?"

"Easy. He never left it. There were a lot of places he could have hidden. Pantry, scullery, coal hole, cellar. Remember, he'd had the run of the kitchen quarters and all the time in the world to construct a foolproof hiding place."

"All right. Then tell me this. Why didn't he leave as soon as Rainey was dead?"

"It may have been a slow-acting poison."

Queen considered the implications of this. He said, "You're making my flesh creep. Do you mean to say he sat there all night watching Rainey die?"

"Watching him die, yes. And making certain that he didn't telephone or call for help. He was twice as strong as Rainey, who would have been getting even less able to resist as the poison took effect."

"It's hard to believe," said Queen. "Though I'll admit there's one thing that supports your theory. The look on his face. He saw death coming and he hated it. No question, we shall have to have an exhumation order. Can you authorise it?"

Jonas said, "I'll ask my partner. She's a much better lawyer than I am."

That evening he rang up Michael Doneval at his home. He felt that Doneval might be more unbuttoned there than behind his desk. He said, "Thank you very much, Michael. The information you gave me has been extremely useful. In fact, it has opened things up to an almost alarming degree. Now I want your help over one more thing."

"If I can," said Doneval cautiously.

"It's nothing I couldn't get myself, but you'll be able to get it more quickly. Could you find out the known details – nothing which isn't in the public record – of the wartime career of a Brigadier Arkinwright."

"Not a common name," said Doneval, "I ought to be able to do that. I'll telephone you some time tomorrow."

"I'm very much obliged to you," said Jonas.

Next morning Sabrina marched into his office with a volume of Probate Court reports and a newspaper. She said, "It wasn't an easy point. There's not much authority on it, because the circumstances are unlikely to arise. However, in *Jepson v. Church 1898* the point had to be considered. Church was sole executor of a man called Ambrose Jepson, who died in somewhat mysterious circumstances which came to light after he had been buried. The police wanted an exhumation order. Church, who was a solicitor, was agreeable. The opposition came from Jepson's sister, his only surviving relative. When the matter came to court, Mr Justice Romer said, 'In many matters the authority of the executor is supreme. But in such a matter as this, which touches the feelings of the family and the intimate friends of the deceased, I consider that the opinion of the senior member of the family – or, if no such person survives, of the residuary legatee to whom the estate has been entrusted – should be regarded as paramount.' "

"If that's right, I can't move in the matter. We shall have to ask Jock Lovibond."

"I'm afraid so. However, my researches into your case have not been entirely negative." She laid the newspaper, folded open, on Jonas's desk. He saw that it was a copy of the *New York Herald*.

"I have an American friend who sends me reports which she thinks I will find interesting."

Jonas had reached a point where he hardly knew what to expect next. The extract was headed, 'Smokers Beware'.

A posthumous confession has solved a fifteen-year-old mystery which puzzled pathologists and forensic scientists and has opened up an alarming prospect for incautious smokers. It seems that a Mrs Sylvester Cramm of Little Falls, Minnesota, lay under considerable suspicion of killing her husband, who had been found dead in the matrimonial home. He had been in good health until that moment. It was public knowledge that he had behaved brutally to his wife and his death was undoubtedly to her financial advantage. For these reasons a very careful autopsy was conducted. However, leading pathologist, Dr Schumacher, was clear in his opinion that death was due to a simple coronary occlusion, precipitated, he considered, by the fact that the late Mr Cramm had been a compulsive smoker. It now appears from the posthumous confession of his wife, a trained nurse, that she had procured some neat nicotine and had injected this into one of her husband's cigarettes. When this was put to Dr Schumacher he agreed that the nicotine vaporised by the heat of the cigarette and inhaled could certainly cause an occlusion of the coronary artery. Moreover, such a matter would be difficult or impossible to detect by normal post mortem examination.

Jonas said, "God dammit – "

"I'm not suggesting," said Sabrina calmly, "that this was the way in which Humbolt was killed. But it occurred to me that the circumstances in his case were very similar. He was a chain smoker. He lived alone in the house. The gardener had access to it and there are plenty of garden sprays from which nicotine could be extracted."

"You know what's wrong with this case," said Jonas crossly. "It's all theory and supposition. I sympathise with Jack Queen. He wants facts and they are in short supply. Certainly Fred *could* have poisoned Dr Rainey. And if he happened to have come across that report – or to have seen the facts reported somewhere else – he might have killed Humbolt that way too. But why? What in the world is the connection between a dentist in Alfriston, a doctor in Shackleton and a jobbing gardener? Yes, what is it?"

Claire said, "I've got a call here from a Mr Doneval. Shall I put it through?"

"Please."

"Short answer to your question," said Doneval. "Brigadier Arkinwright was a sapper. He fought at Dunkirk and got an MC for his efforts on the beaches. Later, being a fluent French speaker, he joined Maurice Buckmaster in the headquarters of the SOE at Baker Street. His job was to equip undercover agents for work in France and Belgium and to debrief them when, and if, they returned. That's the outline. I could fill it in for you a bit more, I expect, if I asked around."

"No," said Jonas. "That's fine. I really am extremely grateful."

Sabrina, who had been listening on the extension, said, "Well, is that your answer?"

"It's a possible answer," said Jonas.

Later that day he reported his findings to Queen who listened, with his face growing longer and longer.

"It now seems possible," Jonas said, "that Fred — his full name my partner tells me, is Frederick Charles Blamey — could have worked, during the war, as an agent in Belgium. He's about the right age and speaks fluent French. Also he struck me, when I met him, as a tough, self-reliant sort of person. And now we find that Brigadier Arkinwright, who had a job at SOE headquarters, thought he recognised him."

"All right. He could have been. It's not impossible."

"Then I'll make another suggestion. That Rainey and Humbolt, who fudged each other's references, came over at the end of the war as soon as they could pack their bags. Because they knew that once the proper post-war investigations got going they would be revealed as undesirable citizens. Collaborators at least. Possibly more than that. They reckoned that they'd be a lot safer in England."

"All right," said Queen, "I can paint the rest of your picture. Blamey, who could have suffered as a result of their actions, gets after them. Waiting, incidentally, for more than thirty years before he went to Alfriston."

"He was a very patient man," said Jonas. "Like all successful secret agents and gardeners. And, anyway, what do we know about what he was doing during that time? Rainey and Humbolt might have been the last names on a long list."

Queen looked at him with something like horror. Finally he drew a deep breath and said, "We started this and I suppose we shall have to go on with it."

"Then you'll have to get your exhumation order. If you discover poison and if it's something which was available to Blamey and if you can dig a convincing motive out of the wartime history, then you'll have some sort of a case."

"That's three 'ifs'," said Queen. "I wouldn't be inclined to bet on our chances."

Three days later, in response to a summons, Jonas went to see Chief Superintendent Whaley. He found Queen with him.

"It's no good," said Jonas. "Jock won't do it. Particularly with a council election coming up. He says an exhumation would simply antagonise public opinion. It would be seen as pointing a finger at Fred. He was a very well liked man. Mrs McClachan, who is Jock's niece by marriage, told him that he was not just a good gardener. An inspired one, she said. Before he worked for her she had been trying for years to grow asparagus. No dice. Then Fred came along and got her a bed of it growing *from seed*. A man with such green fingers, she said, couldn't conceivably have dipped them in anything dubious. You won't change Jock's mind now, however hard you try, I assure you."

As Jonas said this he got the impression that neither of his listeners had any real desire to try.

"Well," said Whaley, "if he won't, he won't. And that's an end of that." The relief in his voice was clear.

When this was reported to Sabrina she said, "Saved by asparagus. What an epitaph for a gardener."

"It's all very well," grumbled Jonas. "You make a joke of it. Whaley and Queen are only too glad to wash their hands of the whole thing. But that's not what I'd call a satisfactory result. I like to know the truth. And now, I suppose, we never shall."

" 'Never' is a long time," said Sabrina. "After all, it only took fifteen years for the facts about the Sylvester Cramm case to come to light. Allow me to give you a quote from your favourite author, Winston Churchill. 'Truth is an uncomfortable creature to keep in the well against her efforts.' "

And in fact it was not fifteen years, but fifteen months before the truth emerged.

It was on an October day in the year following the death of Dr Rainey that Sabrina came into Jonas's office with a letter in her hand.

She said, "Blamey is dead. Cancer of the stomach. When he knew he was dying he wrote me this letter which I will show you on the understanding that it remains entirely confidential."

"Even from Queen and Whaley?"

"Specially from them."

Jonas said, "Very well," and picked up the letter, which was written in a surprisingly firm and educated hand. It opened without any preamble.

I am writing you this to repay certain kindnesses you did me last year. Not only selling my house and making my will for me, but showing me that extract from the *New York Herald*, which was, incidentally, reprinted in the British *Medico-Legal Journal*, available in the public library. A most interesting publication, I found. When you showed it to me I realised that you must have a shrewd idea of the truth and that it was time for me to move. Yes, certainly I killed Humbolt, whose real name, as you may have discovered, was Hervé Maxente. Also Dr Rainey who was René Claude. Both of them deserved to die. They took very large sums of money from the Germans for informing them about British agents for whom, supposedly, they were working. I have no doubt the British Government was paying them as well. This double-cross was carried out so skilfully that very few people knew about it. I did, because I got out of a safe house recommended by Maxente by dropping from a second-storey window. Incidentally breaking my leg in the process. Others were not so lucky. Claude was responsible for one of my closest friends being taken. The Germans were determined to get information from him. It took him eight hours to die. I reminded Claude of this when he was dying. The details are not of great importance. I cultivated Amanita Phalloides, the Death Cap fungus, in a bed against the wall at the bottom of the garden. All that was necessary was to add a few slivers to the field mushrooms waiting for that evening stew. It is a remorseless killer which destroys every liver and kidney cell in the human body, but it takes from six to eight hours to work, so I had to make sure that Claude did not go for help. He finally died just before six o'clock and I let myself out and went home. I had to be back at work by my normal hour, as I needed to root out the remaining fungi, which were in a bed I was supposed to be preparing for tomatoes, and burn them. If I had the time and energy [Jonas noticed that the writing had been growing more straggly, but still quite legible], I'd tell you of one or two other interesting episodes in the years since the war.

*   *   *

Then, at the bottom, "Goodbye and again thanks."

A full minute had elapsed after Jonas had read the letter before he was able to say anything. Fastening on a minor point, he said, "He must have died a rich man. Who gets his money?"

"It all goes to a trust which looks after the dependants of SOE agents."

"I see," said Jonas. But that was not what he really wanted to say. In the end he managed to get it out.

"Did it never occur to you," he said, "that by showing him that cutting, you were warning him that he was suspected?"

"Suspected, possibly. But in no danger when Jock Lovibond accepted my advice against exhumation."

Jonas looked at her speechlessly. Then, "You *advised* him to oppose it."

"Certainly."

"Did you not consider that it was your duty, to the authorities, to the court, to the state, that this matter should be cleared up?"

"As a solicitor," said Sabrina coldly, "my first duty was to my client."

196

THE FREEDOM FOLK

In the four years they had been established in Shackleton the
lunching arrangements of Jonas and his staff had become, like
many other things, a matter of habit. Sabrina took hers at the
Central Café, with others of her sex and totem; more talking
was done than eating. Jonas went to the Conservative Club
and usually managed to get in a rubber of bridge before going
back to the office. Claire brought sandwiches and liked,
weather permitting, to eat them in the open. So far that year
she had been lucky.

It had been an exceptionally mild spring. March was half
over and sunny day had followed sunny day with the wind
blowing steadily from the south-west. Her favourite lunch
place was the Dingle. This was where the Shackle stream
frothed and bubbled its way out to sea over a bed of white
stones.

It was a pleasant spot in any weather. The banks of the little
valley were gradual on the Shackleton side, more sheer on the
far side. The bottom was formed of smooth South Down turf,
through which the stream had cut its bed. On the far side, a
flight of steps ran up to the only human habitation in sight.
This was the cottage of Francis Delamere, a meteorological
hermit, who had roosted up there for nearly half a century,
observing the weather of the Channel coast.

He discouraged visitors, but Claire remembered being
taken up there once with Jonas, who had acted for the old man
in a family matter. He had shown them his vast collection of
weather maps, graphs and statistical records. A monomaniac,
she had concluded, but harmless.

As she was thinking about him she caught sight of a figure

moving on the knoll between the cottage and the cliff edge. Certainly not Delamere. Now that her attention had been attracted she made out that someone had set up an easel and was painting. She finished her sandwiches, crossed the rustic bridge over the stream and climbed the steps to inspect his efforts. Some of the amateur artists who frequented Shackleton in summer disliked being watched at work. Others appreciated an audience.

This seemed to be one of the latter sort. He smiled agreeably as Claire came up and stepped back from the easel.

About forty, Claire guessed. A face tanned by the weather, with wrinkles round the eyes as though he spent much of his time staring into the sun. His short pointed beard, cut in the Vandyke fashion, was beginning to show a sprinkling of grey. He had been painting in watercolour, using a simple palette. It was a composition of sea and sky, a chiaroscuro of blues and whites and greys. Claire knew little about painting, but enough to find the picture effective and attractive.

She said, "I suppose it wouldn't be for sale, by any chance?"

The man said, "You would have to consult Gus Levy about that."

"Gus – "

"He runs the Wardour Galleries. They handle all my work. You may have heard of them."

This was said gravely, but there was a hint of laughter behind it and Claire realised that she had been stupid. This was not the sort of painter who set up his easel on the front and sold his pictures to bystanders for a few pounds. She said, "I'm sorry. Yes, I know the Wardour Galleries. They're in Bond Street, aren't they?"

"Correct. If you know them, do I take it you're a Londoner?" He seemed to have abandoned painting for the moment and wanted to talk.

She said, "I used to work in London, yes. That was some years ago. I've become a confirmed Shackletonian now."

"I can't suppose you've retired."

Definitely he was laughing at her, but she was not annoyed. She said, "My employer, Mr Pickett – he's a solicitor – moved down here from London a few years ago and I came with him."

"Not Jonas Pickett?"

"Correct. You know him?"

"I met him when he acted for me in an unpleasant dispute over the lease of my flat. That was one of the reasons I decided to abandon urban life and bought myself a caravan. A great improvement on a flat in West Kensington, let me tell you."

"As long as the weather stays fine."

"A modern caravan," said the man firmly, "is proof against any vagaries of the climate. I can't imagine why half the populace of our overcrowded, insanitary inner cities don't take to them. They'd be healthier and happier if they did."

"If you can spare the time," said Claire, who found herself liking him more and more, "do please drop in. My name's Easterbrook, by the way. Claire Easterbrook. We're at the far corner of Middle Street. I'm sure Jonas would like to see you again."

"I'll do that. And since there's no one here to effect an introduction, I must do it myself. The name is Wroke. Spelled with a 'W'. Philip Wroke."

When, on her return to the office, Claire told Sabrina about this encounter she said, "You didn't really offer to buy the picture, did you?"

"Yes. But I saw that I'd made a mistake."

"The last time I went to a Summer Exhibition at the Academy," said Sabrina thoughtfully, "there were three Wroke seascapes on view. The cheapest, I seem to remember, was priced at three thousand guineas."

"Then," said Claire, "perhaps it's just as well that he didn't take me up on my offer."

The faintest preliminary ripples of possible trouble had reached Shackleton that morning. The ladies who were lunching together at the Central Café were too engrossed in dissecting the character of the new rector's wife to bother about it, but the stout estate agent who was partnering Jonas at bridge did say, "I hear they had a spot of bother with a nature camp at Portree. Three no trumps."

Jonas was too busy trying to analyse this gross over-bid to pursue the matter. So it was Sam who got the story first.

He took his midday cheese and beer at the Fisherman's

Arms. He was welcomed by the company in the saloon bar, partly from the dignity of his connection with the law ("Crafty old bastard that Pickett"), partly for his Rabelaisian wit and partly, no doubt, from the consciousness that this ex-fairground boxer and strongman could have slung any one of them out of the door with one hand tied behind his back.

On this occasion he was making no attempt to hold the floor. He was prepared to drink his beer and listen, for the conversation had taken an interesting turn.

"Heard about it from my cousin over at Poole," said a gnome-like man who mowed the golf club greens. "Seems they nipped in at Portree. Small place, just this side of Walden."

"When you say they nipped in" – this was a tall fisherman – "you mean they didn't ask no one? They was just trespassing."

"Difficult to talk about trespass, when you don't know who the land belongs to."

"All the land belongs to someone," said the landlord.

"I beg to contradict you," said a thin man whose glasses and manner of speaking had earned him the honorary title of Professor, but who, in fact, kept a live-bait store. "The land below high-water mark belongs to no one."

"Surely you're wrong, Professor," said the landlord. "It belongs to the Queen. Like whales."

"Not so. It is *terra sine titulo*."

Baffled by this display of Latin, the landlord said, "Anyway no one in their senses is going to pitch a camp where the tide can come up and wash it away. Stands to reason."

"From what I heard," said the gnome-like man, "there isn't a lot of reason in anything these people do. They've got a flag with FF on it. Standing, so I understand, for the Freedom Folk, but it could be something different."

A number of alternative suggestions were offered, most of them unprintable. Sam, who had finished his beer, intervened for the first time.

"Diddun I see in the paper," he said, "that Portree had got rid of 'em? How'd they manage that, eh?"

"By force," said the small man. "They're a rough crowd down there. What they did, they turned up one morning early, about a hundred of them, slung out the caravans and tents and pulled down the shacks. Then they ran a fence of barbed wire round the place before anyone could stop them."

"A bit rough," said the landlord. "Wasn't there nothing they could do about it?"

"Well, of course, the man who seems to boss them – Lipitt, or some name like that – he went off to the police. When they arrived they found them camped out beside the road and a dozen tough characters guarding the way back through the barbed wire what they'd put up. The Inspector said, 'We're not going to have any trouble. The first one who starts a fight, we run him in.'"

"Meaning," said the tall fisherman, "that since they were out they'd got to stay out."

"The law," agreed the Professor, "favours the status quo."

"So what did they do?" said the landlord.

"What could they do? They couldn't get back without a fight, so they packed up their traps and moved off down the road. At night they pitch camp on the roadside. Provided they move on each day, no one can do anything about that."

Sam said, "How long ago was it they got turned out?"

"It was last week."

"And Walden's – what – about thirty miles from here?"

The landlord said, "Don't you worry, Sam. The council won't have a crowd like that in here, not in a month of Sundays."

Sam said, "Come to that, I don't suppose Portree wanted them neither."

At the next office coffee break he retailed what he had heard and found an attentive audience.

"I read something about it in the local paper," said Jonas. "Opinion seemed to be divided about the rights and wrongs of it."

"I can't see that it's a question with two sides to it," said Claire. "The people who turned them out were the ones who used force. Surely that put them in the wrong."

"The first wrong-doing," said Sabrina, "was when they camped on someone else's property without permission."

"Apparently it was common land."

"You're using the expression very loosely, darling. If it was what the law calls common land, that only means that the inhabitants had the right to graze their animals on it. It certainly does *not* mean that strangers had a right to come along and live on it."

"I don't think it was that sort of common. It was a piece by the seashore without a private owner."

"If it was above a median tide mark it belonged to the community and came under the jurisdiction of the local council."

Sam said, "That was what they was saying at the pub. They're nothing but a crowd of no-good drop-outs and the council would turn 'em out neck and crop if they tried the same game round here."

"Then I'm afraid, Sam," said Claire, "that your worthy friends in the saloon bar of the Fisherman's Arms are, as usual, talking nonsense."

The tone in which she said this made Jonas look up at her. He said, "Have you got some information that we haven't?"

"You can call them drop-outs if you like. They are people who have got tired of an insanitary overcrowded life in our inner cities" – unconsciously she found she was quoting the artist – " and find a gypsy life healthier and happier."

"Happier for them," said Sabrina. "What about the people they impose themselves on?"

"There should be room in this country for everyone. Wasn't the government telling us, only the other day, that the countryside was over-farmed? The mistake people make is thinking about these people as criminals. Some of them are very poor, it's true. They can't even afford a proper tent, let alone a caravan. They just lean two pieces of corrugated iron together – "

"Claire," said Jonas, "you seem to know a lot more about this than we do. Who have you been talking to?"

"As a matter of fact I happened to run into Philip Wroke again in a café in the town."

"Don't tell me he's one of them."

"He has been with them now for some months, yes."

"That certainly gives them a touch of respectability."

"Oh, he's not the only one. There are several artists, not as well known as he is, I agree. And writers."

"Poets, no doubt," said Sabrina.

"I don't know about poets, but they've got a radio drama-tist. And a pop group. They call themselves The Strollers. They've made quite a few records."

"That was one of the things they told me about," said Sam. "They practise all night. Keep people awake, you see. No thought for others."

Jonas said, "I should imagine it's difficult to discipline a crowd like that. Have they got a leader?"

"Wroke is regarded as second in command. The leader, the man who founded the group, is called Lipsett."

"And what is he?" said Jonas. "An artist, a writer, or a musician?"

"I'm not sure."

"If it's Raymond Lipsett," said Sabrina, "he's a man who writes articles for left-wing publications. I've read quite a few of them. Able stuff, but totally perverted, of course."

"Of course," said Claire sharply. "If his views are left of centre they must be perverted, mustn't they?"

"Children, children," said Jonas. "Don't scratch each other's eyes out." He could see that Claire was losing her temper and that Sabrina would like nothing more than to provoke her. "May I point out that it is now half past eleven and that I, at least, have work to do."

This was true. It was a question of mineral rights at Maggs's farm which had reached the Crown Court at Brighton. Jonas had decided to brief counsel and was drafting a case for Mr Kendrick, QC. It was a complex matter and he had to devote his full attention to what he was dictating, but something was niggling him. He knew his secretary as well as any shrewd professional man would be likely to know a girl who has been working for him for nearly six years, but he had never suspected her of holding strong left-wing views.

Perhaps Wroke had got something to do with this? To date Claire's relationships with the young of the opposite sex had been casual to the point of flippancy. But a forty-year-old artist . . . He realised that Claire had been sitting with her pencil poised for some seconds and wrenched his mind back to the question of the minerals which underlay Farmer Maggs's fields.

*　　*　　*

At a quarter to seven on the following morning a matter which had been of remote interest took a sharp step forward. Jonas blinked his eyes open and picked up the telephone from the table beside his bed.

It was the hermit, Francis Delamere, and he was very angry.

He said, "They've come. You've got to do something."

"Do you mind," said Jonas swinging his legs out of bed and sitting up, "telling me what you're talking about?" He found that he could think more clearly when sitting up, which was as well, because Delamere was almost incoherent with rage.

"Last night," he said, "after dark. Like thieves in the night."

"Your house has been burgled."

"No, no. Worse. Much worse. They're all over the Dingle."

There was no need for Jonas to ask who they were. He could guess only too easily. He said, "I suppose you're talking about those campers."

"A rabble. You've got to move them on."

"I'm very sorry about it. But it's not really my job."

"Certainly it's your job. You're my solicitor, aren't you? Start an action."

Jonas's experience had hardened him to clients who demanded actions on every conceivable and some inconceivable points. He said, patiently, "Just who would you suggest I start an action against?"

"These people. The FF."

"The first difficulty is that they're not, as far as I know, a corporate body. And if we could get over that one, what are we starting an action for?"

"Trespass."

"*You* can't sue them for trespass. You don't own the land."

"You're making difficulties. If the law won't help us we shall have to take matters into our own hands. Like they did at Portree."

"No," said Jonas. "Whatever you do – " But he found that the telephone had gone dead.

He dressed hastily, thought about breakfast, decided that speed was all-important and got his car out. As he was starting it, Sam appeared and jumped in beside him. The quickest approach to the Dingle was along the golf club road. They parked the car in a lay-by and took the track which led down the winding left-hand bank of the stream. As they turned a corner they came on the scene of the action.

A strong fence, three lines of barbed-wire fixed to uprights of angle iron, barred their way. There was a narrow opening through which the track ran. The men standing beside it were clearly both sentinels and guards. Some action was going on in the camp itself. Men and women were crowding round a shanty composed of two corrugated iron sheets. Jonas said, "Good God! Isn't that Delamere? The stupid old coot. He must have wriggled in under the wire at the top end. What did he think he could do?"

The crowd parted and they could see that two men were carrying the old hermit, who was still struggling.

"Better get him out, hadn't we?" said Sam. "Before he hurts himself. Or gets hurt."

He marched up to the gate. The guards said, "You can't come in."

"No such word as 'can't' in my vocabulary, chum," said Sam and marched on. The guards took one look at his formidable bulk and decided that he was out of their class. Jonas, like a small tender being towed by a battleship, followed in his wake.

At the foot of the path they met the carrying party coming up.

"Put that man down," said Jonas, "at once."

"Fuck off," said the leading porter. "He tried to pull down our shanty. We're going to pitch him out on to his head."

"Better put him down," said Sam mildly. "Or get your own head knocked off. Your choice, mate."

The second porter, who had appreciated Sam's potentiality, had already let go of Delamere's legs. His companion had no choice but to follow suit. Delamere fell on to his knees, stopped there for a few moments, then climbed slowly to his feet. He was clearly dazed and shaken. The crowd who had followed him up were standing round, not actively aggressive, but silent and hostile.

They opened out to let a man through. Jonas felt certain that this was their leader. It would have been easier to judge his age if he had not had so much hair on his face. Two bright blue eyes stared out from a forest of beard, moustache and curling side whiskers. Despite all this foliage Jonas thought the man was not much past his middle thirties. He said, "If your name's Lipsett and you're in charge here, I have to warn you that if your people had harmed this man you'd have been in bad trouble. He's nearly eighty and the rough handling he's had might have very serious results."

"He brought it on his own head," said Lipsett. "He came in uninvited and started to pull down this man's shack."

"That was stupid, I agree. But he should have been restrained without violence and removed politely."

"Would you have been polite, if someone had started to destroy *your* house?" It was the voice of an academic, pitched in the upper register, intellectual, relishing controversy.

"I should have sent for the police," said Jonas curtly. And to Sam, "Help this man back to the car. We'll all feel better when we've had something to eat."

When they got back Sam cooked breakfast for them. Delamere had no appetite for food, but drank several cups of sugary coffee, which seemed to revive him. After breakfast, Sabrina joined them. She had heard the news. She said, "They seem to have learnt from their experience at Portree. This time they got their fence up first."

"I've been out of touch with things for a long time," said Delamere. "But when you asked me what action I could take, I seemed to remember – Isn't there something called an action for nuisance?"

Sabrina fielded this one. "You mean the noise they make at night?"

"And by day."

"Yes. I expect you could found an action for nuisance. But it wouldn't do you a lot of good. It'd be a civil action and might take a year or more to get to court. And if you won, you wouldn't get rid of them. You'd simply get an award of damages."

"Oh," said Delamere rather blankly. "Then do you mean there's nothing I can do?"

"Nothing *you* can do, no. But the council could get quick results if it set about it the right way. Normally the court will grant a speedy remedy in a case of aggravated trespass."

When the old man had departed, unhappy, but apparently persuaded to rely, for the moment, on council action, Sabrina said to Jonas, "The present council may do the right thing, but you're not forgetting that we shall soon have a new one."

"I had forgotten," said Jonas. "When's the election?"

"The first week of April."

"And does it worry us?"

"I'm not sure. I've heard some odd stories."

It was one morning, ten days after this conversation, that Admiral Fairlie arrived, by appointment, in Jonas's office. He came to the point with naval promptness. He said, "We've got a crisis on our hands. I've been talking to Bob Rattray. Saul Melford has been taken to hospital with suspected thrombosis. They've started exploratory surgery, but however successful they are he won't be back in action for some months."

"Which means that he can't stand at the next election." Jonas was studying a marked plan of Shackleton and its environs. "He's West Ward, isn't he?"

"Correct. And that's not all. Last time John Benson and Bob Rattray picked up the two Town Wards unopposed. Not this time. They've both got a fight on their hands."

"Their opponents being – ?"

"Lipsett and Wroke."

Jonas took a minute to absorb this. Then he said, "Are they qualified to stand?"

"Certainly. All they need is six residents to support their nomination. There's been no difficulty about that. They've drummed up quite a following already; particularly among the young. Their pop group, The Strollers, have given two concerts. Both of them were sell-outs."

"Yes," said Jonas. "I heard about that." He was making some calculations, none of them reassuring. He said, "What are their real chances?"

"Lipsett won't upset Bob Rattray. Not a chance. But Wroke might oust Benson. He's not wildly popular. And there's more to it than that. You know Desmond Plackett?"

"Insurance broker. Took over the Portsmouth Road Ward when Grandfield was killed in that car accident."

"Right. He's not standing this time. Says he's got too many

business commitments. Actually I fancy he's funking it. Thinks he'd be beaten."

Jonas was scribbling names in two columns. He said, "What about the two Branmere Wards?"

"Greenaway and Forbes have held them for some years now. That part's predominantly commercial. I think they're both safe enough. The trouble is, they don't like each other much. On any important proposal if one of them votes for it the other could easily oppose it."

"What about the Liberties?"

"Florence Fitchett," said the Admiral gloomily. Most men were gloomy when discussing Florence. She might have been described as a supporter of sex equality had it not been apparent that she considered women to be in every respect superior to men.

"You won't rout her out easily," agreed Jonas. "Is that the lot?"

"No. There's the East Ward. In some ways it's the most important. That's where the ragamuffins have pitched their camp."

"Who's the incumbent?"

"Mabel Hanaway. She took it over from her husband, Air Vice-Marshal Hanaway, when he died. We don't know yet who's opposing her. We reckon she's got about a fifty-fifty chance. The campers won't be allowed to vote, of course. But they've been doing a lot of canvassing."

"Who for?"

"Not for anyone in particular. Their line is, turn out the old lady and vote for someone younger and more with it. No doubt they'll persuade someone to stand before the lists close on the fourteenth."

"It's going to be an interesting council, isn't it?" said Jonas. "Let's look at the worst from your point of view. Suppose Wroke gets in, that means that three sets of wards really cancel each other out. The two Town Wards, the two Branmere Wards and, let's say, the Liberties and the West Ward. Correct?"

"I agree."

"Then the two other wards are the ones that matter. Portsmouth Road and the East Ward."

"Exactly," said the Admiral. He sounded, thought Jonas, suspiciously pleased. "That's what I've come to discuss. We've formed a Fighting Committee. Our current idea is that I should stand for the East Ward – that's where my house is, incidentally. And you for Portsmouth Road."

"Hey! Steady on. I've told you once already. I came to Shackleton for a quiet life."

"When the ship's in danger, it's all hands to the pumps."

"But is it in danger?"

"You realise that if things go wrong, we shall be landed with a council that won't move against the campers. They may even give them a lease; then we shall have them with us for keeps. That lovely Dingle turned into a shanty town."

"It makes you think," agreed Jonas. "But please don't bank on me. It's not my line at all."

Next morning he set out on foot to visit Maggs's Farm and discuss mineral rights. It was two miles out of the town. He looked forward to the walk. He thought it might help him to clear his mind. The sky was still blue, but it was no longer a soft blue. There was a hard edge to it. The weather seemed to be changing.

Maggs confirmed this. He said, "Thermometer dropped five points last night. I wasn't sorry. If we're going to have a frost, better now than later. Why? Because if it comes in May, you can say goodbye to your fruit."

When they had finished their business and Jonas was leaving, Maggs said, "Did I hear you was to be our new council member?"

"If you know that," said Jonas, "you know more than I do."

"You'll get a lot of votes if you do stand. I can promise you that. You know who'd be against you?"

"No. Who?"

"Chap called Partridge. You've heard of him?"

"I remember the name vaguely. Isn't he a naturalist?"

"Something like that. He sent us all a bit of paper. I've got it here, if you'd like to read it."

The circular was adorned with the photograph of a young man wearing horn-rimmed glasses and an expression of overwhelming seriousness.

"When I opened it," said Maggs, "I thought it was an advert for a patent medicine, or something like that."

"He does look a bit constipated," agreed Jonas.

"I was going to throw it away, but my wife said better read it. It may be important. I'm glad I did. Some of the things he says, well I ask you!"

Jonas scanned Mr Partridge's electioneering manifesto with interest. He saw that he called himself 'The Countryside Candidate'. His message was that the land belonged to everyone. It must *not* be monopolised by the farming fraternity. Some of it now under cultivation must be allowed to return to its natural state as a habitation for wildlife. Footpaths must be carefully preserved and added to where necessary.

In view of the fact that the majority of the voters in the Portsmouth Road Ward were farmers, Jonas agreed that this bold statement of young Mr Partridge's views would be unlikely to win him many votes.

"You realise," he said, "that most of the things he's proposing couldn't be done by any district council whoever got on it. They can't open new footpaths and they can't change the law."

"No saying what people like that can do once you let 'em in," said Maggs gloomily. "You put your name forward and we'll all vote for you. It'll be a walk-over."

Jonas thought about it as he made his way home. The fact that he would probably win the seat made the idea somehow even less attractive.

He wished he had brought a scarf and gloves – it was certainly much colder.

When he got to the office Claire said, "You've got a caller. I don't know if you want to see him, but he seems keen to see you."

"Has he got a name?"

"It's Raymond Lipsett."

"Oh. Did he say what he wanted?"

"Like most people who come to see you, I imagine he wants help."

She said this so flatly that it sounded like a rebuke. Jonas looked at her for a moment, started to say something, changed his mind and moved off into his office. Lipsett got up politely enough, but did not offer to shake hands. When they were both seated Jonas said, "What can I do for you?"

Lipsett pushed a piece of paper across the desk. Jonas saw that it was a writ issued in the Brighton Crown Court, naming Lipsett as defendant, in a representative capacity, in an action by the council for aggravated trespass. Much what he had expected. He said, "Do I gather that you want me to represent you?"

"That was my idea. It's the sort of thing you do, isn't it?"

"It's the sort of thing I do, yes. But I don't see that I can act for you in this particular case."

"Why not?"

"Well, to start with, I happen to be acting for Delamere. He's considering an action for assault against the people who manhandled him."

"So what? He's not a party to this action."

"True. But you must see that it would make it awkward for me. There are other solicitors in Shackleton – "

"Thank you. I've had some. When I called on Porter and Merriman I wasn't allowed to see the senior partner; apparently he's reserved for people who matter. I was interviewed by a young man who talked as if he'd got a mouth full of plums. He said, 'Sorry, old boy. Rayly it's not the sort of thing we handle, acherly.' So I went on to see R. and L. Sykes. There I did get through to a partner."

"Ronald Sykes?"

"I imagine so. He was at least honest. He said that if he took the case he'd lose half his clients. Do I take it you're going to say the same thing?"

"Not so. I've got more clients than I want. And anyway I'm three-quarters retired. I shall probably retire altogether at the end of next year."

"Then what are *your* reasons, might one ask?"

Temperature heating up a bit, thought Jonas. Better get it over quickly. He said, "I don't want to act in this matter. Simple as that. Anyway, you'll find plenty of firms in Brighton who'll be pleased to help you."

"Shall I really? Then let me tell you something. Most probably I shan't need anyone at all. Because this case is one which isn't coming off." He picked up the copy of the writ,

tore it neatly into four pieces and deposited them in Jonas's
waste-paper basket.

"What makes you think that?"

"Your local rag has conducted a straw poll. It gives us a
majority on the council. I can assure you that the first thing
the new council will do is to abandon this stupid action and the
second will be to grant us a long lease."

"Won't you be a bit uncomfortable, particularly when the
temperature's below freezing point?"

"Be your age. We shan't take a lease on that place. We've got
our eyes on a nice piece of ground behind the front. The
Lammas I believe it's called. I've got a number of friends who'll
join us there. Young keen people with a bit of spunk in them.
Maybe they'll kick up a shindy, but it's what this place wants. It
needs waking up, kicking into the twentieth century." The
words were tumbling out with such force that they seemed to
be generating their own heat. Lipsett's face, as much as could
be seen of it behind its camouflage of hair, was scarlet and his
eyes were snapping. "Maybe the old women of both sexes who
have been roosting here won't like it. Their bad luck. Let
them fly away somewhere else. We shan't miss them. The
future belongs to youth."

As he paused for breath Jonas said, "In fact, you're using
Shackleton as a cuspidor."

"Come again."

"Something you can spit at."

Lipsett looked at him for a long moment. Jonas thought,
now he really is going to burst. Or perhaps he'll throw
something at me. An inkpot and a calendar seemed the most
likely missiles.

In fact, Lipsett rose to his feet, said, "I can see it's a waste of
time talking to you," swung on his heel and went out, closing
the door quietly behind him. He heard his feet in the hallway.
Something was said to Claire. Then the front door shut and his
footsteps went off, crunching the ice on the front path.

When Claire came in Jonas was sitting perfectly still. She
said, 'Not a very successful interview, I gather."

"On the contrary," said Jonas. "Decisive. Could you get me
Admiral Fairlie's number?"

When she came back with it he said, "He's succeeded in

making up my mind for me. I'm going to ask the Admiral to rustle me up six supporters. I'm proposing to stand for the Portsmouth Road Ward. I don't know the first thing about it. I shall rely on you to help me."

"I'm afraid," said Claire slowly, "that won't be possible. I've got a lot of canvassing to do myself."

"For Philip Wroke?"

"No. I'm standing for the East Ward."

After she had left, Jonas sat for a long time staring at the closed door.

After thinking the matter over Jonas decided not to distribute a circular. The one sent round by his opponent must have lost him more votes than it gained. He decided to confine himself to a modified form of house-to-house canvassing. Maggs had produced a list of residents, indicating the cases in which not much persuasion would be needed and those in which he might have to deploy arguments.

That morning he was proposing to visit a corn chandler who had his shop in the tiny village of Moorhampton in the extreme north of his area and who was reputed to be something of a radical. All that week the sky had maintained its steely blue colour and it had been getting steadily colder. The thermometer on the previous evening had recorded a record seventeen degrees of frost. That morning, as he set out in the car, Jonas noticed a change.

It was warmer. Clouds like dirty cotton wool were billowing up from the south-east. As he reached the lane which led to Moorhampton the snow began to fall. Jonas half thought of turning back, but he was now so near his destination that he decided to push on. He found the corn chandler an agreeable enough man who seemed to grasp the advantages of voting for him. When he was leaving, the man said, "Better not waste much time, squire, if you want to get back to Shackleton."

"You think the snow will block the road?"

"It's the ground underneath, see. It's frozen so hard the snow can't sink in. Like as not we'll be cut off by this evening."

It was a difficult drive. The snow was now coming down so thickly that he needed to keep the wipers moving at double speed to clear it and drifts were already forming and threatening to block the road. Fortunately it was downhill most of the way and he managed to keep the car moving, with two hair-raising skids where a patch of ice showed through the snow. When he got to the town the houses gave some shelter and he reached home, tucked his car away thankfully in the garage and went inside.

He found Sabrina and Claire, who lived two or three streets away, with their coats on and their scarves over their heads, ready to depart.

"No clients and none expected," said Claire. "Sabrina and I are getting home whilst the going's good."

"If it goes on like this," said Jonas, "you'd better stay at home tomorrow. Sam and I can cope quite well by ourselves for a day or two."

"An unexpectedly heavy fall of snow on the south coast," said the wireless that evening, in the cheerful voice it reserved for such announcements, "has brought chaos to many areas. Worst hit have been isolated farms on the coastal side of the South Downs. If the snow continues emergency plans are being put in hand by the authorities, involving use of troops and helicopters. However, the snow has arrived so late in the year that the experts are of the opinion that it will not lie for any length of time – "

"Experts!" said Sam. He and Jonas were sitting in front of a roaring fire in the office. "If they're all that expert, why didn't they tell us this was coming?"

"I'm not complaining," said Jonas. He added a generous tot of whisky to each of their glasses. "I don't mind if it keeps it up for a day or so. Makes a nice break."

Next morning it was still snowing, but spasmodically. When it stopped and the wind from the south-west parted the clouds, a sky of the palest blue showed for a few moments. Then the clouds closed in again.

Jonas spent the day in his office catching up with some neglected paperwork. Sam cooked lunch for both of them and retired to his quarters for his afternoon nap. Jonas worked on steadily until the premature twilight forced him to switch on his table lamp.

At that moment the telephone rang. It was Claire. She said, "I thought you might like to know that I've heard from Wroke. He rang me from a call-box. He's moved his caravan up out of the Dingle. It took some doing. Luckily he got some help from a farmer with a tractor."

"What about the others? Are they moving out?"

"Don't sound so hopeful," said Claire. "No. Philip says they're staying put. Actually they're pretty well protected by the banks on either side."

"As long as they've got enough to eat."

"Oh, they're well provisioned. And used to looking after themselves. More so than most people."

Jonas thought she was probably right about that.

At eleven o'clock that night he was having his evening nightcap in front of the fire with Sam when the front door bell rang. Sam ambled out into the hall and came back with Francis Delamere. The old man was wearing a cloak and hood. As Sam helped him out of them Jonas noticed, with some surprise, that although they were wet through there was no sign of snow on them.

"Do I gather," he said, "that it's stopped snowing?"

"The snow stopped at dusk. The thermometer's five degrees above zero already and going up. And it's been raining for the last three hours. You see the importance of that."

"I can see that it must *be* important," said Jonas, "or you wouldn't have come all this way on a night like this to discuss it." He had a suspicion that the events of the last few days might have affected the old man's mind. He added, "Wouldn't it have been simpler if you'd telephoned? Whatever the problem, there's nothing much anyone can do about it at this time of night."

"When you talk like that," said Delamere and there was the snap in his voice of a teacher addressing a backward class, "it's clear that you have no idea at all of what we're facing."

"Which is – ?"

"Disaster. Unless we can clear them out tonight, when the sun gets up tomorrow it's more than likely that there won't be a man, woman or child alive in that camp."

Jonas stared at him. If the man was mad, it was a very convincing sort of madness. He said, "I suppose you know

215

what you're talking about. I haven't got your expertise in these matters. Could you please explain what you're afraid of."

Delamere took a deep breath. He said, "Do you remember what happened at Lynmouth?"

"Lynmouth. That's on the north coast of Devon, isn't it? I do remember they had a sort of flood."

"A sort of flood! It destroyed a complete village. The conditions were similar. First two weeks of rain which water-logged the Exmoor peat. Then a flash storm. Nine inches of rain. The water took the shortest route to the sea. It went down the Lyn River like a tidal wave. Now do you see?"

Jonas was a cautious man, who disliked jumping to conclusions. He started to say, "There's no real certainty about any of this – " when, to his surprise, Sam interrupted him.

He said, in the voice of one who at last sees the answer to a puzzle, "Tilshead."

"That's right," said Delamere. "The Tilshead disaster of 1897. You remember that."

"I can't say I remember it personally," said Sam. "But when I was doing my National Service in the Gunners, we was up at Larkhill and I saw that memorial thing. When I read what was on it I couldn't hardly credit it. The Till's a tiny little stream, normally, that is – sort of thing you could walk across without getting the water over your boots – but one night, it seems, it came roaring down the main street. They show the tide mark twelve feet above the street level. A lot of the cottages had to be rebuilt. They had a public subscription. That's what this memorial's about."

Whilst Sam had been speaking, Jonas had been making up his mind. He said, "Very well. I'm prepared to agree that there's a chance that you're right. The difficulty is what we're going to do about it. If you or I go along to the camp and tell them they've got to clear out before morning, you can guess what they'll say. 'You're just trying to do what they did at Portree. Turn us out and keep us out.'"

"They might listen to you."

"Not in a hundred years. Lipsett knows exactly what I think of him. No. There's only one chance. If we can convince Wroke, he might convince them. Claire told me that he's moved his caravan. I'll try to find out where he's put it – " He

216

was dialling a number as he spoke. There was a long pause at the other end. "I expect she's in bed and asleep by now – "

It was a woman's voice, not Claire's, that answered. The landlady, Jonas guessed. She said, "Yes. Who is it?" Her voice sounded more anxious than irritated.

"I'm so sorry to bother you," said Jonas. "But I must have a word with Miss Easterbrook."

"Oh dear. Are you the police?"

"No. I'm her employer. Mr Pickett."

"I've been so worried. She went out hours ago and she hasn't come back."

"I think I know where she's gone," said Jonas. "Leave it to me." He rang off before the landlady could say anything else. "Ten to one she's with Wroke now. I wish we knew where he's parked his caravan."

"I fancy I saw it as I came past," said Delamere. "There's a lay-by where the path from the Dingle comes out on to the main road."

"Right," said Jonas. "You drive, Sam."

Philip Wroke said, "Yes" and "I see" as Delamere repeated his story. "It did occur to me that there might be danger and Claire and I were sitting up in case any salvage was called for. I must say, we didn't anticipate the sort of disaster you're talking about. We saw the level of the Shackle stream might rise rather sharply, that's all."

"I think," said Jonas, "that we've got to rely on Mr Delamere's expertise. Could you have a word with Lipsett?"

They had found Wroke's caravan without difficulty and were sitting in front of a glowing stove.

Claire said, "He'd listen to you, Philip."

"He might."

"We've got to try, anyway."

"Yes," said Wroke, getting up with a sigh. "I suppose we'd better all go down to lend a hand in case he does agree to evacuate the camp, but to start with I think you'd better keep in the background and let me do the talking."

When he and Claire had put on heavy duty anoraks, they started together down the slippery path that ran beside the stream. Claire and Wroke linked arms. Jonas and Delamere anchored themselves to Sam. They found the entrance blocked with a tangled lump of barbed-wire, but no guards. Sam heaved the barricade aside and they went in.

It was now nearly two o'clock, but there were lights showing in one or two of the tents. Outside one of them a man was digging a trench to lead the melted snow and rainwater away from his shack. He looked up at them as they passed, but said nothing.

There was a light in Lipsett's caravan. When he answered Wroke's knock they saw that he was fully dressed. He saw Claire standing behind Wroke and said, genially, "Come in both of you. You look like drowned kittens." Then he spotted the other three and said, in a very different tone of voice, "What is this? A deputation."

"Sort of," said Wroke. "If you let us in we'll explain."

After hesitating for a moment, Lipsett said, "There's not a lot of room. But all right. Squeeze in if you must. But if you've got anything to say, please say it quickly. I've been spending the early part of the night helping people dig ditches and I wouldn't mind getting a few hours' sleep."

The caravan was smaller than Wroke's and it was a tight squeeze. Wroke said, "I'm afraid we've got to evacuate the camp, Raymond."

"I guessed it would be something like that. Perhaps you'll be good enough to tell me why we should do any such thing."

"Mr Delamere is the expert. I'd rather you heard it from him direct."

For the third time that night the old man spoke. Possibly because he had said it all twice before, or possibly because he was tired, it struck Jonas as less convincing. Lipsett listened with offensive patience and said at the end, "Is that all?"

"Enough surely for precautionary measures," said Wroke. But he seemed less certain than he had been.

"Such as clearing everyone out of the camp," said Lipsett with a smile.

"Well – "

"Then let me tell you a few facts. We have not neglected the possibility of a flood. The level of the stream has been monitored every few hours. Possibly as a result of the surface ice melting, the level has risen by two feet. But when it was inspected an hour ago the level was actually down – "

Wroke said, "But don't you see, Raymond, it's not the stream itself – "

Lipsett disregarded the interruption. He said, "Also we have listened to the weather reports. They were encouraging. A warm front is predicted and by tomorrow evening most of the snow will be gone. So now, if you don't mind – "

Delamere then managed to surprise them. He did not attempt debate. He said, "I have some fifty yards of very good rope. It can be attached to something on each side. Have you any objection if we run it through the camp?"

The stark practicality of this suggestion seemed to affect Lipsett more than any argument. For a moment he hesitated, then he said, "Very well, but no tricks."

It took some time to thread the rope under the barbed wire on each side and attach it. They had anchored it to a tree on the west side and on the other side to one of the council benches which was firmly set in a concrete base. After that Wroke and Claire went back to Wroke's caravan and the other three climbed the steps to Delamere's cottage, where they dozed away the remaining hours of the night in chairs in front of the fire.

Jonas was the first up. He came out of the house as a rim of the sun was showing over the roofs of the town. The warmth of the air had already acted on the sodden ground and the whole of the Dingle was filled with a white mist, through which a row of tent poles poked out like the masts of a sunken ship. Looking across the top of the mist bank he could see Wroke and Claire sitting together on the bench by the far end of the rope. He heard Claire laughing at something Wroke had said.

It was a cheerful and a reassuring scene. The hermit's fears had turned out to be nothing but fantasies. Nevertheless, what they had tried to do was sensible.

Delamere and Sam had joined him and they were standing together when they heard it. It was a rumbling, grumbling sound, like the opening notes of an avalanche as it breaks free and gathers speed. Then a series of sharp cracks, like the opening of an artillery barrage. One or two of the campers just below them looked out of their tents. A woman screamed. Then it hit them.

It was not a flood, it was a tidal wave, ten feet high, frothing grey on the top, brown underneath. It picked up one of the caravans and smashed it into the wire at the bottom, carrying a section of the fence away with it. As the wave subsided for a moment their horrified eyes could see heads bobbing in the water, tangles of grey hair, men and women encumbered by the flapping canvas, trying to claw their way up to the safety of the banks.

Sam had launched himself down the rope. He had already dragged two men clear and had grabbed a girl who was crawling under the wire when the second wave hit them. It was higher than the first and more terrible as it carried a flotsam of broken stuff. A hen coop, half a telegraph pole, the roof of a shed, and bodies. Animals floating on their backs and bundles of rags and human clothing at which Jonas dared not look.

The second wave uprooted what was left of the fence and swung it like a deadly flail across the camp. Frightful though the result of this was, it did at least clear an obstruction from the sides. Sam, at times up to his neck in the water, at times completely submerged, had grabbed two more men and one woman with a child in her arms.

Then the third wave was on them. Higher than the last and awesome in its power, it swept through the little valley like a scythe through corn, carrying everything in its path as it raced to the sea.

As Jonas stood, aghast and helpless, he heard, seeming to come from under the grey waters of the Channel, the sound of a bell. A single piercing note which went on for some seconds as the water level in the Dingle slowly sank.

"There's a lot to do," said the Admiral. He spoke in a brisk and businesslike way, but the horror of what they had seen was still at the back of all their minds, though it was four weeks in the past. He added, "Thank God we've got a council that can tackle it."

It was the last week in April. The elections had brought few surprises. Rattray and Benson, Jonas and the Admiral, Greenaway and Forbes formed an impregnable centre block, able and willing to undertake the work of reconstruction.

Nine of the campers had been dragged from the flood, six of them by Sam. Three more, strong swimmers, had kept their heads. Allowing themselves to be carried out to sea, they had struggled to land a mile down the coast. Seventy, including Lipsett, had died in the flood. To this total had to be added two men, two women and four children from the farms which had been swept away higher up the valley.

A relief fund had been started and the public response, as so often in such cases, was overwhelming.

"Wroke's a good man," said the Admiral. "Though he didn't win a seat on the council he's agreed to head our Appeal Committee. Do I gather, by the way, that he and Miss Easterbrook are engaged?"

"It's high time they announced it," said Jonas. "They've been living together in that caravan for the last month."

"Glad she won the seat. Maybe she'll be able to keep Florence Fitchett quiet. I'm afraid your practice has suffered."

"It hasn't suffered," said Jonas. "It no longer exists. I've decided to retire. Sabrina has joined R. and L. Sykes and they were delighted to have her. The firms have been amalgamated. Sykes and Pickett the new outfit is to be called, so that at least my name will be remembered."

"You've had a pretty good run," said the Admiral thoughtfully.

Jonas nodded, but it was not what he wanted to talk about. It was the first time since the disaster that he had got the Admiral to himself.

He said, "When it all happened, just exactly where were you?"

"On my roof, as I often am in the early morning. Using my telescope. I was too far away to help, but I was perfectly placed to see what happened. Incidentally, I've put up Sam's name for a Royal Humane Society medal."

"Well deserved," said Jonas absently. "What I really wanted to ask you was whether, just after that third wave came

– the final one that swept everything out to sea – did you hear anything?"

The Admiral looked at him curiously.

"What sort of thing?"

"Well – it sounded like a bell. Sam and Delamere heard it too."

"You must have been thinking of that old story. That if another disaster threatened Shackleton the bells of the church under the sea would ring again."

"Something of the sort."

"I didn't hear anything. But the wind was in your direction, not mine. You do realise that even if you did hear it, there might have been a perfectly natural explanation. The old church is still somewhere there, under the waves. Its bells may still be hanging. A heavy piece of wood, brought down by the force of the flood, might have struck against the bell – "

"Yes," said Jonas. "I suppose it could have been that."

But he didn't believe it.

FINE MYSTERY AND SUSPENSE
TITLES FROM CARROLL & GRAF

☐ Allingham, Margery/NO LOVE LOST $3.95
☐ Allingham, Margery/MR. CAMPION'S QUARRY $3.95
☐ Allingham, Margery/MR. CAMPION'S FARTHING $3.95
☐ Allingham, Margery/THE WHITE COTTAGE
MYSTERY $3.50
☐ Ambler, Eric/BACKGROUND TO DANGER $3.95
☐ Ambler, Eric/CAUSE FOR ALARM $3.95
☐ Ambler, Eric/A COFFIN FOR DIMITRIOS $3.95
☐ Ambler, Eric/EPITAPH FOR A SPY $3.95
☐ Ambler, Eric/STATE OF SIEGE $3.95
☐ Ambler, Eric/JOURNEY INTO FEAR $3.95
☐ Ball, John/THE KIWI TARGET $3.95
☐ Bentley, E.C./TRENT'S OWN CASE $3.95
☐ Blake, Nicholas/A TANGLED WEB $3.50
☐ Brand, Christianna/DEATH IN HIGH HEELS $3.95
☐ Brand, Christianna/FOG OF DOUBT $3.50
☐ Brand, Christianna/GREEN FOR DANGER $3.95
☐ Brand, Christianna/TOUR DE FORCE $3.95
☐ Brown, Fredric/THE LENIENT BEAST $3.50
☐ Brown, Fredric/MURDER CAN BE FUN $3.95
☐ Brown, Fredric/THE SCREAMING MIMI $3.50
☐ Buchan, John/JOHN MACNAB $3.95
☐ Buchan, John/WITCH WOOD $3.95
☐ Burnett, W.R./LITTLE CAESAR $3.50
☐ Butler, Gerald/KISS THE BLOOD OFF MY HANDS $3.95
☐ Carr, John Dickson/CAPTAIN CUT-THROAT $3.95
☐ Carr, John Dickson/DARK OF THE MOON $3.50
☐ Carr, John Dickson/DEMONIACS $3.95
☐ Carr, John Dickson/THE GHOSTS' HIGH NOON $3.95
☐ Carr, John Dickson/NINE WRONG ANSWERS $3.50
☐ Carr, John Dickson/PAPA LA-BAS $3.95
☐ Carr, John Dickson/THE WITCH OF THE
LOW TIDE $3.95
☐ Chesterton, G. K./THE MAN WHO KNEW
TOO MUCH $3.95
☐ Chesterton, G. K./THE MAN WHO WAS THURSDAY $3.50
☐ Crofts, Freeman Wills/THE CASK $3.95
☐ Coles, Manning/NO ENTRY $3.50
☐ Collins, Michael/WALK A BLACK WIND $3.95
☐ Dickson, Carter/THE CURSE OF THE BRONZE LAMP $3.50
☐ Disch, Thomas M & Sladek, John/BLACK ALICE $3.95
☐ Eberhart, Mignon/MESSAGE FROM HONG KONG $3.50

☐ Fennelly, Tony/THE CLOSET HANGING		$3.50
☐ Freeling, Nicolas/LOVE IN AMSTERDAM		$3.95
☐ Gilbert, Michael/ANYTHING FOR A QUIET LIFE		$3.95
☐ Gilbert, Michael/THE DOORS OPEN		$3.95
☐ Gilbert, Michael/THE 92nd TIGER		$3.95
☐ Gilbert, Michael/OVERDRIVE		$3.95
☐ Graham, Winston/MARNIE		$3.95
☐ Griffiths, John/THE GOOD SPY		$4.50
☐ Hughes, Dorothy B./THE FALLEN SPARROW		$3.50
☐ Hughes, Dorothy B./IN A LONELY PLACE		$3.50
☐ Hughes, Dorothy B./RIDE THE PINK HORSE		$3.95
☐ Hornung, E. W./THE AMATEUR CRACKSMAN		$3.95
☐ Kitchin, C. H. B./DEATH OF HIS UNCLE		$3.95
☐ Kitchin, C. H. B./DEATH OF MY AUNT		$3.50
☐ MacDonald, John D./TWO		$2.50
☐ Mason, A.E.W./AT THE VILLA ROSE		$3.50
☐ Mason, A.E.W./THE HOUSE OF THE ARROW		$3.50
☐ McShane, Mark/SEANCE ON A WET AFTERNOON		$3.95
☐ Pentecost, Hugh/THE CANNIBAL WHO OVERATE		$3.95
☐ Priestley, J.B./SALT IS LEAVING		$3.95
☐ Queen, Ellery/THE FINISHING STROKE		$3.95
☐ Rogers, Joel T./THE RED RIGHT HAND		$3.50
☐ 'Sapper'/BULLDOG DRUMMOND		$3.50
☐ Stevens, Shane/BY REASON OF INSANITY		$5.95
☐ Symons, Julian/BOGUE'S FORTUNE		$3.95
☐ Symons, Julian/THE BROKEN PENNY		$3.95
☐ Wainwright, John/ALL ON A SUMMER'S DAY		$3.50
☐ Wallace, Edgar/THE FOUR JUST MEN		$2.95
☐ Waugh, Hillary/A DEATH IN A TOWN		$3.95
☐ Waugh, Hillary/LAST SEEN WEARING		$3.95
☐ Waugh, Hillary/SLEEP LONG, MY LOVE		$3.95
☐ Westlake, Donald E./THE MERCENARIES		$3.95
☐ Willeford, Charles/THE WOMAN CHASER		$3.95

Available from fine bookstores everywhere or use this coupon for ordering.

Carroll & Graf Publishers, Inc., 260 Fifth Avenue, N.Y., N.Y. 10001

Please send me the books I have checked above. I am enclosing $_____
(please add $1.25 per title to cover postage and handling.) Send check
or money order—no cash or C.O.D.'s please. N.Y. residents please add
8¼% sales tax.

Mr/Mrs/Ms _____

Address _____

City _____ State/Zip _____

Please allow four to six weeks for delivery.